CROSSED SKIS

CROSSED SKIS

An Alpine Mystery

CAROL CARNAC

With an Introduction
by Martin Edwards

Poisoned Pen
PRESS

Introduction © 2020 by Martin Edwards
Copyright © 1952 by The Estate of Carol Carnac
Cover and internal design © 2020 by Sourcebooks
Cover image © NRM/Pictorial Collection/Science & Society Picture Library

Sourcebooks, Poisoned Pen Press, and the colophon
are registered trademarks of Sourcebooks.

Published by Poisoned Pen Press, an imprint of Sourcebooks,
in association with the British Library
P.O. Box 4410, Naperville, Illinois 60567-4410
(630) 961-3900
sourcebooks.com

Originally published as *Crossed Skis* in 1952 in
England by Collins Crime Club, London.

Library of Congress Cataloging-in-Publication is on file with the publisher.

Names: Carnac, Carol, author. | Edwards, Martin, writer of
    introduction.
Title: Crossed skis : an alpine mystery / Carol Carnac ; with an
    introduction by Martin Edwards.
Description: Naperville, Illinois : Poisoned Pen Press, [2020] | Series:
    British Library crime classics series | "Originally published as Crossed
    Skis in 1952 in England by Collins Crime Club, London"--Title page
    verso.
Identifiers: LCCN 2020014723 (print) Subjects: GSAFD: Mystery fiction.
Classification: LCC PR6035.I9 C76 2020 (print) |
    DDC 823/.914--dc23

LC record available at https://lccn.loc.gov/2020014723

Printed and bound in the United States of America.
SB 10 9 8 7 6 5 4 3 2

To our party at Lech am Arlberg, January, 1951
BARBARA
MICHAEL
JEAN
MICHAEL
MARY
TONY
PATRICIA
DICK
DIANA
FRANCIS
MARGARET
GEOFFREY
JUNE
RICHARD
JOHN
With thanks for their help and advice,
and happy memories of their charming company.
May they never Cross their Skis.
CAROL

CONTENTS

INTRODUCTION

Crossed Skis, originally published in 1952 under the legendary imprint of the Collins Crime Club, is the first Carol Carnac novel to be published by the British Library. But Carol Carnac was a pen-name of Edith Caroline Rivett, who is already familiar to fans of the Crime Classics series under her original pseudonym, E. C. R. Lorac. The author was known to family and friends as Carol (and Lorac is Carol, spelt backwards). The Lorac books feature Inspector Macdonald, whereas the usual lead detective in the Carnac novels is another likeable Scotland Yard man, Julian Rivers.

When this book first appeared, Carol (it seems simplest to refer to her by that name) was in her late fifties but an enthusiastic skier. Indeed, she dedicated the novel to her fifteen fellow members of a ski-ing party at the Austrian mountain resort of Lech am Arlberg in January 1951 "with thanks for their help and advice, and happy memories of their charming company. May they never Cross their Skis."

Carol frequently used thinly disguised versions of real people, names, places, and events in her fiction. *Crossed Skis* illustrates this technique, since it concerns the misadventures of a party of eight men and eight women who travel to—Lech am Arlberg, for the ski-ing. Crime writers who fictionalise people whom they know are taking a risk (especially if they base their murderers on their own acquaintances) but this is a book which derives an important part of its appeal from the authenticity of the background. Carol's particular strength as a writer lay in her ability to capture the atmosphere of a place. Examples in the Lorac canon include Devon (*Fire in the Thatch*), London (*Bats in the Belfry*) and Lunesdale in north Lancashire (*Fell Murder*). Here she conveys the excitement of the skiers and the beauty of the Alps with her customary skill as well as with the benefit of first-hand experience.

One of the main characters in the book, and the oldest member of the ski-ing party, is Catherine Reid, known as Kate. It doesn't seem unduly speculative to suggest that Kate is in essence a self-portrait. There are several clues in the text; for instance, we're told at the start that Kate wants to paint during the holiday, and Carol was an accomplished artist. Kate "was interested in all human beings," like her creator, and during the course of the story she also indulges her instinct for amateur detection.

Crossed Skis is a book in which two distinct storylines gradually converge. Once we have been introduced to the ski-ing party, the scene switches to Bloomsbury. After a fire at a decaying boarding-house, a man's body is found. Inspector Brook, a detective at the scene, is puzzled by an impression in the mud, before realising that it is the same size and shape as the ring and point made by a ski-stick—"a very character-istic mark: once you'd seen it you remembered it." But what connection can this incident possibly have with ski-ing? He reports to Chief Inspector Rivers of the C.I.D., who is sure that they are dealing with a murder case. Rivers is a skier (he says of international ski-running "it's one of the best things I know"), and he is convinced that so is the culprit: "I've never been after a skier before. I wonder where he's gone."

The reader will have little doubt that the answer to this question is to be found in Lech am Arlberg, but Carol maintains suspense with conspicuous skill, running the police investigation in tandem with the story of the skiers' activities on the other side of the Channel. She strikes a pleasing balance between mystification as to the culprit's identity, description of Rivers's low-key but relentless methods of detection, and an account of the pleasures of ski-ing which even those who wouldn't be caught dead on the snow-covered slopes are likely to find engaging.

The first novel to appear under the Carol Carnac name, *Triple Death*, was published in 1936. She'd made her debut as Lorac only five years earlier, with *The Murder in the Burrows*, but ten more Lorac titles were in print by the end of 1936, and she probably adopted the alternative pen-name to avoid giving the impression that she was flooding the market. In all, there were twenty-three Carol Carnac books; the last to be published in her lifetime was *Long Shadows*, a.k.a. *Affair at Helen's Court* (1957) while *Death of a Lady Killer* appeared posthumously in 1959.

At the time she wrote *Crossed Skis*, Carol Rivett was settled happily in the rural village of Aughton in Lunesdale. She had moved there during the war, to be near her sister Maud and her brother-in-law John Howson. Today she is remembered in Lunesdale as someone who loved the local community, and was in turn embraced by it as if she were a native-born countrywoman. Thanks to Lena Whiteley, who knew Carol, I have been given a picture of a typical day in the author's life. She would do her correspondence in the morning (often receiving fan mail from readers in the U.S.), and take her letters to the post office. In the afternoon, she would garden and let her mind wander as she thought up her stories. In the evening she would bathe, dress for dinner, put on make-up. and an evening gown, and often dine on her own, before writing later on.

She travelled around England, and also went to Austria, Switzerland, and Italy. A sociable woman, she was an active member of the Detection Club, and served for several years as its Secretary. Her fellow crime writers called her "the Lady of the Lizard" because she liked to wear a brooch of a turquoise-spotted lizard with ruby eyes. Her other pastimes included embroidery and art and she had a keen interest in heraldry. She created her own illustrated bookplate and also a logo for the Detection Club which is still in use today. Despite her considerable body of work, and the success which she achieved during her lifetime, her fiction spent decades out of print until the recent resurgence of interest in classic crime fiction led the British Library to be persuaded of the merit of reprinting selected Lorac titles. This particular book seems to be the first Carol Carnac novel to have been reprinted in Britain since her death in 1958. It is a pleasure to welcome the reappearance of a name that has been missing from the bookshop shelves for far too long.

—Martin Edwards
www.martinedwardsbooks.com

Chapter I

1

"By the Golden Arrow arch at Victoria Station, continental side, at twelve noon, tomorrow, New Year's Day, and don't be late," said Bridget Manners patiently. "You can't mistake the Golden Arrow arch, and anyway all the porters know it. Yes, I know the B.B.C. has given gale warnings for Portsmouth, Dover and Thames, but you'll just have to bear it. Bring your Kwells and don't be late."

She put down the receiver and threw up her arms in a gesture of despair. "Jane, I shall be raving before we start. Everybody's ringing up all day, as though I hadn't told them everything. Oh, Hades, who's that?"

"It's all right. That'll be Pippa, she's a sensible wench," said Jane, as the door bell rang. "She just wants to hear about the last man, and probably to try on her ski-ing trousers. She's borrowed them and she's in a panic in case she can't sit down in them. I'll go to the door."

"And I'll go and powder my nose—it's priority," said Bridget.

Phillipa Brand (commonly called Pippa), a tall bonny lass in her twenties, came into Bridget's sitting-room with Jane.

"I can't believe it's true!" she exclaimed. "Do you really think we shall get off tomorrow? I've been panicking for weeks. First it was on and then it was off, and it's just been too hair-raising. Winter sporting! I've never wanted to do anything so much, and I simply can't believe it's true we're going."

"Well, we are going," said Jane firmly. "Sixteen of us. Eight men and eight women. Biddy's got everything taped—tickets, reservations, couchettes and hotel, and she's worked like a Trojan over it. If anybody falls out now, it'll be just unforgivable. What with Raymond getting married and Nigel having an appendix and Charles going broke over a new car, it looked as though we should be an eighty per cent hen party. But it's all right and everything's in order. Oh lord, that's the phone again. You try on those bags while I answer it. There's generally lashings of room in them and you're not that buxom."

"I'm bigger than I look—there," said Pippa, as Jane lifted the receiver and began to chant: "By the Golden Arrow arch at Victoria Station, continental side, at twelve, noon... oh, it's Daphne. Yes, I know you know, but we're just making sure. What? Oh yes, Bridget's got the last man. Nigel raked him up. Oh, Nigel has got an appendix. Yes, jolly bad luck. Twelve o'clock tomorrow. Cheers."

Bridget, with nose duly powdered and curly hair brushed into order, came back into the room. Bridget was very pretty, but her clear-cut face was purposeful, her eyes intelligent as well as beguiling. She gave an expert glance at Pippa's ski-ing trousers.

"Hallo, Pippa. Those are all right... quite snappy in fact. Sakes, what a time we've had. But I don't think there can be any more crises now, and I saw Veronica this morning. She said Lech is all one can wish—jolly good ski-ing, not too remote and nice places to dance. So it sounds all right."

"It sounds a dream," said Pippa. "I've wanted to ski all my life and now it's really going to happen. Do tell me about the others. It's all been changed so often I've just lost count."

Bridget sat down by the fire. "You know several of them," she said. "Eight females—you, Jane and me. Catherine Reid, who's a friend of Jane's. She wants to paint, I believe. Meriel Parsons—you remember her, she paints, too, and she was on the land during the war. Martha Harris is coming with her brother—he's a doctor. It's useful to have a doctor in the party. By the way, have you insured your legs? I have. You never know with ski-ing. Who else? Oh, Jillian Dexter. She's Ian's sister and quite a lovely, I'm told. Daphne Melling was in the Wrens with me, and she comes to our Reel parties. That's all the girls—Jane, Pippa, Catherine, Meriel, Martha, Jillian, Daphne and me. It'll be simpler to use front names. We can all learn each other's surnames as we go along."

"Do you know them all?" asked Pippa.

"I know most of the shes and some of the hes," replied Bridget. "Malcolm Perry's coming, he's a schoolmaster and he was ski-ing somewhere last year. Tim Grant's a pilot, I believe, and Derrick Cossack's in the Navy. Frank Harris and Gerald Raine are both doctors. There's an Irishman named Robert O'Hara, I don't know anything about him except that he's a very good dancer, and I don't know Ian Dexter either. He's only just down from Cambridge. The last man is Neville Helston. Nigel raked him up for us at the last moment. I don't know the first thing about him, but Nigel says he's O.K., a pretty fair skier and keen on dancing and he's travelled a lot. He rang me up, and he seemed very keen to come, so that's the lot."

"I think it's marvellous of you to have organised it all," said Pippa, and Jane put in:

"I think it jolly well is. Nobody knows what a sweat it is getting a party together like this. People say they'll come and then say they can't, and you book rooms and cancel them, and wrangle about reservations, feeling all the time that it's all quite futile."

"And when you've just about decided to drop the whole thing, it all starts taking shape and people behave beautifully," said Bridget. "I do hope it's fun. We had a gorgeous time at Scheidegg last year, and I'm dead keen to do some more skiing. It should be rather amusing to have a party who don't all know one another."

"Are we all meeting at Victoria tomorrow?" asked Pippa.

"No, not quite all," replied Bridget. "Timothy Grant is flying to Zürich, his airline's giving him a lift. The Irishman may be travelling by a later train. He seemed a bit vague, but he knows his way about, so I left him to it. Most of us are going second class and I've got couchette reservations for twelve, so we shan't have that awful business of sitting up all night. Two of the men are travelling third class to save money. It'll be pretty grim for them, sitting up all night on hard seats, but I suppose they think it's worth while. I'd rather them than me. It's a perishing long journey to Austria, and those continental thirds are simply grim."

"Do we go right through in the same train?" asked Pippa. "Calais to Lech, wherever Lech is."

"It's in Austria," said Jane, "and the station for Lech is Langen. We drive from Langen to Lech, it's higher up than Langen. We leave Calais at half-past five and get to Basle about seven the next morning. We change at Basle, and get a Swiss breakfast on the Austrian train. Cherry jam and croissants. Glory, how nice! I adore meals in Switzerland."

"Talking about meals, Jane and I are taking some food with us," went on Bridget. "Dinner on the train costs an awful lot, no matter what currency you pay in. You can get food tickets this side and pay in sterling if you want to, but the tickets cost fifteen shillings, and fifteen bob for a meal on the train always seems a bit steep to me."

"Fifteen bob for dinner? Save us," groaned Pippa. "I'll bring my own food, sandwiches or something."

"Don't cut sandwiches, they get dry," said Bridget. "Bring a loaf and some butter, and some hard-boiled eggs and ham if you can get it. And a big Thermos with lime juice ready mixed, because the trains are frightfully hot and you'll get terribly thirsty. We shall have lunch in the train when we leave Victoria, and you can get tea on the boat."

Pippa gave a wail. "Lunch on the boat train just before a Channel crossing with the worst gale of the year blowing? What a hope."

"It's only about an hour's crossing and there's no need to be sick," said Jane firmly. "Take a Kwells and make an act of faith…"

"Mountains…" murmured Pippa. "Faith may move them, but it won't make my lunch stay put if—"

"Don't be morbid," said Bridget firmly. "And remember, twelve o'clock at the Golden Arrow arch. We've got our registered baggage to cope with, and it always takes longer than you expect, so although our train doesn't leave until one, we're going to meet at twelve. So now trot home and sleep well and dream of ski-ing down the nursery slopes at Lech."

"Heaven!" cried Pippa.

"—or head first in a snowdrift," said Jane. "Until you've tried ski-ing, you've just no idea how many different ways there are of falling, or how many places on your anatomy you can collect bruises. You have been warned!"

2

New Year's Day, 1951, was as dreary a day as an English winter can devise. It dawned with a bitter wind, while rain and sleet drove in a mixture of perishing misery across the drab London streets. At nine o'clock, a half-hearted pallid light shone on throngs of office workers who battled their way through slush and gale or stood in depressed queues at bus stops. After that half-hearted effort at daybreak, a sort of sullen deterioration set in, and by midday a yellow gloom was deepening to obstinate darkness.

Jane Harrington and Meriel Parsons stood nobly by the Golden Arrow arch at Victoria, counting up their party, giving advice and information about registered baggage, while everybody said the same thing: "Thank heaven we're getting out of this, into the sunshine."

The thought of sunshine over the mountains in contrast to the filth and gloom of London animated the whole party as they made their way to the boat train platform, all laden with miscellaneous baggage. All had boots slung around them somewhere, some had skis, though most of the party intended to hire them. Bridget was busy handing over railway tickets and introducing everybody to everybody.

"Jane, Meriel, Pippa, Daphne... Oh, do you know Malcolm Perry and Derrick Cossack? Jane, have you seen Martha and Frank? Oh, and there's Gerald, and that must be Jillian and Ian... How many's that? We've got seats all together in the same coach. Do get in, everybody. Jane, count them in. Is this one of us?"

"Miss Manners? I'm Robert O'Hara. What a day, it's like night with the lid on. I only just made it. I thought my taxi would never get across."

"Is that the lot?" murmured Jane to Bridget, who was still standing on the platform.

"No. The last man hasn't come yet... I do hope he's not letting us down," said Bridget. "We're rather a pleasant-looking crowd, aren't we? The Irishman's a big lad, isn't he? and I like those tweeds of Pippa's."

"You'd never know he was an Irishman, he doesn't sound like one," said Jane.

"He may be a North American Indian for all I know about him, but he looks all right to me," said Bridget. "Who's this? Our lost lamb? He's cut it pretty fine."

A tall dark fellow came running up the platform. "Miss Manners? I'm Helston. Sorry I'm late, my other train was held up in the fog. Nigel sends this with his love." "This" was a box of chocolates.

"Thanks a lot, get in, we're all in here," said Bridget.

The other flashed her a grin: "Awfully sorry if I held the party up. It was just one of those things. But it's all right now."

They scrambled in, and Bridget and Jane set to work on further introductions: "Neville Helston, Malcolm Perry—Jillian and Ian Dexter, Martha and Frank Harris... Robert O'Hara. Glory, we're off, we've really done it! Fifteen of us on this train and the sixteenth flying. I never believed we'd really get off."

"I'm very grateful to you for letting me come," said Neville Helston to Jane, who replied:

"We were very glad you could come. It squared the party, and we all think it's better to have even numbers of hes and shes, for dancing as well as sociability. You do dance, don't you?"

"Yes, rather," replied Neville, and Jane added: "Oh, good. That's the dining-car men. They're going to give us our lunch in here, it saves trailing along to the dining-car. I'm simply starving. Goodness, what's that?"

There was a crash farther along the coach, and the dining-car boy had started laying the tables, and Ian Dexter gave a howl of woe.

"My bottle of rum—Hell! it's smashed. I do call that a perishing shame. I brought it to cheer the party en route."

"Bad luck," called one of the others, but Ian turned indignantly on the dining-car attendant:

"Look here, you smashed it. You jolly well ought to provide another one."

"I never touched it, sir, it just rolled off the table," said the boy, looking thoroughly scared.

Bridget Manners intervened here, in a voice of cheerful common sense: "Don't be an ass, Ian. I saw it happen. It just rolled off. The boy never touched it, it's not his fault at all."

The boy gave Bridget a grateful glance, and she turned again to Ian: "I think it's plain bats to take drinks from England to France. Drinks are about the one thing which are certainly cheaper in France than England."

"Oh, I know," said Ian, "but the rum was a Christmas present. I thought it might act as a restorative to anybody who feels a bit dim after the Channel. Glory, don't I just about reek of the stuff?"

"Smells fine, but lord, what a waste!" groaned O'Hara, as the aroma of rum filled the coach, sweet and stimulating and yet a little sickly.

"Is that bad joss?" inquired Helston, while Malcolm Perry sniffed the warm smell with an appreciative grin.

Jane turned to Helston: "Of course it's not bad joss, it's baptising the party, like christening a battleship."

"I think we're going to have fun on this trip," murmured

Malcolm, as Battersea Power Station slipped past and the train gathered speed on its way southward.

"South for sunshine, south for ski-ing, south for snow," said Bridget, and the Irishman added: "South for steak, south for sirloin and south for sufficiency, or a surfeit. Eat till one busts and meat at all meals. How I do loathe what's called the meat ration."

"That's the last thing I want to hear about the meat ration until we come back to England," said Jane firmly, studying the big Irishman with a thoughtful eye.

Neville Helston smiled at Bridget. "We drown all our cares in the Channel. Once over, everything's glorious," he said.

Bridget rather liked the half-shy smile on his thin dark face, and sensing that Helston still felt a bit shy among all these vociferous travellers, she said:

"Well, we had a glorious time at Scheidegg last year, and I don't see why this shouldn't be just as good. Have you grasped everyone's names yet? I'm still in the state of hoping I'm giving the right name to the right person."

"Don't you know them all?" he asked. "I thought you were all friends."

"Well—friends of friends," replied Bridget. "There are several I'd never met before: Robert O'Hara, and you and Derrick Cossack, and the man who's flying—Timothy Grant. He's probably got there already and bagged the best bedroom. We haven't all got rooms in the hotel, some of us are parked out in chalets. Are you particular about 'sleeping-in'?"

"Not a bit. Park me out," he replied. "Now let me see if I can cope with all these names. Front names permitted?"

"Oh, yes. It's so much easier," she replied.

"Right. Now, three dark girls—Bridget, Pippa and Catherine—or Kate."

"Kate. She paints, I believe."

"And three fair girls, Jane, Daphne… and…"

"Jillian. She's the youngest of us all. Jane shares digs with Meriel and Daphne lives in the country. You're doing rather well."

"And two midway girls… the 'Ms'—Meriel and Martha. I haven't got the hang of the men yet, but who's the big tough?"

"Robert O'Hara, an Irishman, and Malcolm's pretty large, too."

"O'Hara," murmured Neville. "He doesn't look like one, or sound like one."

"No, and I don't think Malcolm looks like a schoolmaster," replied Bridget, "and neither do you look like a Civil Servant, although Nigel says you work in Whitehall in a government office."

"A government office? Not this trip, anyway," he laughed, and Bridget replied:

"It's like being let out of school, isn't it? I think we all feel the same—and getting away out of this foul weather's just too good to be true."

"It's good… and it's true, too," he replied.

3

By the time they reached Dover, most of the party had got to know each other's names and compared notes on previous winter sports experiences. Those who knew the ropes explained to those who didn't how the ski-ing schools were organised, about nursery slopes and ski lifts, about hiring equipment and reckoning currency, about costs of this, that and the other in Swiss francs and Austrian schillings. Jane said afterwards that she felt more and more with every minute that passed that ordinary work-a-day conditions of life had become unreal and far away. The immediate present seemed to blot everything else out. It was difficult to believe that half the party had only met the other half a couple of hours ago, because they seemed to be making a whole already, a group of happy excited people who took one another for granted and whose conversation turned on what they were going to do in Austria rather than what they did at home. The general effect was of spontaneous light-heartedness, a desire to please and be pleased.

By the time they reached Dover, the sky was heavily clouded, and the promised gale was blowing all right. When they queued up for passport inspection, they could see the cross-Channel steamer at the quayside swaying and tossing even in the shelter of the harbour, and there were anticipatory groans from many in the queue who knew what sort of crossing they were in for.

The inevitable wait, while the queue moved slowly past the passport officials, gave Jane a chance to study some of her less known travelling companions. Jane, who could still look a teen-ager in ski-ing kit, was twenty-seven, an observant, thoughtful, sensible lass who knew her way about, but she had a gift of laughter—and her laugh was a charming sound—as well as a keen sense of the ridiculous.

Everybody was clutching passports and heaving hand luggage along as best they could. Jane was quick to notice that Robert O'Hara's passport had a green cover, and she thought to herself, "So he is Irish, after all. I should never have guessed."

O'Hara grinned down at her—he was a very big fellow. "Why are passport photographs invariably such blots?" he observed. "Mine might be anybody—except me. It's a cross between a pugilist gone to fat and a reformed criminal."

"Mine doesn't even look reformed," said Jane. "It's like something from the staff of Belsen. Why are some people photogenic and some not? Biddy's is utterly ravishing, and Malcolm's has got that soulful sixth-form look which is so misleading—the hope of his side and the winner of the Head's personal prize for the most helpful boy in the school."

"Hi, it's quite a few years since I was in the Sixth," protested Malcolm, and Neville Helston put in:

"If you want a star-turn passport photograph, mine beats the band. It's frankly revolting. I feel indignant every time I'm identified by it."

"But the chaps hardly look at them," said O'Hara. "They get so blasé with the blinking things they just look at the date and stamp them. If Neville and I exchanged passports I don't suppose they'd even notice. What about trying it on?"

"Not me," replied Neville. "I'm going to Austria, and none of your Irish humour. If you want to get quodded, you can do it without any help from me."

"Quodded? Well I'm dashed, what a rotten suggestion," said O'Hara indignantly, as they lifted their suitcases again and staggered on towards the passport office while the wind howled louder and louder and the clouded sky grew darker, and the prospect of the Channel crossing grew ever more unattractive.

Chapter II

1

At the time that Bridget's ski-ing party was queueing up outside the passport office at Dover, Mrs. Mabel Stein was returning home by trolley bus from a visit to her married sister in Highgate. The fact that New Year's Day had fallen on a Monday had been very satisfactory to Mrs. Stein; she had a house off Red Lion Square which she let out in rooms, providing breakfasts also for those who liked to pay for them. Two of her lodgers were elementary school teachers, and they were away for the school holidays. The other two lodgers were young men, and both had told her that they were going out to parties to welcome the New Year in, and that they did not expect to be back to sleep, so the matter of breakfast did not arise.

Consequently, Mrs. Stein had treated herself to the unusual indulgence of a week-end away with her married sister. They had had a party, too, and had kept it up nearly all night, until the beer and stout and gin had all been lowered, and the melancholy of satiety had followed the merriment of indulgence. Mrs. Stein had gone up to bed about five o'clock in the morning and had not unnaturally slept until midday. She awoke with a bad head and a dry mouth, and a feeling that somebody else was to blame. Since Gert and Bob, Mrs. Stein's sister and brother-in-law, awoke with similar feelings, the mixed meal which followed had been an acrimonious one. Gert had called the meal "breakfast," but Bob expected dinner—his usual midday meal—and there had been some plain speaking. Mrs. Stein had rashly intervened on her sister's side, and had only been abused for her pains, and told a few home truths about Syd. Syd was Mrs. Stein's son, and, as she said, "Boys will be boys"—even though Syd did go a bit far.

As Mrs. Stein went home on her trolley bus, she reflected sadly that one had to pay for one's pleasures: her head "ached shocking" and her feet, encased in new shoes, ached worse than shocking. She looked out of the bus window at the dreary streets, her eyes rather blurred and uncertain. At one of the bus stops the street lamps lit a hoarding, and Mrs. Stein gazed at a big poster designed by a continental touring company. "Winter Sports", it proclaimed, and the words accompanied a vivid picture of snow peaks against a too-blue sky, with figures of skiers rushing down a gleaming slope.

"My, ain't that pretty," thought Mrs. Stein. "Must be a fair picture. Reminds me of something... can't remember what. Lor, my head does ache."

She alighted at Southampton Row and made her way eastwards. This was a neighbourhood which had suffered badly in the blitz of 1940, and the big rubble-covered spaces were now sparsely clad with grimy snow. Mrs. Stein had only walked a hundred yards from the bus stop when she saw a familiar figure approaching her and she said:

"Hallo, Syd. Had a good time? I shan't half be glad to get home. Me shoes are just about killing me."

"Say if we go out and have a nice cuppa," suggested Syd. This unexpected invitation was not welcome to Mrs. Stein; she knew her Syd too well.

"Not me," she replied. "I'm that tired I could drop. If you've got anything to say, you can tell me at home."

"Now don't you be awkward, Mum. I don't often ask you out," he protested.

"No, you don't," retorted Mrs. Stein, "and when you do, I know you been up to something. You come along home."

"What's the hurry?" he countered, and Mrs. Stein's aching head reinforced her dawning suspicions. She stood still and faced him.

"What d'you mean? What you been up to?" she demanded shrilly.

Syd took her by the arm. "Don't stand about in this per-ishing wind," he grumbled, but Mrs. Stein refused to budge until she realised that a policeman across the road had turned to look at them. Then, with a sinking heart, she tottered on in her high-heeled shoes. If Syd couldn't stand being looked at by a copper, he must have been up to something pretty bad. She walked on heroically for another hundred yards, then she said:

"I'm going home, and that's that. So just you don't be silly. Either tell me straight out, or else come home and talk it over. And if it's money again, I tell you I'm not having any. I'm not straight yet after your last little flutter."

"Better not go home yet," he said.

"Why not?"

"The house is on fire. Now don't start creating, Mum. There's no one at home, and you're insured, see?"

"Insured? You wicked…" She started forward, but her ankle turned in her unaccustomed shoe and she fell heavily, screaming with the pain of twisted ankle and the impact of kerb and pavement.

"Now then, what's all this?" demanded a gruff voice.

Mrs. Stein sat dizzily on the kerb stone, her aching head in her hands, while Syd replied to the constable:

"Turned her ankle, that's what she done, all along of this blasted snow. Got new shoes on, too. Here, Mum, up you gets. I'll find you a taxi. It's them shoes of yours."

Mrs. Stein let Syd pull her to her feet. She felt bad, but she had recovered her presence of mind. She'd always been respectable, and no copper had ever given her a dirty look, and she wasn't going to give this one a chance.

"That's right," she said. "Twisted me ankle. Silly of me. Ought to've been more careful. No. I'm not hurt, just a bit shaken up. Give me an arm, Syd. We'll soon be home."

"O.K., Mum," said Syd obligingly. "You've got some pluck. A real whopper you came. Why, there's a taxi. Better get in. You'll feel shaky after that. Better go to a chemist's and get a pick-me-up."

"Get a bandage round that ankle, ma'am," admonished the constable, as he assisted Mr. Stein's bulk into the taxi.

"Thanks a lot," she shrilled, as Syd said: "Shaftesbury Avenue and stop at a chemist's."

2

Mrs. Stein sat with her face in her hands for a moment. Then she pulled herself together.

"You'd better tell me, and no lies, mind. If you don't tell me straight, I won't help you out. One lie and I've done with you."

"I don't need to tell you lies," he said doggedly. "I been at Monty's—you know—and I was there until three o'clock, along of all of them. I went home, thinking I'd light the kitchen fire for you if you wasn't back. I knew as soon as I opened the door—full of smoke it was. I got out pretty quick. There wasn't nobody about, not a soul, and I suddenly thinks, 'Why not let it burn? Mum's insured, and we can get the insurance and start again somewhere else. Go to Australia or that.'"

"Get the insurance—and who's going to believe that?" she stormed. "Houses don't go setting themselves on fire. If you done this, Syd, you've got to face it and no help from me. That's fraud, that is, and it'll mean gaol if they prove you did it."

"I tell you I didn't do it. I couldn't've done it," he argued sullenly. "I was at Monty's till three, and when I got home the upstairs part was all burning. It hadn't just begun, I tell you."

The taxi-driver pulled up at a chemist's shop, and Syd helped Mrs. Stein across the pavement. Her ankle hurt her badly, blood was running down her calf from a cut knee, and her head was aching and confused. "I'd better get tied up and ask for a drop of something," she thought to herself. "This is going to take some sorting out, and Syd may be a wicked boy but I'm all he's got. I've got to help him."

The chemist was a kindly man; he bandaged Mrs. Stein's ankle, bathed her knee and plastered the cut, and finally gave her a draught. "You go straight home and lie down, ma'am," he advised her. "I don't think you'll have much trouble, but if the ankle's not better tomorrow, you see your doctor or go to the out-patients.'"

"Thanks ever so," said Mrs. Stein. The draught had steadied her and she felt herself again. She counted up the money in her purse, decided she'd got enough for the taxi fare and gave him the address. As the taxi moved off, the clanging bell of a fire engine sounded down the street and Mrs. Stein shuddered.

"Whatever did you do it for, Syd?" she groaned, as the taxi started.

"I tell you I didn't. I ain't done nothing," he protested sullenly. "Ain't done nothing" had been Syd's response to trouble since he could first speak. Mrs. Stein made no answer. She'd heard that one before.

3

Number 13, Lioncel Court, Mrs. Stein's home, was a corner house. It had been one of a row of six handsome, if decrepit, Georgian houses until October, 1940. Then a land mine had dropped five houses away. Two houses had been totally demolished, two more were pulled down by demolition squads, and two remained. Number eleven had been gutted by fire, but its sturdy party walls still helped to support number thirteen, which apart from broken glass had survived intact. Across the road the remaining houses were still boarded up, the blast having disposed of glass, plaster, doors and any other items less stable than the excellent Georgian brickwork. One day, numbers two to twelve were to be reconditioned, but at the time of the fire in number thirteen there were no neighbours to observe the beginnings of the catastrophe.

By the time the Fire Brigade arrived, the roof of number thirteen was flaming to high heaven, while sporadic snow hissed faintly on the blazing rafters. It was obviously in the top storey of the house that the fire had originated, and the firemen broke in on the ground floor and satisfied themselves that no inmates were in the two lower floors of the house.

By the time Mrs. Stein and Syd arrived on the scene, the fire hoses were reducing the flames to occasional splutters, and the neighbourhood reeked with the sour distressful fumes of charred and sodden woodwork. Mrs. Stein put on a very creditable act of amazement and despair. She would have rushed into the house, but police and firemen prevented her.

"Not that there's anybody in there, thank God!" she declared. "All gone for holidays, and me and Syd took the week-end off. I'd never've believed it could happen, not to an empty house. It do seem hard, it's me living, that house is, and right through the blitz it was never touched and now going a-catching fire because I took the first holiday I had in years."

"Might have been worse, Mum. It's only the top floor's burnt out. Your bits and pieces downstairs'll be all right when they've dried out. It's the water does half the damage," said a friendly fireman.

They took Mrs. Stein and Syd along to the nearby police station, because it was impossible for them to re-enter their own house yet. Even though the fire was under control, the smoke and heat and fumes made it dangerous—and the sergeant wanted a few details, as was always the case, the police explained. When Mrs. Stein was offered a chair in the comfortably warm fug of the charge-room, she slumped down in it and burst into tears. Her tears were quite genuine: she was so upset that a good cry was inevitable.

The big policemen were kindly souls: they produced a cup of tea, hot and strong, and put plenty of sugar in it, while Mrs. Stein sobbed out her story: how she hadn't had a holiday in years, letting rooms did tie you to a house, what with beds to make and breakfasts to cook and all the cleaning to do single-handed.

"Quite true, ma'am. Now you have that cup of tea. It'll

help pull you together," said the sergeant. "You've had a nasty shock, coming home and finding the place on fire."

"Not half I haven't, thanking you kindly," said Mrs. Stein, kicking her smart shoes off with a sob of relief. "I beg pardon, I'm sure," she said, "but I couldn't stand them any longer. I been at my sister's—Mrs. Lewis, that is—out by Highgate Archway. Saturday morning I went there, me own house being empty and everyone away and not coming back till tonight, or so they said. Gert was having a party and somehow we made a night of it, you know how it is..."

The police were patient and kindly, quite accustomed to dealing with Mrs. Steins. They knew already that she was a widow, that she took lodgers, and was known to be respectable. They noted down Gert's address and heard a few details about the party and being late to bed and oversleeping and not feeling too good after the party. "And your son was with you at your sister's house?" inquired the sergeant.

"Syd? Oh, no. Syd likes young folks. He didn't want to come to his auntie's," said Mrs. Stein, and Syd took up the story.

"I went and stayed with a friend, Mr. Monty White—got a flat off Euston Road, he has, and we went out dancing to the Euston Palais, and came home to Monty's and had a party, him and some of the boys. So I stayed the night there, and hadn't been home until I came along with Mum. I met her near Southampton Row and meant to take her out to tea, but she'd slipped on the snow and twisted her ankle and so I got a taxi for her."

The sergeant didn't think much of the look of Syd, nor of the way he gave his evidence, either.

"Yes. I see. You'll have been at work today, I take it?" he inquired, his experienced eyes on Syd's pasty face.

"No. I'm out of a job—having an 'oliday between jobs, so to speak," said Syd. "I was at Monty's till tea-time. Fact is, I'm not used to dancing half the night, and I knew I could have me sleep out, so I didn't bother."

"Just so," said the sergeant. "Where was your last job?"

"What's that got to do with you?" asked Syd truculently, but his mother cut in:

"Now that's no way to speak, Syd. The officer's been very kind and polite, and you mind your manners." She turned to the sergeant. "He was in Hardy's, in the Tot'n'am Court Road, up till Christmas. A packer, he was, but he found the work too heavy. Never been real strong, Syd hasn't. He was going to get a lighter job, and I said, 'Do you no harm to have a week off. You look peeked and that, and we can manage somehow.'"

"Thank you, ma'am," said the sergeant politely. "Now you just sit here and have a bit of a rest, and I'll see how things are shaping at your house."

He went out, leaving a constable in charge, and the latter found a stool for Mrs. Stein to rest her bandaged ankle on, and poured her out another cup of tea. "That's real kind, that is," she said. "I never been in a police station before, and I'd never've believed you'd be so kind. I felt that bad, what with one thing and another."

4

The sergeant returned with another officer: the former said to Mrs. Stein: "I'm afraid I've a nasty shock for you, ma'am. You said you believed the house was empty. That was not so. There was somebody in the second-floor front room. I'm sorry to say he died in the fire."

Mrs. Stein gave a cry, then she put her face in her hands

and sobbed. "...Couldn't've been. He went out Saturday, before I did. Mr. Gray that was. Said he wasn't coming back till tomorrow."

Still very patiently, but persistently, the police got the facts they needed from Mrs. Stein. She stopped crying and made a real effort to answer the questions sensibly. She had four lodgers, all men. Two school teachers, Mr. Bell and Mr. Rawlinson—they were away at their own homes. Mr. Stephen, in the top-floor back, was a commercial. Away a lot, he was, and she didn't expect him home tonight. Mr. Gray, he hadn't been with her long, he was a writer or newspaper man. Always quiet and well behaved and paid up regular.

"Do you know where he came from, or where his people live?" asked the sergeant.

"Now let me think," said Mrs. Stein, pressing her hands to her aching head. "He once said something about Liverpool, but I think he was an Irishman. What was it he told me... something about being able to get things in Ireland you can't get here. But I never asked him no questions. I don't believe in asking questions."

"How did he hear about you having a room to let?" inquired the sergeant.

"Oh, Mr. Barker sent him along. Mr. Barker at the newspaper shop. I always tell Mr. Barker when I've got a room to let. People asks at newspaper shops, along of them putting up notices for you—things to sell and that. And Mr. Barker's a good judge—he knows I don't want no married couples with children, and it saves trouble in the long run if you only take men... and I've always had a good name and kept the house respectable." Again Mrs. Stein put her face in her hands and wept. "I'm that tired," she sobbed. "Parties never did agree with me, and what with all this upset I just can't help it. D'you think he got drunk and came home mixed and set fire to 'imself? Not that I've ever known him mixed. But it was the New Year and that…"

5

It was the police who made arrangements for Mrs. Stein to stay the night at Mrs. Barker's—the newsagent's wife.

Mrs. Stein's house wasn't fit for her to go back to, they said, not tonight. Mrs. Barker, with the everlasting good nature of a real Cockney, said Mrs. Stein could sleep with her, and Syd could double in with Mr. Barker—it'd do for the night, wouldn't it, and both the police and Mrs. Stein agreed promptly that it would.

Having disposed, so to speak, of the problem of Mrs. Stein and Syd, the borough police were then free to concentrate on the results of the fire at number thirteen, in consultation with the officers of the Fire Service.

Inspector Brook of E Division accompanied the Senior Fire Officer, Captain Grant, up the malodorous stairs of Mrs. Stein's house, up the blackened, sodden, reeking stair carpet to the second floor, where the plaster had fallen in a discoloured shroud, mingled with charred remains of laths; up above the attic roof at the top of the house showed blackened beams, between which snowflakes fell dispiritedly from the dark skies. Police officers and fire officers alike are inured to grim sights and smells, but both men were glad when they were able to leave that reeking burnt-out bedroom and the remains of humanity which had fallen face forward against an old-fashioned gas fire.

Captain Grant produced a flask and the inspector swallowed a drink thankfully, while he coughed his lungs clear of smoke and wiped his stinging eyes. "What d'you make of it?" he inquired.

The fire officer snorted—a sound combining both physical and mental discomfort.

"I don't like it," he said. "You can argue that deceased was sitting in front of the gas fire. There was a bottle of Scotch on the floor—or the fragments of a bottle. Maybe he lowered the lot. The P.M. should tell us that. Maybe he was dead drunk. He fell asleep, and drunks sleep heavily. He tumbled forward, his face against the gas fire—and he never woke up. That it?"

"Might be," said Brook. "Or on the other hand, he was rendered unconscious and then shoved forward... and his clothing caught fire and the lino caught fire and then the bed and the cupboard or whatever it was in the corner."

"I'd like to know what there was in that cupboard, or on top of it," mused the fireman. "Stacks of newspaper and a few other combustibles by the look of it. Did you notice the curtains—or what was left of them, on the rings? Old-fashioned wool repp, still lined with black-out material. Wonderful the way that repp wears—more than a lifetime. And it takes a lot to make it burn. It doesn't flare, it just smoulders. Those curtains were drawn across the windows, you know. Makes you think."

"Umps... you mean the room could have smouldered for hours and nothing would have been seen outside. Assuming the chap fell forward, with his face against the gas fire, he'd have been suffocated pretty fast. He could have lain there, and his clothes would have caught fire. Cloth doesn't flare much. And we don't know how long the gas fire was alight. It's a shilling in the slot meter, but no knowing how much gas was left, or when the last shilling was put in."

"True enough," agreed the other. "Well, you've got a

corpse, unidentifiable: you've got a room in which most of the furniture is charred and all the fabrics virtually destroyed. Nothing like fire for destroying evidence. I'd give it as my opinion that the fire started in the way I suggested, and it burnt slowly. The chap's clothes may have smouldered for a long time before the fire got a real hold, and when it did get hold it was the inner corner of the room that burnt first—it was that cupboard which led the flames, as it were. Well, it's up to you."

"Was there a typewriter in that room?" asked Brook suddenly.

"I didn't see one—but it was still too hot to examine things properly. Why?"

"Mrs. Stein said he was a writer or a newspaper man," said Brook. "Our chaps know all about Mrs. Stein. She's been there for years and she's a good name as an honest decent sort of body, but that son of hers is a ne'er-do-well. Can't keep a job."

"I see," said Captain Grant.

That was all. Neither man needed to enlarge on what they "saw": their understanding was tacit but complete.

Before he took any further steps, Inspector Brook had a word with Mr. Barker, the newsagent. Barker was a stout wheezy soul, obliging and not unintelligent. The Inspector asked him about Mr. Gray, whom the newsagent had sent round to Mrs. Stein.

"Middle of November it was," said Barker. "Young chap came into the shop and asks about rooms, furnished or unfurnished. It's perishing hard to get rooms in central London, as you know. Mrs. Stein wasn't quite his cup of tea. He was a gentleman. But her house is clean and she's honest. You might go farther and fare worse, I tells him. Maybe it's shabby, but there's no livestock, you'll be treated straight, and it's respectable—if that's what you want. He grinned—nice-looking young chap, he was: 'That's what I want,' he says—and that's all there was to it. He ordered a *Mail* and a *Telegraph* and paid regular, but I hardly ever saw him again."

"Can you describe him?" asked Brook.

"He was tall, on the thin side, dark hair, good teeth, about twenty-five or six, I'd say. What you'd call a nice-looking young gent. Good class, too. It's a shocking thing, this is. He must've been tiddley—drunk as a lord, as they say."

Brook went back to number thirteen, thinking hard. He'd left a constable outside, and he found the man sheltering under the projection over the front door which served as a porch. The constable had his torch light directed on to the ground, and he was examining a mark in a muddy depression where a flagstone had broken away.

"What is it?" inquired Brook.

"I was just wondering what made that impression in the mud, sir. Like a wheel of sorts, laid flat."

Brook had a look. It was a small circle, about five inches across, with a sharp dented hole in the centre and four other marks, spaced within the ring as the spokes of a wheel might be placed. Brook scratched his head. "Reminds me of something... can't remember what," he said. "Find something to cover it up with. You never know..."

He went upstairs again, into the burnt-out bedroom, and deliberately considered possibilities. Then he sent one of his men to telephone to the gas office. It was just when he had given this order that a recollection flashed into his mind. Perhaps it was the desultory snow which helped the reminder. Last winter Brook had watched the Norwegians ski-jumping on Hampstead Heath... imported snow, he remembered. "That's a funny thing," he said. He had realised that the impression in the mud below Mrs. Stein's porch was the same size and shape as the ring and point made by a ski-stick. It was, he recollected, a very characteristic mark: once you'd seen it you remembered it. "Ski-ing," he said slowly. "Who… and why? About the last thing you'd connect with this place."

Chapter III

1

While Inspector Brook ruminated over the impression which a ski-stick might—or might not—have left in the mud outside the front door of Mrs. Stein's house, Bridget's party settled down in their reserved compartments on the Calais-Basle express. The Channel crossing was behind them: it had been about as rough as a Channel crossing could be, and the party of fifteen had broken up into small units and chosen their own way of surviving "La Manche". Some stout-hearted souls had sat in the saloon and eaten toasted buns—young Cossack upheld the tradition of the Navy in this way, accompanied by "the last man," Neville Helston, and the Irishman, O'Hara. Cossack had never done any ski-ing, and the other two seemed to know all about it, and could discuss the famous Swiss ski-runs as well as the trials of beginners. While these three ate a solid tea, Malcolm, the schoolmaster, sat in the bar with the two doctors; Ian Dexter found a private corner and was seen by nobody else in the party during the hour and a half that the sturdy vessel banged her way through the ill-tempered sea. The girls of the party scattered to various parts of the ship, but at Calais everybody seemed in good health and excellent spirits, and none had the loathsome greenish pallor of the recently sea-sick.

Bridget had distributed the reservation tickets for the Basle train without bothering to sort out the parties. It had been vaguely intended that the girls should share one compartment and the men the other, leaving two men to their purgatorial hard seats in the third-class compartment elsewhere in the train, and one man—the Irishman—to fend for himself, since only twelve couchettes had been available. As the final arrangement worked out, however, Kate Reid (the oldest of the party) and Meriel Parsons found themselves sharing sleeping quarters with Frank Harris, Malcolm Perry, Ian Dexter and Neville Helston. Malcolm, being well provided in the way of French currency, decided to have dinner in the restaurant car, and Dr. Harris went with him, so Meriel and Kate unpacked their food parcels and invited Ian and Neville to join them in a picnic meal. They were just starting to feed when they saw O'Hara in the corridor, and invited him to join them, too. Nothing loath, he came in, a tall strapping dark fellow with a rather endearing grin.

"Jolly nice of you," he said. "I'm in rather a poor way. Having joined the party at the last moment, I haven't got any sleeping reservation. I've been walking up and down the train trying to induce one of the conductors to find me a sleeper or couchette or something. The train's pretty full and it looks as though I'm going to have a poor night."

"I feel rather bad about this," said Helston. "I'm really the gate-crasher. I didn't tag on to the party until a few days ago. You really ought to have my couchette, O'Hara."

"No, rather not. You've got Nigel's reservation, that's fair enough," replied the Irishman. "I don't want to pinch anybody else's place. I shall find something."

Kate Reid observed the party with lively amusement. She, like Meriel, had not met any of the three men previously, and it was entertaining to see how five strangers could settle down together over a picnic supper as though they had been friends for a long time.

"What part of Ireland do you come from, Robert?" asked Ian Dexter. The latter was a fair lad, rather quiet and serious at first glance, Kate had noticed, but he had a mischievous smile which altered his face completely.

"County Kerry," replied O'Hara. "Why? D'you know it?"

"No, but I've been in Dublin," replied Ian. "If you're a southern Irishman, why do you speak like an Englishman? There's nothing Irish about you."

"Well, I went to school in England," replied O'Hara, and Neville Helston put in:

"The Irish and Scots are all alike. They adore their own countries. They can hardly speak of their dear homelands without tears in their eyes, but they take jolly good care not to live in said homelands."

Kate laughed. "That's perfectly true," she said. "All the enterprising Scots come to London, or else emigrate to the Commonwealth, because there's more money to be made outside Scotland than there is in it. But they all join hands and weep and sing 'Auld Lang Syne' on the steps of St. Paul's on New Year's Eve, and the Irish are just as illogical. Own up, Robert: you despise the English, don't you—in comparison with the Irish—but your Irish parents sent you to an English public school so that for the rest of your life you'd sound like an Englishman."

"I don't believe he is Irish," said Ian mischievously. "It's just an affectation. He was probably born in Wigan."

"Have another egg," said Meriel hospitably. "What does it matter if he's Irish or not? He says he can ski. If he can't, that'll give him away. It's awfully dangerous to say you can ski, especially if you haven't done it for some time. You try to demonstrate a Christie, muff it and cross your skis and then you're sunk."

O'Hara took the egg in one hand and produced his green passport with the other. "Do you know what this is?" he demanded.

Ian Dexter promptly seized the passport and studied the photograph in it. "Glory, what a tough!" he said. "I don't believe that's a photo of you at all, Robert. This chap must be double your weight."

"I've lost weight this past year," said O'Hara. "I've been farming, and you can't get enough food in England to keep your weight up if you're doing heavy work."

"That's definitely phony," said Meriel. "Farming may not always make money, but there's always plenty of food on a farm, good times or bad."

Neville Helston had seized O'Hara's passport from Ian. "It's not a bad photograph," he said. "Apart from the fact that he's thinner, it's really quite like him. Those big lamps he wears change his dial a bit, but otherwise I'd say it's a truthful representation of an ingenuous countenance."

"Is it?" said O'Hara wrathfully. "What's yours like?"

"Oh, mine's slanderous," replied Helston. "It has all my bad points and none of my good ones. I showed it to Nigel and he said it showed every known facial symptom of mental defect—but the chap at Dover and the French bloke on the boat both seemed quite satisfied with it." He drew the passport out of his pocket and Ian Dexter opened it and gave a yell of joy.

"But this one's utterly frightful. It's sub-human," he said.

O'Hara promptly seized it. "On the contrary," he said. "It's a perfectly good likeness. It's got that half-baked look which is the hallmark of the English gentleman. It's worthy of a place in a museum, I admit. By the way, weren't you at Cambridge?" he added to Helston.

"No. I was at Oxford—Univ.—but before your time."

"Did you row?" asked O'Hara, and Dexter began to laugh.

"That was the most unkindest cut of all," he said. "Anyway, Oxford hasn't rowed for years. They paddle, instead."

"When everybody's finished insulting everybody, say if we decide about the bunks," put in Kate. "The man's just coming round to fix them up. There are three each side. Meriel and I have bagged the bottom ones. Ian and Neville have the next choice."

"I'll have the top floor facing the engine," said Ian. "The top ones are the only ones you can read in, because the lower ones don't get any light. Who's going to deal with the windows? That's the chief problem. If you keep the window shut everybody dies of heat, the temperature by midnight will be simply terrific, but if you open the window the people in the top bunks die of cold—and it's still freezing hard outside."

"You'd better leave me to cope with the window," said Kate. "I'll open it at intervals, when the heat gets really unbearable."

"Can't we leave the corridor door open?" asked Meriel, but Kate replied:

"If you do, nobody will sleep at all. The light shines in, and people go to and fro all night. You won't sleep much anyway, but lying down is better than sitting up—and no night lasts for ever, as Swinburne didn't say. Now we shall have to heave everything off the luggage racks, because they convert into the top bunks. Wake up, Robert, get your traps down: glory, we do seem to have got a lot of junk between us. Who's is the rucksack?"

"Mine," said Helston. "Here, leave it to me, it weighs a ton… Sorry, Dexter, you should keep your head out of the way."

The next few minutes were a confusion, as the attendant pulled the upper bunks down from their brackets, arranged blankets and pillows and chattered in a medley of rapid French and incomprehensible English. By the time his job was done, the only thing to do was to "go to bed," since it was impossible to sit on the lower bunks because the next tier allowed no head-room. Malcolm and Frank came back from the restaurant car, and Robert O'Hara had to find quarters elsewhere. Helston called out to him: "If you come back here in about four hours' time we could change over—you can have my bunk and I'll take over any place you've managed to scrounge."

"Well, O'Hara had better be careful he comes to the right compartment," said Frank Harris. "Remember the lights will be out, and if you go climbing the ladder to the top bunk in the wrong compartment your motives may not be clear to the occupant. It's all very well to laugh, but it wouldn't be so funny if it really happened. It's very confusing once the lights are out."

Meriel broke down into hopeless giggles. The whole situation looked so bizarre to one fresh to the continental couchette. Malcolm had already climbed up into his middle bunk and was removing shoes, coat, collar and tie methodically, while Ian Dexter sat on the bunk above doing likewise, draping his belongings about him while he said: "You could write a glorious farce about mistaken identities. Some chappy getting on to somebody else's bunk while the occupier goes for a walk."

Kate had already rolled herself on to her lower bunk, turned her face to the wall and was pretending to go to sleep, while the train banged its way noisily over a track which seemed much bumpier than an English permanent way. She knew she wasn't going to be able to sleep—the heat, the stuffiness, the noise and the vibration all combined to make sleep difficult. About half-past nine Frank Harris turned the lights out and everybody settled down to get what sleep they could. Kate had a short nap and woke up feeling half-boiled and desperately thirsty. She had a drink from Meriel's big Thermos, and then crept cautiously out of her bunk and let the window down a little, breathing in the cold air gratefully. She decided to leave the window open a bit and got back on her couchette and tried to sleep again. It was about midnight that she heard someone move in one of the upper bunks: the occupant climbed cautiously down the ladder and crept to the door. As the door was opened the light from the corridor shone across the compartment and Kate turned her face to the wall and asked herself—as all continental travellers ask themselves at some stage of the journey—if it was really worth while coming away at all. Then one of the men in the upper bunks began to sneeze; remembering the snow outside, Kate got up again and closed the window—this always happened, she thought. You've either got to be too hot or too cold. Rolling back again on to the bunk, she resigned herself to hours of wakefulness—and then fell asleep, her slumbers interspersed with awareness of jolts and bangs and thirstiness and the odd smell of French trains.

2

It was about five o'clock that Kate finally decided she would give up pretending to be asleep, and would make the best of such washing accommodation as French trains provided. Collecting her sponge bag and towel from the grip on the floor beside her, she staggered cautiously to the door and got out into the lighted corridor, where she found quite a number of travellers who were preparing to get out at Mulhausen. The train was due at Basle about half-past six, and Kate reckoned she had time for a leisurely wash before the queue of later would-be washers formed up. The plumbing looked better than she had hoped, but in contradistinction to English trains the cold water did not run at all and the hot water was boiling so hard that it only emerged in spasmodic drips and splutters—but any water was better than none at all, and after sponging her face she tidied herself up and felt better. Emerging from the exiguous toilet into the corridor, she found, as she had expected, that a number of other people had had the idea of getting up early. Robert O'Hara was one of them, and he looked distinctly disillusioned and the worse for wear.

"Hallo, what sort of night have you had?" inquired Kate.

"Pure H," he replied. "I sat bolt upright for hours and about two I couldn't bear it any longer, so I stood and I strolled and I cursed and I swore and other people swore back at me. However, we're nearly through. Breakfast at Basle. Glorious thought!"

"Why didn't you come and take turns on Neville's couchette?" she asked. "I believe he cleared out about midnight, probably expecting you to take his place."

"Did he? I didn't really think he meant it when he made

the offer. Anyway, I was miles down the train. Some people got out at Lille and I thought I was going to have several places to myself, but it filled up at the next stop. The chaps you really ought to sympathise with are those two in the thirds—the slums, so to speak. They look properly browned off. Sitting bolt upright on hard benches for twelve hours is sheer purgatory. Hallo, here's Dexter. Sleep well, little man?"

"Not all that. Those couchette things give me claustrophobia," said Dexter. "What hopes of a shave? Do the taps run?"

"The hot one only: it issues boiling water in occasional drips," said Kate. "I wish you luck with it."

3

It was still dark when they reached Basle, and they felt anything but their best as they trooped past the passport office windows and were inspected by officials who didn't really seem to take much interest in them. The Swiss officers were so accustomed to these parties of English skiers that they regarded them with benevolent amusement and the formality was soon over. Bridget counted her party into the Arlberg express with a sigh of relief. This train took them right through to Austria, and Bridget said to Jane:

"Well, that's that. We've got them here and not lost anybody en route and we shall be at Langen by two. Now for breakfast. Coffee! Lovely thought!"

By the time the fragrant coffee was being poured into the big thick cups, the dawn was breaking and the whole party brightened up. It was Frank Harris who said:

"I feel as though we've been let off the lead. For the next few weeks we can disregard everything but ourselves and our skis. No newspapers, no radio, no letters unless we really want them. The international situation can be forgotten, the Labour Government can be ignored: unofficial strikes, ration cards and the fuel crisis need not affect us. It's quite an awe-inspiring thought."

"No newspapers, no radio," murmured Daphne Melling. "It's quite a thought. My revered Papa insists on listening to the news thrice daily almost as though it were a religious obligation. We live in an atmosphere conditioned by Korea, United Nations and the Iron Curtain. Is it really true that I shan't have to hear about them? I don't mean to be flippant, but I don't see that it really helps the world if I am depressed three times a day. Oh, look—what's that river?"

"The Rhine, my child. You may have heard of it," said Frank, and Jillian, the youngest of the party, said:

"It's rather marvellous. Anything can happen while we're away and we just shan't know."

"If you really want to know, you can doubtless order an air-mail copy of *The Times*," said Frank. "If you're homesick, you can put a personal call through to Much Binding in the Marsh and a patient telephone operator in Vienna will connect you for the sum of about two hundred Austrian schillings. For myself, I'm prepared to make an act of faith that my country, my family, my patients and my dog will continue to thrive without me."

"And if they don't, it'll be just too bad," said Ian Dexter, his eyes lighting up with a sort of mischievous zest. "For myself, I shall forget all embarrassments, debts, peccadilloes and serious offences. The answer to all callers is 'Gone abroad. Left no address.' If anybody wants me, they can come and find me—on skis. If pressed too hotly, I vanish into Russian occupied territory. It won't be so far away, you know."

"Who on earth wants to go into Russian occupied

territory?" asked Derrick Cossack. "Lots of people want to get out of it, but that's a different story."

"Mittel Europa," said O'Hara. "We could get anywhere—they can't patrol all the mountains. Ski into the unknown."

"And land up head first in a snow drift some hundred yards from your starting point," said Harris.

Meriel called from the next table: "He says he can ski. Perhaps he'll enter for the International Ski Race at Lech—or change identities with a Czech. Can you talk Czech, Robert?"

"He can't even talk Irish," retorted Ian.

Chapter IV

1

"So it seems to be our pigeon, Brook," said Chief Inspector Rivers.

The C.I.D. man was talking to Inspector Brook of E Division about the case of the dead man whose body had been found in Lioncel Court. Scotland Yard had been consulted in the matter and Rivers had gone over the evidence with Brook and the Fire Service officers. The Chief Inspector's first suggestion had surprised Brook a little, for Rivers had had the slot machine of the gas fire in the burnt-out bedroom opened by the gas people and the coins in it examined for fingerprints.

"It may be quite futile, but the only hope of identifying deceased for certain is by getting his fingerprints in the hope that we may get something to compare them with," said Rivers. "The hands of the dead man are too badly burnt to give us prints, but it's to be assumed that he put the coins in the meter himself, so we ought to be able to get his prints."

The result of this intelligent idea had been so successful

that Rivers had been almost apologetic when telling Brook about it: one of the things which endeared Julian Rivers to the men who worked with him was his diffidence—he always spoke deprecatingly of his own brain-waves.

"It was one of those flukes," he said to Brook. "There was about one chance in a few millions that his prints were in our records, and it happened to come off. It's an odd story. We've got the fingerprint record though we don't know the chap's identity. We only know we want him—badly. You remember the Post Office case—in Beacon Lane?"

Brook nodded. The whole of the Metropolitan Police knew the Beacon Lane case. It had been an exceptionally daring and skilful robbery from a small City post office, shortly before Christmas. The post office was in a building otherwise occupied by offices. Access had been gained by the roof, and Rivers described it to Brook.

"It was pretty certain that two men at least co-operated on the job. The chap who opened the safe was a pro, an oxyacetylene expert, but the chap who did the breaking in was a new practitioner so far as we are concerned. He did a piece of climbing which I should have said was impossible, especially when you remember the fall of snow we had. I went over the most probable approach with Deakin, and I tell you we were roped pretty carefully. It was one of those ancient rabbit warrens in which old buildings and new are muddled up together; the tilt of some of the roofs was enough to scare the skin off a cat, to say nothing of shinning up pipes with hardly any handhold and no foothold to speak of. I've done a bit of rock climbing and any amount of roof scrambling and I tell you I was scared stiff, and that was in daylight after the snow had melted. Our devil-may-care lad did the same thing at night, with a few inches of treacherous frozen snow over everything, and he got in by the skylight. If it hadn't been for his subsequent behaviour I'd have felt a sneaking liking for him. He'd got the sort of nerves and fortitude you found in the Commandos. It must have been hell on those roofs the night he did it."

Brook nodded. "Wonderful what they'll do rather than earn an honest living," he said. "So you got his fingerprints?"

"Yes—by a bit of sheer bad luck for him. They didn't leave any prints on the job—they were much too spry for that, but sometime, during the course of that climb, a packet of cigarettes must have fallen out of his pocket. It bounced down the slope of the roof and landed in a dry spot under a jutting-out coping stone. I saw it lying there, and I went down that damned roof after it, with slates skidding and my heart in my mouth—it was as ramshackle a bit of roof as you like. I got it—and got the prints, too. Clear as say-so. They're the same prints we got from the coins in the slot meter." Rivers paused. "D'you believe in luck, Brook?"

Brook scratched his head and refused to be drawn. Abstractions were not his long suit and he was a bit wary of Julian Rivers' agile mind. "I don't know, sir."

"Well, I admit that I believe that luck, or chance, holds the final trump," said Rivers. "Take the chap who did that climb. He studied his terrain all right. He started his climb from a garage roof two blocks away, and he went up and down, traversing, gaining here a little and there a little. It wasn't luck that got him to the skylight in Beacon Lane: it was skill and judgment, physical endurance and fortitude. He reached the skylight, forced it, got in—swinging like a monkey: he went downstairs to the basement, unbolted a heavy door and admitted the pro who tackled the safe. The pro walked out by the basement door, which was bolted again by the climber.

The latter went up to the skylight again, got out, took the trouble to screw down the skylight from the outside, so that it appeared secure from inside, and retraced his route over the roofs. Somewhere he dropped his packet of cigarettes: he probably didn't notice it at the time. It was a whitish packet and would have looked like the snow. That was just sheer bad luck—and his bad luck held. The packet fell in a dry spot, so we got his fingerprints."

Brook grunted. "They think they can foresee everything," he said. "They can't."

"No, fortunately for us," said Rivers. "Without the element of chance I might be out of a job. Well, having regained the ground, our lad had a nasty shock. He found himself face to face with a porter who was on his way to Covent Garden. Our lad hit him—scientifically and efficiently, dead on the point. The porter went down like a log, as the saying is, and the back of his head hit the stump of a cut-off railing and disorganised his cervical vertebrae just where they're most vulnerable. He died in hospital some hours later, but he recovered consciousness enough to tell us what he'd seen." Rivers paused, and then went on: "It adds up, doesn't it? Fingerprints on the cigarette carton: manslaughter or murder, according to the way the jury looks at it: and now the prints on the coins in the gas meter, added to your impression of a ski-stick in the mud. I like that last bit," he added. "It fits in with the picture. A climber who wasn't afraid of frozen snow on steep tilted roofs: he probably liked the snow. It gave him a feeling of confidence because he was used to climbing above the snow line. And he was a skier—ever done any ski-ing, Brook?"

"No, sir. I saw those Norwegians ski-jumping, though. I thought it the hell of an exciting business. Climbing and ski-ing—nerve, balance, and then nerve again, that it?"

"That's it. Apart from ski-jumping, there's ski-running. In the international races they come down the slopes about forty miles an hour, crouching, balanced to a degree that's miraculous, every muscle, every ounce of weight coordinated to keep them at one with their skis as they swing and turn, using their sticks to add to their momentum, and at the bottom they brake in a few yards, grinding the edges of their skis in to bite the snow, while their knees and ankles take the strain of that sudden deceleration. Gad, it's one of the best things I know."

"So you're a skier, too, are you, sir?" asked Brook, almost startled by the sudden liveliness of Rivers' grey eyes. He was a sleepy-looking chap as a rule, thought Brook, but he didn't look sleepy now. Rivers laughed, his face resuming its normal placidity. "I've done a bit," he said. "I went to Scheidegg every year in the '30s, and I went to St. Anton last year, and to Carinthia in '48. It's a thing you never quite forget, like swimming, but I floundered like a beginner for an hour or two when I started again in '47. This is a new one on me, Brook. I've never been after a skier before. I wonder where he's gone."

2

"Gone, sir?" Brook looked at the Scotland Yard man with some astonishment. The E Division Inspector was a very competent officer—he would not have been appointed Inspector in that division otherwise—but he preferred to keep in line with his evidence and not get ahead of it. "You mean you suspect the deceased is not the man who lived in that room and who put the coins in the slot meter?"

"That's just what I do mean, Brook," said Rivers. "I don't often make psychic bids, and when I do I generally keep them to myself, but you recognised the print of that ski-stick and you had the imagination to realise it might mean something. That was imagination, you know. It may be the crux of the whole case and not one man in ten would have registered the impression and recognised it, so it seems only fair to tell you what I make of the bits and pieces if you'd like to listen."

Brook suddenly grinned. "I'd like to all right, sir. I'd never thought of myself as having imagination. I'm careful, I'll say that. I know it's often a very small thing which sets the whole thing going—but anyway, if you'll tell me what you do make of it, I'll hold it as a privilege and I tell you so straight."

"And you can tell me straight when you think I go off the rails," said Rivers. "I'm thinking of this lad who went roof climbing—Gray, he called himself, though I bet it wasn't his name. It wasn't the first time he'd played that game. We've had one or two robberies up and down the country which were assumed to be inside jobs because the premises showed no signs of having been broken into. It's possible we might have come to the same conclusion about this one, because the skylight had been screwed down very securely and anyway it was the deuce of a business reaching it from the leads. My own idea of Gray is that he's some anti-social young limb who's gone off the rails and who took to stealing to make good his debts or defalcations. And then, with the loot on him, he found himself face to face with a working man who guessed he'd been up to no good. Gray hit him, and the chap died—we broadcast, asking for witnesses, and Gray would have seen how he stood."

"But he'd have thought there was nothing to connect him with it," said Brook.

"Would he?" asked Rivers. "He'd got a sense of detail, you know. The way he screwed up that skylight showed that. He used an old rusted screw and turned it right in and saw to it there were no splinters. Oh yes, he used his brains all right. A chap like that would remember he'd had a packet of fags in his pocket. And they'd gone. He wouldn't have known where he lost them, but he'd have known his fingerprints were on them. He knew he'd killed a man, though he didn't know how much that man told us before he died."

"Yes. I'm beginning to get you," said Brook.

"Well, that's the picture," went on Rivers. "A fellow who was capable of climbing those roofs and making no mistake while doing it: he'd got courage to the verge of recklessness and skill and judgment in physical exploits. If he were caught, he faced a long term of imprisonment—a life sentence, maybe—or the chance of being hanged for murder. As I see it, Gray wasn't the sort of lad who'd got the other variety of courage which we call moral courage. He couldn't face up to what he'd done and the thought of imprisonment was too much for him. Maybe he was claustrophobic—the prospect of being locked up maddened him. In my experience, men with his sort of reckless physical courage and hardihood do fear imprisonment. My guess is that he determined to get away while the going was good, and in the getting he killed somebody else, started the fire to make his victim unidentifiable, and walked out."

Brook pondered. "You're thinking the victim tried to cash in on Gray's loot, sir. They got away with a lot of cash in that post office job, and taking your reconstruction of Gray's character, he was one to hit first and think afterwards. Not a good chap to threaten."

"There's that," admitted Rivers, "but my argument's along another line. It's the impression of the ski-stick I'm thinking of. There weren't any ski-sticks in that burnt-out bedroom, and Mrs. Stein had never seen any skis or ski-sticks in that room. She knows what skis are—she's seen them at the flicks. But someone brought a ski-stick to that house."

Brook's orthodox mind was beginning to be infected by the livelier mind of the C.I.D. man: up till now, Brook had been plodding away at familiar issues, motives and actions which were the commonplace of police experience. A burglar, just getting away with the doings in his pockets, often turned violent if someone got in his way: that same burglar, sitting pretty on the proceeds of his coup, might turn nasty if some snooper butted in and demanded a rake-off: that was all according to Cocker, but the Chief Inspector was thinking along different lines. In retrospect, Brook visualised those Norwegian skiers: something outside routine altogether, something almost fantastic. For the first time in his official career, Brook leapt ahead of his evidence and propounded a fantastic theory to a superior officer.

"Some other bloke turned up at number thirteen, complete with skis and ski-sticks and all the doings, and Gray laid him out, pinched the skis, and went off to Norway as cool as brass—or wherever it is they do go?" he hazarded madly.

Rivers chuckled. "Bravo, Brook. That's the sort of stuff we want to work on. And it's not so plumb crazy as you're thinking it is. We've got a few items of evidence to encourage us."

"Have we, sir?" asked Brook hopefully.

"Let's look at what we have got," said Rivers placidly. "First, that newsagent described Mr. Gray, who applied for rooms, as 'a gentleman'. Now I know that word is unpopular in these democratic days, but elderly London newsagents of the type of Barker do use the word with precision. They mean something by it: most often a professional man as differentiated from a tradesman, and men like Barker are often very acute at diagnosing the difference. Very well: Gray, as he called

himself, though I'm quite sure it wasn't his name, was a gentleman, possibly a public school or university man. It's the
ski-ing element that made me suggest a public school. Ski-ing
isn't everybody's sport. It didn't come my way as a youngster."

"Nor mine," said Brook feelingly.

"It's not uncommon for the public schools to organise
parties of boys who're taken winter sporting with a school
master in charge," went on Rivers, "and having suggested that
point, I'll tell you how it may suggest a plan of action to us. It
isn't often that educated fellows turn into cat burglars. The
fact that this fellow behaved as he did implies some sort of
story behind it—a build-up, so to speak. My guess is that he
got himself into trouble of some kind, like getting into debt,
gambling to retrieve it, and then helping himself to money
not his own. Forging a cheque is quite a likely offence as a
suggestion. Now we haven't got any record of his fingerprints
apart from those on the cigarette packet, so he has never been
sentenced. My idea is that he got himself into trouble but
wasn't prosecuted."

Brook nodded. He was on familiar ground again now.
This was the sort of reconstruction he could follow. "Yes, I've
known that happen," he agreed. "A good old firm of lawyers
or stockbrokers, for instance; they know the young fellow's
parents and refrain from prosecuting to save the parents dis-
tress. The thief is sacked, of course, and in my experience
such young fellows go from bad to worse."

"Of course this is all guess work," said Rivers cheerfully,
"but I think we've got enough data to send out an all stations
inquiry. We give the best we can in the way of a description,
based on information from Barker and Mrs. Stein: we add
the probability that the chap was a climber and a skier, and
that he may have left his job or been summarily dismissed

within the last year. It's pretty thin, but it's surprising what odd items of information come the way of the police force one way or another."

Brook agreed—he knew that last bit was true—and then he returned to the subject of the ski-stick and its impression in the mud. "What's your idea of how that ski-stick came to be set down, sir?"

Rivers laughed. "I could make you up a dozen explanations, with chapter and verse. My most probable explanation is this: that another fellow came to call on Gray and brought the ski outfit with him. He may have come to borrow some odd bit of equipment he hadn't got, or to ask advice from Gray as an old hand. He put down his stuff on the doorstep when he rang the bell and that was how the impression of the stick was made. I don't think Gray would have done it. As I said, he's got a sense of detail."

Rivers paused while he lit another cigarette. "I'll admit I've been suggesting a lot of possibilities for which there is no evidence at all. What I'm going on is my own assessment of the character of the man who climbed over those roofs. He reached his objective, as they say. He doubtless got away with at least a thousand pounds in cash, assuming they divided the loot. I just don't believe that the chap I believe Gray to be, got drunk and went to sleep in his room, so that he fell into a gas fire and never woke up. It's out of character. Neither do I believe that he let another chap dope him or bat him over the head, though I'm willing to believe the converse."

Brook nodded: he was thinking very hard, and he added his own suggestion. "The converse," he said slowly. "Gray murdered another man. He must have had a pretty strong motive to do that. Did the other chap know what Gray had already done—or did Gray think we were after him, and try to put us off by leaving a corpse which could pass for his own?"

"I think the latter is a point worth considering," said Rivers. "Have we got some information filed away somewhere which could lead us to Gray? I'll consult Records about that one. Meantime, we've got a lot of routine stuff to do. We want information about anybody seen in the neighbourhood carrying skis, or a taxi-man who picked up a fare carrying skis or ski-sticks."

"New Year's Day. It was a beast of a day," said Brook. "Came over dark as pitch and snowing a blizzard. Not the sort of day people do notice things. It's a pity that house is so isolated. No neighbours, nobody passing. There's one thing I'd meant to tell you, sir, but maybe you won't think it's relevant."

"Let's have it. If it's something you've noticed it may be worth a lot, Brook."

"That son of Mrs. Stein's, sir. Syd, she calls him. I reckon Syd's a wrong 'un. He got sacked from his last job for suspected theft. Nothing proved—just here's your money and quit. And he's in with some nasty flash friends. I'm not satisfied in my mind about Syd. If it hadn't been for all this other stuff we've been discussing, I'd have been giving Syd the biggest roasting I dared."

"Why not?" said Rivers. "What sort of a chap is this Syd? Amateur pugilist, or anything of that kind?"

"Lord, no. He's a wretched little weed," said Brook. "One of these snivellers. But I'm not satisfied with his account of how he spent the afternoon. It seems to me he might have gone home before he said he did. You see, his mother was well covered by insurance."

"I see," said Rivers. "That's an old story. But what's your theory about Syd? Do you believe he started the fire? If that's the idea, we shall have to begin thinking all over again."

"No, sir, I don't think he started the fire," said Brook, in his careful way. "That fire started in Gray's bedroom, and from what we know of Gray, he wasn't the sort of chap Syd could have tackled. Apart from his poor physique, Syd's not the violent type. He's a sneak thief if ever I saw one. My idea is that Syd might have gone home earlier in the afternoon, realised the house was on fire and decided it wasn't a bad idea to let it burn and cash in on the insurance. And I'd say he was an inquisitive cuss. Maybe he went and had a look to see which room was burning—anything in this for me? so to speak. Pinch what he could before the fire got too fierce. Anyway, there's a chance he knows something useful if we could only get it out of him."

"That's quite an idea," said Rivers. "Let me have all the details about him you've got, and we'll do the roasting together. Two of us will be even more impressive than one, though I should say you've got quite a technique of your own with the Syds of this world."

"I've had quite a bit of practice, sir, and I'm well up in local conditions," replied Brook. He grinned—a pillar of the Metropolitan Police, blossoming out under the encouragement of Chief Inspector Rivers, C.I.D. Julian Rivers generally got the best out of the men he worked with, because he worked with them and not over them.

Chapter V

1

The six or seven hours in the train between Basle and Langen were the pleasantest part of the long journey for Bridget and her party. Crossing Switzerland in daylight was a very different matter from rumbling across France at night. Once they were beyond Zürich the mountains seemed to close in on them, and in the latter hours of the journey they had the thrill of seeing others doing what they had come to do themselves, as they watched the tiny figures of distant skiers come flying down the slopes with the precision and speed of animated toys. The party was broken up into small groups in different compartments, and the travelling companions of the night found themselves talking to those whom they had previously known only by sight and by a hopefully guessed front name.

Jane Harrington sat next to Malcolm Perry; the latter was a schoolmaster at Sherbury, and Jane felt that here was somebody who conformed to type in the pleasantest sense of the word. He was a classical scholar, but not oppressively scholarly, Jane decided: at least his erudition (which she was prepared to take for granted) sat lightly on him. His eyes were amused and amusing and he sat back with a comfortable indolence, neither restless nor impatient nor excited, but "definitely not missing much," as Jane put it.

"Have you got everybody sorted out yet?" she asked him.

"I think so. Fifteen of us, nobody married. Everybody with a job, highly individual and professional."

Jane considered the smiling eyes, and decided the look of indolence was but a cloak to a character in which the critical and analytical were well developed.

"If one were married one couldn't come dashing away for jaunts like this," she observed.

"True. It has its points," he rejoined.

Kate Reid put in a word here. "How did you find out that nobody's married?" she inquired.

"None of the girls wear a wedding ring and none of the men has mentioned a wife," he replied.

"Do they always?"

He laughed and turned to study Kate's quizzical face: she was considerably older than the rest of them and was quite obviously a person who was capable of taking what Malcolm would have described as a "disinterested interest" in any topic she pursued, without regard to what her vis-à-vis might be thinking of her. "The answer to both is in the affirmative," he replied, and then added: "in my experience, that is."

She laughed. "Very wise of you to add the proviso. I don't jump at conclusions myself, although I knew you were a schoolmaster within five minutes of meeting you."

"Why?"

"Because you said 'last term'. All school people do it, whether they mean to or not."

"I suppose we do," he agreed. "Have any of the others similar identifying habits?"

"Nothing that's quite so like a reflex," she replied. "Doctors are always easy to talk to because they're conditioned to it. Ian talks about Cambridge—incidentally, he's older than the average undergraduate, isn't he?"

"Yes. He didn't go to the university until after he'd done his term in the Army. He was in Burma." He broke off, and then added: "I might have used the expression 'last term' deliberately, you know. If a chap wanted to pass himself off as something he wasn't, it'd be quite a good tip. Much easier than saying, 'Last time I was with an Everest expedition' or, 'That time we were in the Antarctic, one of the met. fellows went mad.'"

"I think Everest's too well documented," suggested Kate. "I don't think you'd get away with that one: there's always the chance that the person you're talking to had read all the climbing books and remembered the personnel."

"Meaning that you've read them," he replied, laughing back at her. "Can you remember the names of everybody in the base camp? I didn't say anything about climbing Everest, you know. And how long is it since you read a climbing classic? We haven't had any Everest expeditions for many years." He caught Jane's eye and said: "You've got that calculating look on your face, Jane. Mental arithmetic going on furiously. Query, how long is it since an attempt was made to climb Everest, and how old should I have been at the time?"

"Yes," said Jane calmly. "I won't go into details, but I think it's quite possible. You'd have been between twenty and twenty-five at a guess—just about the right age. Did you enjoy it, Malcolm?"

"Yes and no." He broke off, laughing. "I believe I could

keep it up—against any bowling—for quite a while, because I do read those books. I bought them. And even if Kate's well briefed, which I'm prepared to believe, she can't check up on anything because she hasn't got her reference books with her, and she can't get any books while she's on this jaunt. Alpensports hotels don't run to English libraries. Hallo, where's this?"

"It's Buchs," said Jane. "I believe it's the last stop before the Austrian frontier. That'll be passports again. I don't know anything about Austria. Are they fussy, like the Italians used to be? The Italian Customs people always liked to poke round in your luggage. The Swiss are such sensible people: they never fuss."

"Nobody fusses when it's a party of English skiers," said Malcolm. "They're too used to them. Not one of us has even been asked to open a suitcase or rucksack and the passport examination is only perfunctory. Getting back to my Everest ramp, did you read those books of Millar's—*Maquis* and *Horned Pigeon*? One of the things which fascinated me about them was the way these chaps memorised their cover stories. If the Gestapo put them through it, they not only had to have the details of their own lives off pat—place of birth, parentage, school, occupation and all the rest—they had to give names of schoolmasters and school friends, the officers under whom they served during their military service and any amount of similar details. They had to learn all this by heart, so that they almost lived themselves into the characters."

"I suppose if you know that your life's going to depend on it, it does provide a spur," said Kate reflectively. Then she went on: "You were quite right, Malcolm, and I was quite wrong. An Everest expedition would make an awfully good background story. The personnel is so limited: you could learn it quite easily, and the chance of being bowled out by anybody would be infinitesimal, because you could overcome all ordinary doubters by sheer authority and determination. You could count on the fact that the chance of meeting anybody who *had* been on an Everest expedition was exceedingly remote."

"Quite true," he replied smilingly, and Jane put in:

"We still don't know for certain that Malcolm hasn't been on an Everest expedition in one capacity or another, Kate. I'm certain there's a leg-pull in it somewhere and the laugh's on us."

"I have no further comments to make," said Malcolm serenely. "It makes the whole expedition much more intriguing to have an element of mystery about one's associates. Now I'm going to stroll along to the slums and see how the poor unfortunates are getting on. I think Derrick is feeling disillusioned and I prophesy that he will never again want to cross Europe in a third-class compartment. By the time I get back it'll be about time to assemble our luggage and look out for Langen."

Kate turned to Jane with a slightly perturbed face after Malcolm had gone into the corridor. "Have I put both feet in it simultaneously? D'you think Malcolm is somebody famous and that I ought to have taken him seriously when he mentioned Everest? Perry... Have I heard of anyone named Perry?"

"What does it matter?" asked Jane. "Anyway, I don't believe he's anybody famous. He may be a climber, although he doesn't look like one to me."

"Why not?"

"He likes his comforts," replied Jane, "and he's got that happily indolent look. I can't see him doing anything that would involve him in quite so much discomfort as an Everest expedition. But I still think there's something in the way of a leg-pull brewing. Malcolm had an expression on his face like a cat that's snaffled the cream."

"I've still got an idea that I've seen a photograph of him somewhere," said Kate. "He's got an interesting head. I'd like to do a portrait of him sometime."

Jane laughed. "You won't get a chance this trip, not unless it snows so hard that we can't ski. We shall all be out all day, and in the evenings we shall dance."

"It doesn't sound particularly indolent to me," said Kate. "Jane, I've got an idea. If there is any funny stuff being devised, it's not for our benefit. The men are all much too nicely behaved to rag us on such a brief acquaintance. If they rag anybody it'll be the Irishman—Robert."

"Why? I rather like him. He's amusing."

"He's been throwing his weight about too much as an Irishman—everything Irish is right and most things English are wrong. It'll be the equivalent of an apple-pie bed for Robert. Ian Dexter and Neville whatever-his-name-is were ragging him last night. I hope they don't go too far. We don't want to have any feelings."

"Oh, we shan't have any feelings," said Jane happily. "When you're ski-ing you don't have time to think about anything else. Besides, Malcolm's a sensible creature. He's older than Ian and Co. and he'll see to it they don't go haywire. This is rather a well-balanced party, really. It's better to have one or two people who've reached years of discretion."

2

The party clambered down out of the train at Langen station, conveying a surprising collection of properties across the snow-covered track—suitcases, rucksacks, picnic baskets, skis, ski-sticks, ski-boots, extra coats and rugs. It was Martha who observed: "We look like a pack of displaced persons, carrying all their worldly possessions," but Jane retorted:

"Considering we've been travelling for twenty-four hours I think we look a credit to ourselves. How do we go on to Lech? I do hope it's by sleigh."

"Do you? I hope it isn't," said Malcolm, close behind her. "Horse sleighs are all right for an hour or so: after that you get steadily colder and colder and colder. You may not feel cold, Jane. It's because the air's so dry, but you've got to remember it is cold—a much lower temperature and a much higher altitude than you're used to."

She grinned at him. "Speaking as one having authority?" she laughed. "Malcolm, it's lovely and the cold air's like wine."

It was lovely: even on the railway track and on the long low platform they were conscious of the snow peaks rising gloriously into the soft blue of the afternoon sky, of the crisp powdery dryness of snow which had a totally different quality from the squalid soiled snow of London streets. In the intense light, reflected back from white ground and roofs and slopes, everybody looked different: dark was darker, fair was fairer, colour was brighter. Clearly defined, sharp cut, brilliantly lit, everything had a quality of vividness and vitality which was exciting, so that fatigue was forgotten and laughter bubbled up in a world which was as lovely as a fairy tale.

"It's like arriving in a new world," said Kate. "A world that's clean and young. Only twenty-four hours, and it seems like going from an old life to a new one. I suppose it's the air and the light: it makes me feel light-headed."

"Light-hearted, you mean," said Neville's voice behind her. "Twenty-four hours be damned. It's no time or all time. Can I heave those traps for you? You've got some registered baggage to collect, haven't you? It all came on the train with us—you'll find it along there. I'll go and dump this in the bus. It's a motor-bus, not sleighs."

Kate and Jane found their baggage at once: replied to questions with a mixture of negatives. "*Rien à déclarer.* Nothing at all. *Nein. Nicht. Niente,*" they laughed, and the station officials seemed satisfied with their light-hearted denials and porters loaded the suitcases on to a sleigh and whizzed it off to the waiting bus. Frank Harris was one of the last out from the Customs officials and he mounted the step of the bus.

"Hi, you there! There's some more traps which they say belong to our push. Jillian, you've left your grip behind. Daphne's got another suitcase to clear and there's something of Neville's. Pull yourself together, do, this outfit's going to start in a minute. No. Skis go in the rack outside, Ian, not in here. Lord, what a lot of trippers we look."

Some of them scrambled out again as Harris sat down beside Jane. "All these bus and station chaps are used to this sort of thing. I expect it's the same with every train. The mad English forget all their valuable baggage the minute they step on to real snow. Who said they felt light-headed?"

"I did," said Jane. "I do, too, but not so light-headed that I'm capable of forgetting my luggage with my best nylons and my long frocks. Oh, look at Neville—what a super line in suitcases, with his name painted right across it. Fancy forgetting that. Oh, goodness, now I've got to get my Austrian currency out. How much is an Austrian schilling worth? It's dizzy-making. I've coped with French francs and Swiss francs and I haven't conditioned myself to the Austrian variety yet."

3

The loaded bus, with chains on its big wheels, ground up the snowy ascent from the little station and made its devious way up the "Flexenstrasse", the mountain road which coiled up and up in a great series of hairpin bends and wide curves into the mountains above Langen. Sometimes they could see the road right above them, bracketed out from the mountain side: sometimes they ran through tunnels, whose approach showed them the sheer precipice below. They saw the timbering set in the mountainside to keep avalanches from blocking the road, and they began to realise the extent of the engineering feat which had built this road to the remote mountain valley of Lech, all for the benefit of the winter sports trade, it appeared. It was an exciting drive, and Jane began to wonder how often the road got blocked by snow. Tremendous though the achievement in engineering it, she could not help feeling how small was the man-made effort in comparison with the vast forces of weather and mountains.

"Does the road ever get blocked?" she asked Malcolm.

"Quite often, I should think," he replied. "It depends how long the snow comes down without a break. I believe they keep the snow ploughs going night and day, but if the snow falls heavily for more than four or five days they're defeated."

"And then you're cut off?"

"That's it. But it's nothing to worry about. The hotel people must always be prepared for a few days when they're cut off and they're awfully good at looking after their visitors."

"I wasn't worrying," said Jane, "but it must feel rather odd to know that you couldn't get away. The railway's there, but you couldn't reach it."

"You could ski," put in Neville Helston. "There are always ski routes apart from the road, and the guides know them."

"I don't know if you've ever skied in a blinding blizzard," said Malcolm. "It's not my idea of enjoyment, and if there's been a heavy fall, it's dangerous, too. You can set off an avalanche and get buried under tons of snow, or take a header in a snowdrift which is too deep to get out of."

"Perfectly true," said Neville, "but aren't you regarding ski-ing merely as a sport, something which you pursue for enjoyment only? Ski-ing was first developed in Scandinavia, as the sanest and safest and fastest way of travelling on snow slopes. When it's regarded as a means of progression and not as a sport you don't expect it to be comfortable all the time."

"It was the English who turned it into a sport," put in O'Hara. "I believe it was they who introduced it to Switzerland as a sport: the Norwegians were just practical over it."

"Have you ever skied in Norway?" asked Malcolm, and O'Hara replied:

"No, but I do know that the Lapps and Finns and Scandinavians have skied time out of mind—before the Christian era, I believe. They hunted on skis, so, as Neville says, they didn't always expect it to be de-luxe."

"Was it really the English who introduced ski-ing into Switzerland?" asked Kate, and Neville put in:

"Not quite. In 1883 a traveller gave the monks of St. Bernard a pair of skis and the monks saw the sense of them and became adepts at it. It's true that it's the English and Americans who have done most to popularise it as a sport, mainly because they were wealthy, but it didn't originate in Switzerland at all. Hallo, we're arriving somewhere. Is this place Lech?"

They could see snow-covered roofs, wooden houses with

great wide eaves and balconies, and skiers began to pass them on the road, going down the smooth hard surface of beaten snow with the apparently effortless speed which is one of the charms of ski-ing. Frank Harris, who spoke German, was talking to the driver. "It's not Lech," he said. "It's Zurs. Lech is a few miles farther on and not so high up. We run down from here."

The bus pulled up and the driver got out to deliver packages at an hotel. O'Hara, who was an impatient and restless soul, said: "Look here, if other people are ski-ing back to Lech, why can't we? I'm tired of this bus. Neville, you've got your ski-boots on, what about it. You can ski, can't you?"

Helston grinned, his dark face lighting up with a daredevil look. "All right, Irishman. I'll take you on, and if I get there first the drinks are on you this evening."

They jumped out of the bus, though Frank Harris protested: "Don't be in such a dashed hurry. You'd far better wait until you've had some practice runs. It always takes a bit of time to find your balance."

The other two did not heed him, and a moment later they had collected their skis from the rack at the back of the bus and were strapping them on, and before the driver came back the two men had got away, walking rather than ski-ing, pushing their skis smoothly forward until they reached a gradient to give them their first run. It was some minutes before the bus started up, and a little while later Frank Harris said: "There they are—going rather well, by Jove. O'Hara's quite swell... Gad! First toss! Who was it? Helston?"

"It's the Irishman who's the expert," said Bridget, but Ian Dexter put in:

"Is it? Did you see the way Neville fell? Half the skill of ski-ing is falling the right way... He's up again. What a lark. I wish I'd done it, too... skied, I mean. Rather snappy to finish the journey on skis."

4

By the time the bus disgorged passengers and luggage outside the Kronbergerhoff Hotel at Lech, Neville Helston and Robert O'Hara were already there, standing with rather self-conscious grins, and declining to give any information about the number of falls they had experienced en route. Just before they all crowded into the lounge of the hotel, Kate Reid took one good look at what she could see of Lech and was well satisfied. It was an Austrian village, set in a wide Alpine valley, with a stream racing in torrents between snowy banks. Cradled on all sides by the embracing snow slopes, dominated by mountain peaks, Lech yet retained the charm of a village. It had the comely wide-eaved wooden houses familiar to travellers in Switzerland, which clustered round an enchanting little stone church, whose tall rather gaunt tower was crowned by an onion-shaped cupola, glowing golden in the lucid light. Neither the hotels, nor the polyglot crowds in ski-ing kit, destroyed the impression that Lech was an Austrian mountain village, which had its own way of life, its own character, developed and bred in the mountains: something picturesque and yet sturdy, colourful and independent, to which the winter sports crowd was but an incident in a life of sturdy independence, whose ways and traditions had developed in its mountain environment.

5

Entering the modern swing doors of the hotel, the party stepped into another world. Outside was the white light from the snow, and air so cold that it seemed crisp: inside was electric light, the fierceness of continental central heating, and a crowd of people packed around café tables or standing about in ski-ing kit. French, German and Italian were being babbled furiously, and the English party were but an inconsiderable item among this volume of vociferous Europeans. Then followed a considerable debate about rooms: the hotel manager, a fair young German who spoke admirable English, explained that owing to various accidents (including inevitable ski-ing casualties) only a few rooms were available in the hotel itself, though there were rooms for all in different houses in the village. Eventually Kate and Jane agreed to share a double room in the hotel: Timothy, who had flown to Zürich, was already installed there. The others were all scattered about in other houses, and their luggage was piled on to sledges and they went out again across the snow to their various establishments.

Kate and Jane went upstairs, their one desire to get out of their travelling clothes and wash away the grime of their long journey.

"We shall all be feeding together, so the party will still feel a party," said Kate. "Personally I'm thankful to have a room in the hotel. Trailing over the snow in a long frock and boots isn't my idea of bliss. Jane, we're rather an amusing lot, aren't we? It's going to be fun to sort people out."

"Yes," agreed Jane. "I think it's going to be quite a lot of fun."

Chapter VI

1

After his discussion with Brook, Julian Rivers did some concentrated thinking on his own account. This case was beginning to fascinate him, for it gave play to those faculties which generally had to be relegated severely to the background of a detective's mind. In this case, it was the usual humdrum of routine which could be disregarded for a while, and the creative faculty given rein. Rivers was in process of creating the personality whom he sensed as his quarry and there was fantasy as well as fact in his mind. Snowy ice-bound roofs, the mark of a ski-stick: the ability to hit hard, keep a cool head, and take advantage of chance: all these were woven together in the Chief Inspector's awareness of the man who had called himself Gray, and who had left his fingerprints on the coins he had put in a gas meter.

Thinking over his conversation with Brook, Rivers decided to let Syd wait for the moment. The Syds of this world could always be fielded by the police when they were wanted, and indeed were often more useful late rather than soon. "I'll have a smack at one of the schoolmaster blokes who lodge chez Stein," said Rivers. "They may be able to produce a few items about Gray."

It was in the early afternoon of January 3rd that Rivers arrived at a very modest little bungalow on the outskirts of Harpenden in Hertfordshire, in search of Mr. George Bell, assistant master at the Hackney and Spitalfields Primary School, Mr. Bell now being on holiday with his parents, who were retired shopkeepers. Rivers drove from London to Harpenden through the half-light of a dreary snowy day. It was bitterly cold, with a vicious east wind blowing, and Rivers thought the chances were that any sensible schoolmaster would be at home by the fire on such a day.

The Chief Inspector proved to be right. The front door of Restharrow was opened by a fair young man of an amiable countenance who said "That's me" when Rivers inquired for Mr. George Bell.

"Sorry to bother you when you're on holiday," said Rivers. "There's been an accident at 13 Lioncel Court—a fire, to be exact, and I'm a C.I.D. man, making a few inquiries."

"C.I.D.—gosh, that sounds a bit spectacular," said George Bell. "Come in. We'd better go in the dining-room. The old folks are snoozing over the fire in the sitting-room. There's a gas fire in here, so we needn't freeze."

The dining-room was very small, very neat and very "utility". George Bell lit the fire, turned a chair round for Rivers and then said: "What's the trouble? No one badly hurt, I hope?"

He was a likeable young man, Rivers decided: fair, sturdy and clean-looking, with a plain square face, very big hands and a cockney voice with no affectation about it.

"I'm afraid there was," replied Rivers. "The fire broke out in the upper part of the house, and we found a dead man in the room occupied by Mr. Gray. The presumption is that deceased is Gray, but the remains are too badly damaged to be identifiable."

"Lord, I am sorry. What a ghastly business," said George Bell. He sounded genuinely sorry, and Rivers went on:

"Yes. Death in a fire always seems ghastly, but it's sensible to remember that fire victims are nearly always rendered unconscious by the smoke, and are probably asphyxiated by fumes. Well, our trouble is that we can't find out anything about Gray's home or people. Was he a friend of yours?"

"Well, no. Not exactly," said George Bell, rumpling up his stubbly fair hair. "We just happened to dig in the same house, and I saw him occasionally. I don't mean I didn't like him, but he'd only been at Mrs. Stein's about a month, and I wasn't quite his sort, if you get me."

"I don't quite, but I want to," said Rivers. "What sort was he?"

"Oh, I should say he was a public school type," replied Bell, speaking quite easily, his candid face rather earnest. "I don't mean that I know anything about public schools. I was at the Hackney Central myself, but in the Army some of our officers had got voices like Gray's. Jolly nice voices. I'm a cockney myself, and proud of it, but I like to hear voices like that sometimes."

"Agreed to all that," murmured Rivers, taking out his cigarette-case. "Do you smoke? and may I?"

The C.I.D. man was quick to realise that it was no use hustling George Bell: the latter had a careful but not a quick mind, and this was one of the occasions when leisureliness might earn a premium.

"Oh, thanks very much, of course," said George, accepting a cigarette and providing an ash-tray. "I don't often smoke, but it does help sometimes. I suppose you really want to find out about Gray's people. I'm afraid I can't help. He never mentioned his family or his home."

"I want to find out anything of any kind about Gray," said Rivers. "At present our information is almost minus. Do you know if he had a job?"

"He was a journalist—free-lance," said Bell. "He said he did a bit of reporting and wrote film criticisms and dramatic criticism."

"Did he ever mention what paper he wrote for?"

"No. I don't think he'd got a regular job, not on any particular paper, I mean."

"Did you ever hear a typewriter going in his room?"

"Oh yes. Quite often. Oh, did I tell you he was an Irishman? I think he said he came from Southern Ireland, but I don't know exactly where."

"Did he speak like an Irishman?"

"Oh no. Not usually. You couldn't say he'd got an accent—unless it was B.B.C.—but he could put on an Irish accent good enough for a music hall. I've heard him trying it on Mrs. Stein—wheedling something out of her, you know."

"When was that?"

"Oh, at breakfast. I didn't often see him at breakfast, because I always have mine at eight sharp, except on Sundays, and I sometimes saw him then. He was a very nice chap, not condescending or anything like that, although he must have been used to a very different sort of living conditions. I once said something of the kind to him, and he said he liked number thirteen and Mrs. Stein. He was interested in people and said he was out to get experience of all kinds. So

I asked him—but I expect I'm wasting your time, burbling away like this."

"You're not wasting my time. I want to hear everything you can remember about Mr. Gray," replied Rivers. "If you want to know why I'm so interested, I'll tell you one reason. Both you and Mrs. Stein say that Gray was a writer, a free-lance journalist. You say that you often heard a typewriter going in his room. There was no typewriter in the bedroom of his when we examined it after the fire. That fact seems a bit odd to us. A typewriter can't be burnt up completely in a fire."

"I see," said George Bell, and then added sadly: "Oh, dear. That doesn't look too good, does it? I'm glad I haven't got to sort that one out, Inspector. I hate the look of it."

"All you've got to do is to tell me everything you can remember about Mr. William Gray," said Rivers. "You were just going to say you asked him something."

"Oh yes, about my boys' club. Do you mind if I explain about it?"

"Of course not. Explain anything you like."

"Well, I told you I was at school in Hackney. Then I had a job in a warehouse for a bit and then I was in the Army. When I was demobbed I applied for admission to an Emergency Teachers' Training College. I'd always wanted to teach, particularly London lads—real toughs, you know. I was a tough myself."

Rivers laughed a little: he was beginning to see George Bell in the round: an earnest, conscientious and not unintelligent young man: George must have done well in the Army to get taken at an Emergency Training College after starting his career in a warehouse, but his prevailing characteristic was philanthropy: George obviously wanted to help his "toughs".

"So you work at a club for your toughs," said Rivers.

"That's it; we see they get games and P.T. and boxing and all that," said George. "Gray was a well-built chap, obviously the athletic type, so I asked him if he'd come and give us a hand at the club some time, coaching games or boxing—but he wouldn't take it on. Just laughed and said he was born lazy. I was disappointed. I thought he might be the type—but he wasn't."

"What type was he?" asked Rivers bluntly. Then he added: "Look here. You haven't been exactly featherbedded during your life, have you? A warehouse, the Army, and then a primary school teacher in a tough district. You ought to be able to sort out the sheep from the goats."

George Bell flushed. "I hate making judgments like that," he said slowly. "I tend to like people, and I take them at their face value, if you see what I mean."

"I know just what you mean," said Rivers. "You're an amiable unexacting sort of chap and by nature you're an optimist. But if you were only that, you wouldn't be much use in that boys' club of yours. To be any good at that job, you've got to be able to tell an honest boy from a habitual liar. Otherwise they make a fool of you and you don't do any good."

"Too true," murmured George Bell. "I can sort out the boys all right: I know a bit about them, the homes they come from, the jobs they go into, the companions they go about with. I don't know any of those things about Gray. And if he was killed in that fire, I don't think I'm all that keen on sorting him out."

Rivers remained silent, and George Bell studied his companion with troubled, thoughtful eyes. "You mean you're not certain that the dead man is Gray," he said slowly.

2

"Having looked all that in the face, and realising we can't afford to take anything for granted in my job, say if you try to answer my question," said Rivers. "What type was he?"

The C.I.D. man had given George Bell no information. He had simply repeated that the dead man was unidentifiable, but George was not at all stupid. He worked out the obvious possibilities for himself, and his square face looked very troubled.

"What type was he?" he repeated slowly. "It's difficult for me to say, because I was out of my depth with him. For one thing, he was a gentleman. I know it's a word that most people fight shy of these days, and to most chaps it doesn't mean anything—like esquire on an envelope. It used to mean something, but now it doesn't."

"Perfectly true," said Rivers patiently.

"My dad taught me to respect the word gentleman," said George Bell slowly, "but I don't think I use it quite the same way he did. I just know that men who have been brought up with a certain sort of background and been to certain sorts of schools have an easy kind of attitude, no matter what company they find themselves in. They're not shy or clumsy, and they know all the answers when it comes to talking to chaps who are different to themselves. We get some University blokes at the club sometimes—Oxford or Cambridge, I mean— and they've all got that easy way. But it doesn't mean they're better chaps than the others—the dockers and porters and railway men. I mean the one sort isn't more truthful or more reliable or more honest."

"Of course they're not," said Rivers. "Now getting from the general to the particular: in your opinion was Gray truthful and reliable and honest?"

George Bell flushed and looked unhappy. "He wasn't truthful," he said slowly. "As for reliable—I don't know. And he wasn't honest in the way I've been taught to be. He was all for black market and cheating the Government, thought it was all right—though all sorts of chaps do the same."

"I know they do," said Rivers. "Cheating the Government seems fair game to lots of people who are honest with individuals. When you say Gray wasn't truthful, can you give me an instance?"

"Yes, but it's rather a silly one," said George. "I went to that film on ski-ing—a documentary. It was marvellous. I happened to sit just behind Gray, and he got talking to the bloke in the seat beside him. The bloke was a German and they talked in German. I understood some of it, because I mugged up German when I was in the Army, in Cologne."

"Did Gray talk German fluently?"

"Oh yes, like a native. They talked about ski-ing and famous ski-runs and places in Switzerland and Austria, Carinthia and the Julian Alps. They both got awfully excited about the ski-jumping in the film. I understood enough to know that Gray must have done a lot of ski-ing. But when I mentioned ski-ing to him next time I saw him, he said he'd never done any." George Bell looked apologetically at Rivers. "It sounds silly, doesn't it? Perhaps Gray thought I was being a nuisance, talking too much and all that, but he could have shut me up without telling lies."

"Did you tell him you'd seen the film?"

"Yes, but I didn't say I'd seen him there, and I certainly didn't say I'd listened in to him talking German. He may have thought I was going to worry him about the club again, asking him to give a talk on ski-ing," said George ingenuously. "Our toughs like chaps who can do things. But he needn't have said he'd never skied in his life," he ended sadly.

"I quite agree," said Rivers. "When did you go to that film?"

"Just before the end of term. About December 17th. It was a Friday."

Rivers sat and thought for a moment. It was on the night of December 17th that the Post Office robbery had occurred. Then he said, "Did you ever go into Gray's room?"

"No. Never. We often had a word if we met on the stairs, and I sometimes saw him at breakfast on Sundays. That's the only meal Mrs. Stein serves. I told you I wasn't really a friend of his. I'm just somebody he talked to because I happened to live in the same house he lived in. I think he thought I was an awful mug. I don't drink, and I'm not interested in betting and all that."

"Was Gray interested in betting?"

"Well, he knew all the answers. Mrs. Stein puts a bob on occasionally, nothing much, just for a bit of fun, and Syd's keen on horse-racing."

"Syd," said Rivers reflectively. "What do you make of Syd?"

"He's not got much backbone," said George Bell unhappily. "I'm afraid his mother spoilt him when he was a kid. He was an only child and his father died when he was small and his mother adored him. I can see how it happened."

"I'm asking you what you make of the result," said Rivers, and to the latter's amusement George Bell suddenly turned on him in wrath.

"Look here, sir, you jolly well do some of your own summing up. I don't see why I should do the dirty on everyone."

Rivers laughed. "Fair enough—but we always try to get our conclusions checked. I gather that Syd is a potential ne'er-do-well."

"Well, yes, that's true enough," said Bell soberly. "It's just what I feel myself, but I don't think he's gone very far on the downward slope. I've been doing my best to influence him, but these weak-kneed chaps are sometimes harder to deal with than the real bad 'uns." He paused, and then added: "Are you thinking of that typewriter?"

Rivers nodded. "Yes. If Syd went into that room at all, he might be able to tell us something useful."

"May I have a go at him, sir? It's like this. If you tackle him, he'll tell lies right away, and you'll know they're lies and believe he's worse than he is. I might get the truth out of him."

"I said you were an optimist," said Rivers. "One thing puzzles me a bit though. It's plain enough that you were 'brought up honest' as they say. From what you've said of Gray, he wasn't particularly honest, but you said you liked him."

"Good lord, sir, if I disliked chaps because they weren't straight, I might as well throw my hand in right away," burst out George Bell. "The only way you can help some of these boys with criminal tendencies is by liking them. If you don't like them, you'd better keep away. As for Gray, he was just an ordinary sort of chap in the way he told bloomers and picked winners and told Mrs. Stein how she could get beef steak from Ireland. All that didn't prevent me liking him." He stopped and then added abruptly: "Anyway, Gray was the sort of chap you couldn't help liking. He'd just got something about him. Even Rawlinson liked him—and that's saying a lot."

"Rawlinson? oh, your other fellow lodger," said Rivers. "Why? Is he a misanthrope?"

"He's a communist," said George Bell. "I'm not giving anything away. Everyone know he's a communist. He's one of the die-hard variety, hates everybody who isn't red. He thinks I'm poisonous, helping to bolster up a rotten system. He says Gray's a capitalist parasite—that's because he wore good clothes—but even Rawlinson liked Gray."

"Where does Rawlinson live?"

"Barnsley. His father's a miner. He's very bitter, but you can't blame him for that. He's got plenty to remember which makes for bitterness."

Rivers nodded. Then he said: "Say if I sum up the gist of what you've told me and you can add anything else that occurs to you. Gray was a gentleman: he had an attractive voice and easy manners and wore good clothes. He told you he was a journalist. He talked fluent German, was enthusiastic about ski-ing though he told you he couldn't ski. He had a typewriter and you heard him using it. He told you he came from Southern Ireland, but he didn't sound like an Irishman. That the lot?"

George Bell sat very still, apparently thinking hard, his face very troubled. Then he said: "Will you tell me this, sir? Have you any reason to suppose that Gray ever broke the law? That is, if he's still alive, would there be any charge against him?"

"Yes," replied Rivers, "and if I read you aright, you're not surprised to hear it."

"That's quite true," said Bell slowly. "I knew he was phony. I've got no proof, but he just didn't fit. Chaps like him don't stay in houses like number thirteen without a reason, not unless they're very hard up, and he wasn't hard up. I've known one or two newspaper men, and the first thing they always tell you is the paper they write for. I think Gray said he was a newspaper man because he was often out at night." He paused and then added: "The only other thing I can tell you about him is that I saw him in the Hackney Public Library on the Wednesday after Christmas. I came up to change my own books, and I just caught sight of him in the Reference Library. I didn't speak to him and I don't think he saw me."

"Do you know what he was reading?" asked Rivers. "Book? Newspaper? Periodicals?"

"He was looking at a map," said George Bell. "I think it was the big *Times Atlas*. It's a huge thing." He broke off. "I suppose I had to tell you," he said miserably. "I'm sorry, because I liked him. You couldn't help liking him." He looked at Rivers, his face troubled and thoughtful, and then added: "I feel a bit ashamed of myself over it, but I can't help being frightfully interested in all this. Detection's such a scientific business these days. I suppose you'll go through that atlas for fingerprints."

"I dare say we shall," said Rivers easily, "so if yours are in it, perhaps you'd like to say so now."

George Bell looked startled, then he grinned. "No. I've never touched it," he replied. "It's true I'm inquisitive, but not indecently so. It never occurred to me to snoop or try to find out what Gray was looking up. I wasn't even interested."

"Well, I'm glad you were sufficiently interested to notice what he was studying," said Rivers. "It's my job to find out all that I can about Gray, and you've been very helpful. One other thing: what happens to letters when the postman leaves them at number thirteen?"

"They fall on the floor in the hall and the first person who notices them picks them up and puts them on the hall table. In the mornings it's generally me, because I'm always downstairs one of the first. Mrs. Stein isn't interested in letters, she never writes any, and Syd stays in bed until the last possible moment."

"Did you ever notice any letters for Gray?"

"Very occasionally: generally typewritten envelopes. That's all I can tell you about them."

"Do you know if he ever had any visitors, or brought anybody home with him?"

"Not to my knowledge, but I'm out quite a lot myself. I

never heard him talking to anybody in his room." Again he paused, evidently thinking hard in his conscientious way. "There's one thing I should like to say, sir. About Mrs. Stein. She's honest: what I call a decent good sort. I know she's stupid in some ways, especially over Syd, but she's straight herself. You can trust what she says."

"Thanks. I'm very glad to have your opinion over that," said Rivers. "Incidentally, I think you'd better leave Syd to me. I'll sort him out. And many thanks for all the trouble you've taken."

Chapter VII

1

While most of Bridget's party spent all the daylight hours with the various classes of the ski-ing schools, Catherine Reid preferred sometimes to get away from both the crowd of earnest learners, the electric ski-lifts, and the perspex cabin slung on a cable which carried skiers high above the snow-laden conifers to the upper slopes. Unfashionably, Kate simply walked. She followed the smooth tracks worn in the snow and studied the life of the farming folk away from all the apparatus and elaboration of "Alpensports".

Less than a mile away from the hotel she found herself in another world, where life was no longer conditioned by sport. Here, in the long Lech valley, small wooden farmhouses stood above the turbulent stream, and from their barns and byres came the fragrance of hay and cattle. Kate spoke very little German, but the farming folk were courteous and friendly, and she soon found herself invited into the byres to see the beasts in their winter quarters. It was an enchanting sight to one interested in beasts: behind the double doors of the byres was a wide clean gangway: to one side mild-eyed cows stood contentedly; *café au lait* in colour, they were beautiful creatures, accustomed to being handled and quite confident of the good intentions of human beings. On the other side of the gangway, sheep, pigs and goats were grouped in their separate pens, and hens roosted on the beams. Kate enjoyed seeing this aspect of an Austrian winter and was much impressed by the good condition of the animals.

Coming out of the warm fragrance of the byre, the crisp cold air of the mountains was almost breath-taking, and Kate found herself pausing for a breather on her way up the valley. She glanced up the slopes to her right, where the sun still shone dazzlingly bright on the white snow peaks, though the valley was now in shadow, and she saw two skiers coming down the mountainside in long traverses: a rapid swoop, then a turn, and another swoop in the other direction. Both men were going beautifully, driving in their ski-sticks with the rhythmic purposefulness which bespoke expert skill. To Kate's disappointment—and sympathy—one of them fell as he took the turn and his skis stuck up at the comic angle which makes every ski-ing tumble look exaggerated. In a flurry of snow he got up again, while the leader sped on along the slope, and Kate recognised the man who had tumbled as Robert, the Irishman of the party. He waved to her, and began to come down to her level, sliding and side-stepping rather than ski-ing, as though the fall had shaken him up a bit. She hailed him when he came within earshot.

"Bad luck! Have you hurt yourself?"

"Only me pride," he called back, the brogue sounding in his voice for once. "I always do it," he said mournfully. "I'll keep going for a dozen turns, all out of the book, and then

I'll take a toss for no reason at all. 'Twas the divil himself invented ski-ing. What have you been doing, all by yourself?"

"Making friends with the farmers on two and a half words of German," she laughed. "Do you like cows?"

"Shure and I do. Wasn't I brought up with them?" he replied.

"I often wonder where you were brought up, Robert," she replied. "You're not cut to one pattern, are you? But if you like cows, come and see the ones in there. It's like Noah's ark inside, but the cows are lovely. Quite a parlour they've got, double doors to keep them snug and windows to let the sun in. Come and look at them."

"I'd like to. Just wait while I take these damned things off. That's Neville on ahead, and Ian's going strong not far behind. How I hate them."

"Never mind," she said. "They won't see the cows. I think it's an awful pity to come to a place like this and see nothing but crowds of skiers and ice bars and luxury hotels. I love these farms, with the cattle housed amidships, keeping the whole house warm. They look so snug."

He bent down and loosed the ski-straps and picked the skis up. "Of course you're right," he said. "This is real—the farms and the stock. It's not just exhibitionism and wanting to be clever, like our stuff. And the farm people all use skis sensibly, as a practical way of getting about their business. I say, you do seem to have made yourself at home," he added, as Kate slipped the latches and opened the doors of the cattle shed. She called softly: "Cusha, lass. Cush, cush, cusha lass," and the cows turned their heads and murmured back. "It's an international language: all cows understand it," she said. "Do you remember 'High Tide on the Coast of Lincolnshire'?

'Cusha, cusha, cusha calling
'Ere the early dews were falling
Come up Whitefoot, come up Lightfoot…'

We still call the cows in like that."

"I remember," he said. "Jove, they are fine beasts. Do they like apples?"

"All cows like apples. You must know. You're obviously used to them," she replied, noticing the way he leant against the cow's flanks, with one arm over her broad back.

"Not to Austrian cows," he replied. "I say, I think you're jolly sensible, coming and seeing all this."

"I think it's lovely. I've never seen sheep and goats and pigs and cows all wintered together like this. How hard the farm people must work with all these creatures to feed all through the winter," said Kate, as she rubbed the creamy neck of the cow beside her.

"Jolly good sort of work, though," he replied. "I wish I had a farm like this. It's a good life. We waste so much time on elaborations. What did that poet chap say—spending our lives making more and more money because we're for ever discovering we need too much. It's quite true. New things are invented, so of course we think we need them. Do you ever get to loathe money and all the elaborations, Kate?"

"I don't make enough money to loathe it, and I'm not really elaborate," she replied. "But we couldn't have come to Lech without money. Travelling isn't exactly cheap."

"Too true," he said ruefully. "I just about bust the bank to come, and I've done such a damn'-fool thing. I've lost most of the money I brought to spend."

"Lost it? How on earth?" she asked. "Do you mean dropped your wallet in the snow?"

"No. I suppose it's been stolen. I changed a traveller's cheque for £10 at the hotel the day we arrived—I hadn't any Austrian currency with me. I put the notes in my suitcase in my bedroom and they've just disappeared."

"Did you lock your suitcase?"

"I thought I did," he said ruefully, "but I may not have. Anyway it wasn't locked when I went to it again. I know I'm a careless devil, but I did think I'd locked it. Anyway those locks on suitcases open with almost any key."

"How simply sickening," replied Kate. "What are you going to do about it?"

"Nothing. What can I do?" he answered. "Do you know the house where I sleep? It's that largish chalet, away up the slope beyond the bridge. It's kept by two old girls named Braun. They're awfully nice, both of them. I'm certain they're honest. I'm not going to the hotel manager to say my money's been stolen. It's like accusing the Fräulein Brauns."

"Who else is in the house?"

"Ian Dexter and Tim Grant, of our party, but there are other bedrooms let. I believe a German left yesterday and another chap came. People are always coming and going. It's hopeless to check up. I shall just have to give it up, but it means I've got very little money for drinks and jaunts and all that, and it makes me feel a fool."

"It is rotten luck," said Kate, "but I do feel you ought to be able to do something about it. Have you told the others? Ian and Tim?"

"No. I don't like to. It's pretty beastly, you know. Look here, Kate, I'm sorry I told you: I didn't mean to worry you. I suppose I just felt shirty about it, and wanted a bit of sympathy. Sorry. Forget it."

"Don't be an ass, Robert," she retorted. "It's a sickening

thing to have happened, but apart from it's being bad luck on you, I don't think you ought to be so casual about it. If there's a thief about, it's only fair to warn the others. The same thing might happen to them."

"Oh, no, it won't. They're all more careful than I am. They carry their money and passports about with them. Look at Harris and Cossack. They simply bulge with documents and common sense."

"You could do with a bit more common sense yourself," she replied. "Why did you get your traveller's cheque made out for ten pounds? Two or three pounds is much more convenient, and traveller's cheques don't get stolen, because of having to produce passports and sign the cheques. Have you got your passport all right?" she asked suddenly.

"Yes. At least, the hotel's got it: they asked for them all to check up on."

"Yes. I remember. Look here, Robert, I think you ought to tell the manager about losing those notes. He speaks perfect English, so you can explain everything, and tell him you're certain it's not the Fräuleins. He'll be grateful to you for telling him, because hotel people always have to be on their guard against thieves."

"The blond type?" he queried. "I don't like him. I can't cotton on to Germans."

It was Robert who had nicknamed the hotel manager "the blond type," scornful of the extreme fairness and the look of un-English grace about that very elegant young German, and the name had caught on among the rest of the party.

"Oh, don't be silly. That's just prejudice," replied Kate. "If you're going to dislike foreigners, you'd better not come abroad."

"I don't dislike foreigners," he retorted, "only Germans. I like Austrians."

"How do you know the difference?" she asked. "You can't even speak German, can you? Look here, Robert, if we're going to have tea at the Schneiderhof we'd better get back."

"Yes, rather. But I'm awfully glad I had that tumble and you brought me in here," he said. "I've enjoyed it. It's one of the things I shall remember."

They left the farm, calling "*Guten Abend*" to the old lady, who waved at them from the kitchen door murmuring, "*Bitte schön,*" while the children round her called "*Grüss' Gott*"—the invariable greeting of the country folk.

"They *are* nice people," said Kate, and Robert nodded.

"I know they are."

2

The sun had disappeared behind the peaks, and the valley was faintly blue under a luminous sky. Robert called Kate's attention to two figures on the snow track in front of them. "That's Neville and Ian. They're walking back. Neville's a swell skier."

"He's not as good as you are, Robert. I've seen him muff some quite simple runs, and he took several tosses before he got the hang of it. And he came quite a mucker when you and he set off from Zurs, the day we got here. Didn't he hurt his hand rather badly?"

"Sprained a finger or something, but it doesn't seem to cramp his style much. I say, Kate, thinking it over, I don't think I want to raise a stink about that money being pinched. It's all a bit awkward."

"Why is it?"

"Well, most of you know one another at home, or you're friends of friends or something. I tagged on rather at the last moment, and nobody knows me. I know Ian and Tim will feel fed up with me if I start creating about losing money. I was an ass to tell you about it, but you're such a sensible soul."

"More than you are," said Kate, who had been doing some quick thinking. "Look here, Robert. You must have got some reason for not wanting to say anything about that money. Is it that you've got an idea in your head about who might have taken it?"

He was obstinately silent, and Kate went on: "If it's that, it is a bit awkward, but I still think you ought to say something. Will you let me discuss it with Frank Harris? He's a wise sort of person, and his advice would be worth having."

"I'll think about it," he replied, "but I do know it's the sort of thing which can wreck a party like this one. We're all matey, and the chaps go in and out of each other's rooms and digs, as you'd expect, and I don't want to be the one to muck it up. Look, the other two are waiting for us. We shall have to catch them up. Don't say anything now."

3

Ian and Neville were feeling very pleased with themselves, having accomplished their run without a fall, and Ian was full of ambitious schemes for a longer excursion on their own, without a guide.

"Neville and I have been studying the map. We're thinking of ski-ing over to St. Anton," he said. "I believe it's rather a good place and there are some shops there."

"He's panting to spend some money," said Neville. "In my opinion it's just waste of money buying things to take back to England. By the time you've paid Customs duty, you might as well shop in England—or in Ireland, as Robert's always reminding us."

"You've got to take something back in the way of presents when you come abroad," said Ian, "and as for Customs—well, they don't search you. And the small sort of things I might buy won't upset international economics."

"Now, now: it's the principle of the thing," said Neville, "so don't start that; but I'm all in favour of going over to St. Anton, just for the run. It isn't difficult: the gradients seem easy, and it's not too far. We can come back by train if we've had enough ski-ing."

"Is St. Anton on the railway then?" asked Kate, and Ian replied:

"Yes. It's the next station beyond Langen on the Vienna line, or you can get on to Villach by changing somewhere. I believe there's some fine winter sports places in Carinthia."

"Yes, but you have to go through Russian occupied territory or something, so it's not so good," replied Neville. "Anyway, we're not going for a railway journey, but I think it's worth trying the run to St. Anton. We could have a meal there and sample the local bars. We'll look into it. What were you doing up the valley all by yourself, Kate?"

"Seeing the farms and the way they winter the stock, and the hay they feed them on," said Kate. "It's lovely sweet-smelling stuff. Lots of clover in it, or vetch. I wonder if they grow any root crops. I do wish I talked more German."

"Why? Are you interested in farming?" asked Neville, in his quick interested way.

"Yes. I was brought up on a farm, and I live in the country," she said. "Didn't somebody say you used to live in the north of England, Neville? Were your people farmers?"

"At one time," he replied, "but I've lived in London for

some time. I like farming though. I should like to see the cattle here. I suppose they're in the buildings all the winter. Do they turn them out into the meadows as soon as the snow melts? Funny to think of this place without snow over everything."

"I believe it's marvellous here in June, knee deep in flowers," said Ian. "The blond type was talking about it. I should rather like to come here in the summer."

"Too hot and too many flies," said Neville. "This is a winter sports place, not a summer resort."

"I should rather like to see it without the snow," said Kate. "It'd be lovely to see those cows out at pasture. What sort of farm was yours, Neville?"

"Oh, mostly dairy farming and a spot of arable. It's a long time ago, you know, and one forgets."

"Maybe it is, but you never forget a farm you've been brought up on," said Robert, in the rather opinionated way which generally roused a retort from his English companions.

Ian grinned. "Nostalgia, Robert? Do you remember all the cows by name?"

"I do, actually," said Robert, who nearly always rose to a bait. "They were little black Kerries. Do you know them, Kate?"

"Yes. Our postman keeps them. He's got a fell farm, and Kerries are good doers, as we say up north."

"How bovine you are," said Neville, and Robert put in:

"Well, what sort of milking cows did you keep on your ancestral acres? Something large and opulent? Pedigree Herefords at least."

"I don't think they were pedigree, but they were Herefords, as a matter of fact," said Neville.

Ian interrupted him. "Oh, for the love of Mike, don't go on to stock breeding. Give me dancing every time. They've got rather a good band at the Schneiderhof. Kate, do you think they'd play some reels for us? Tim's brought the band parts and we could do two eightsomes."

"They might. Get Malcolm to talk to the band leader: he really can talk German," said Kate.

"What's the matter with Robert?" put in Ian. "He's laughing like a hyena, all to himself."

"I have a few private jokes," retorted Robert, and Kate said quickly:

"If you want to laugh, you should tell other people what you're laughing about."

"Well, you know," said Robert, "and the other two wouldn't be amused."

Chapter VIII

1

After tea at the Schneiderhof, including a surfeit of cream cakes which cost an amazing amount when translated into English currency, Kate left the others to their dancing and walked back to the hotel with Frank Harris. A blue dusk seemed to caress the snow: stars were beginning to gleam above the mountains and the valley shone with golden specks from lighted windows. The sound of sleigh bells and the soft thud of horses' hooves on the beaten snow tracks combined to make enchantment of the Austrian village.

"Oh dear, it's so beautiful. I know it's silly to go on saying it, but there is a something here," said Kate.

"There is. One couldn't wish for more," said Frank Harris, his quiet voice sensible and sympathetic. "Are you worried about something, Kate?"

"Yes. I am. How did you know?"

"I suppose it's practice. Most of the people doctors deal with are worried," he replied.

She laughed. "I'm not ill, Frank."

"I know that," he returned prosaically. "I never saw anybody look less ill. Professionally, you are totally uninteresting."

"I'm delighted to hear it. But I should like some advice, unprofessionally."

"I'll do my best. Come and join me in the bar about half-past six. It's always empty then. Malcolm and Tim generally come along about half-past seven, but at half-past six teas are over and sundowners not begun."

"I'll be there," she replied.

Kate indulged in the luxury of a bath—baths were expensive in Austria—and changed into a long frock, enjoying the leisureliness and the sense that it was worth while to dress up in this place, with the prospect of a superb meal, served with ceremony, and an evening in a ballroom to round off a day spent in the sunshine. "What a lovely life—just for a little while," she mused. "I couldn't go on like this indefinitely, but it's glorious for a holiday."

She went downstairs into the bar, which was at one end of the hotel ballroom. Frank Harris was already there, sitting at a table in the shadows. The ballroom lights had been put out, and the only light came from the bar.

"How pleasant and peaceful," she said.

"Yes. It's pleasing to be out of earshot of a babel of mixed foreign tongues competing with a dance band," he said. "What'll you drink, Kate? Kersch? Cinzano? Cap Corse? or a good old-fashioned whisky and soda? I think I prescribe the latter."

"Thank you very much, though I scruple to let anybody stand me a whisky here," she said. "It's the most expensive drink they've got and currency isn't unlimited. If I have one on you now, will you have one on me another time?"

"Thanks. I will," he said sedately, and got up to fetch the drinks from the bar.

"What's it all about, Kate?" he inquired, after they had raised their glasses each to each.

"May I put a hypothetical case, Frank? I want to keep names out of it. I admit I'm breaking a confidence, but I feel I want advice."

"Go ahead. No names needed," he replied.

"Suppose that in a party like this one, somebody discovers that he or she has been robbed of a wad of Austrian notes, is it sensible for them to say nothing about it, or would it be wiser and fairer to warn the rest of the party that there's a thief around?"

He considered for a moment. "The latter, in my judgment. Why doesn't he—or she?"

"Because they're afraid of spoiling the party. There seems to be no evidence about the theft, and mentioning it might cause a feeling of constraint among a set of people who are very happy together."

"Can you give me some more facts, Kate? Was the money stolen in the hotel or out of it? From a coat pocket or bag, from the cloakroom, or out in the open?"

"From a suitcase in a bedroom, not in the hotel. It just disappeared."

"I see." Again he paused, and then asked: "Other nationals in the same annexe, or British only?"

"Both."

"It's a bit difficult," he said. "First, I'd give it as my opinion that the staffs, in the hotel and out of it, are known to be honest. Nothing is more of a nuisance to a hotel proprietor than complaints of theft. Hotel-keeping in places like this is a highly organised profession, relying on integrity and the recommendations of satisfied clients. Hotel managers are very careful only to put people of known honesty in charge of annexe sleeping quarters."

"I entirely agree with you there," she said, "so, incidentally, does the person who lost the money."

"Good. That's quite sound, I think. Hotel staff ruled out. Look here, Kate. I'm not speculating about personalities, and I've agreed to leave names out of it, but you've got to admit that I'm justified in assuming that it's one of the men in our party who's lost his money. If it was a girl, you wouldn't have come to me about it. You'd have gone into a huddle with Bridget and Jane, both of whom have got plenty of sense."

"All right. I'm glad to see you've got a detective instinct, Frank, though I admit nothing and deny nothing."

"Agreed. Now the thing I don't like about the business is this: the very fact that the aggrieved party hasn't made his loss public looks to me as though he's got an idea as to the identity of the thief and doesn't like to come into the open about it. And his idea may be right or may be wrong."

"I thought of that, too, Frank, and to some extent I sympathise with him. It's a beastly thing to suspect one of a party like this of thieving."

"Admittedly. Incidentally, if this had happened to you, what would you have done?"

"Oh, I should have come into the open about it," replied Kate. "I'd have told the others exactly what had happened in order to safeguard them. But I should be quite certain that none of the girls in this party would have done it. Although I didn't know them all personally before we came away, I should back my own judgment over that."

"Well, I'm glad to hear you say so," he replied dryly. "For myself, the longer I practise, the more profoundly sceptical do I become of my ability to judge anybody. Human nature's too damned complicated. But I don't want to undermine your belief in your fellow beings. Now look here: will you leave me to deal with this thing in my own way? I'll mention no names, but I think it's only fair to warn other people to be on their guard."

"All right. I'll leave it to you. After all, I only came to you because I felt something should be done about it. Oh, here's Malcolm. Hallo, had a good day?"

"A very good day, thank you," said Malcolm. "I was promoted to class three, went up the ski-lift without falling off, and came down the long slope, taking exactly two and a half hours over the descent which the international ski-runners do in three minutes, ten seconds, so I've every reason for complacency. Won't you have another drink, Kate?"

"No, thanks very much," she replied, watching Malcolm as he strolled across to the bar and thinking how very nice he looked in his dinner jacket. "Complacent?" she thought to herself. "Perhaps he does look complacent; it's that effect of effortless ease, either on skis or off. There's something about an Englishman abroad which marks him out from other nationals. Good tailoring, good figures… and complacency. What was it Jane said, 'Like a cat who's got at the cream'…"

2

The party of sixteen "Englische" had been given their own private dining-room, in which one long table seated them all. There were no fixed places. The party sat with the girls and men alternating, but tended to group themselves to some extent. Robert and Neville were generally somewhere near Jane and Kate, Ian and Tim more often near Bridget and

Meriel, while Frank Harris occasionally presided at the head of the table. He sat there tonight, and when the last course had been served and the Austrian waitresses had left the dining-room, Harris said: "Shut the door, will you, Neville? I want a word in confidence with the assembled party."

All heads were turned in the doctor's direction as he raised his voice a little to make this unexpected announcement. Kate guessed what was coming, and it was only by an effort that she kept her eyes from glancing round the faces which were turned towards Harris.

"It's not that war's been declared, or anything of that nature," he began, his voice cheerful and prosaic, "but a problem has arisen which I feel I ought to tell you about. Somebody—shall we say the authorities—have warned me that they suspect a thief is at large. It's an awkward situation, because places like this can suffer a lot from imputations of this kind. So I'll ask you not to repeat anything I'm saying. Next, if any of you have any currency, please don't leave it in your bedrooms. You've all got pockets in your ski-kit, so keep any notes in your pockets—Austrian notes, that is. Next, about English pound notes. We've all got some, I know that. You're not supposed to change them on the Continent, so presumably you won't want them till we go back to England. Between us, we've got quite a sum in English currency, and it's up to us to see that it's not lost."

He paused, and Kate thought: "He's doing this jolly well. It sounds most convincing."

Frank Harris went on: "I don't know how you feel about this suggestion, but if you like to put your English notes in sealed envelopes with the name and amount on, I'll see that the whole lot are put in the safe until we leave. It'd be simpler than individuals doing it."

"Jolly good idea," put in Derrick Cossack, the naval lieu-
tenant. "Is this a new sort of currency racket, Frank?"

"I'm sorry, I can't tell you," said Harris, "but, as you know,
the English pound note is accepted as valid anywhere on the
Continent, so you can see the implications. Now I'm going to
ask you all to count your English notes some time this evening
and make sure you've got what you ought to have got. I know
that when one comes abroad one tends to ignore one's English
money, and even to forget it is money, because you don't use
it out here. So just check up." He glanced round and added:
"Some of you chaps may be wondering why I was picked on
as a responsible representative of this party. It's partly because
of my misleading appearance of advanced age, partly because I
speak German. Anyway, I've taken the job on on your behalfs,
so to speak. Now if any one of you finds that you've lost any
valuables, will you please come to me and tell me?"

He faced them squarely, a reliable-looking, sensible fellow,
and there were quick murmurs of "Of course"—but that was
all. Harris went on after a short pause.

"And it's not only money, of course. It's not for me to guess
whether those things some of you girls wear round your necks
are real pearls or not. In some cases I rather imagine they are."

Kate heard Neville laughing, and realised that she had
almost unconsciously put her hand up to her neck, and that
Jane Harrington had done the same. Both of them wore
"pearls," and Ian Dexter joined in Neville's chuckle. Ian had
a delightful laugh, unusually mirthful, but his face was impish as he called to Jane: "A fair cop, J. I always rather fancied
those beads of yours."

"That's enough of that," said Frank. "If you girls must bring
things of that sort away with you, don't leave them in your
bedrooms. Wear them, under your jumpers for preference.

Well, ladies and gentlemen, you have been warned. Please take this seriously, and don't chat about it in public places. I have been told that the British are satisfactory to deal with because they have a sense of responsibility. I rather liked the sound of that one. Finally, if you have anything to report, please come to me. Agreed?"

"Passed nem-con," put in Tim Grant. "I don't know if it's up to me to do it, but I should like to propose a vote of thanks for Presidential speech. I consider it was very tastefully done."

"I second that," put in Derrick Cossack.

"Thank you for your kind attention," said Frank Harris. "What about an eightsome? I'm told that Tim has explained the intricacies of the Scots Reel to a Viennese bandmaster on two words of German and several Lagers."

"Very clever of you, Tim," said Jane, as they moved out towards the ballroom. Pippa linked her arm in Kate's as they moved along the corridor.

"Do you read Galsworthy, Kate?"

"Yes: or rather I did. He wrote for my generation. I thought he was a marvellous storyteller, but the odd thing is I can't read him these days. The world's changed such a lot."

"I suppose it has, but I haven't any standard of comparison," said Pippa. "I live in the country, near Winchester. Perhaps my parents are a bit Galsworthy-ish, but I was thinking of that phrase 'A dark disharmonic young man'. Don't you think it describes Tim Grant rather well?"

"Yes: perhaps it does," said Kate, glancing at Pippa with a feeling of surprise. Pippa was fair and gay and beautiful, but Kate had not previously credited her with being thoughtful. "I think that's rather acute of you," said Kate. "Disharmonic... meaning not quite in tune with the world, as though there was something sombre in the set-up?"

"Yes. As though the world's let him down, or he's at odds with it."

When they entered the ballroom, Kate and Pippa did not go down at once on to the floor. They stood on the gallery in front of the bar and looked down at the dancers. Kate said: "The thing which astonishes me is that the lads and girls of Tim's age and yours don't look more 'disharmonic'. It's only six or seven years since you were in the hell of 'all that,' particularly the lads, and they hardly show a mark of it. Tim was a pilot, wasn't he? Ian was in Malaya: Neville was a Commando, I believe. I think the recuperative power of young humanity is incredible."

"I suppose it is," said Pippa, "but faces often don't tell the real story. Robert often looks much more—what was the word you used?—sombre than any of the others, and he wasn't in the war at all. Look at him now."

"Yes, he does look hipped," agreed Kate, "but Irishmen are moodier than Englishmen. He'll be all right when he starts dancing. He's a lovely dancer, just as he's a lovely skier, although he's out of practice. You'd better go and dance, Pippa. Do your stuff and leave me to meditate. Hallo, surely the men aren't packing up?"

Ian and Neville had come back from the dance floor and Neville stopped to murmur in Kate's ear as he passed her: "Ian and I are going to check up on you know what. We can't bear the suspense any longer. We're neither of us in the plutocrat class."

"We shan't be a brace of shakes," said Ian. "Cossack's gone, too. He's a careful chap."

3

It was during the first "old-fashioned" (which was a Strauss waltz) that Robert came and sat by Frank Harris. Robert usually danced every number, and more than one of the girls of the party raised their eyebrows at him. With Ian and Neville busy on their own devices, and Harris showing no inclination to dance with anybody, the girls were having a dull evening.

Robert muttered in Frank Harris's ear. "Thought I'd better tell you. Ten quid's worth of Austrian notes were pinched from a suitcase in my bedroom either last night or this morning."

Harris's face didn't alter at all, and his voice was completely casual as he replied: "Right. I'm not surprised. I'll look in on you on my way back to bed. I'm in Walterhof, so I pass your shack. Say between eleven and twelve?"

"O.K.," said Robert, sulkily rather than cheerfully, and Harris added:

"We'd better go and dance, or we shan't be popular. See you later."

It was some half-hour later that Neville Helston came and sat down beside Frank Harris and said: "Sorry and all that, but my English pound notes have gone. Dexter and Cossack and I went across to check up."

"Where did you leave the notes?" asked Harris.

"In a drawer, under my clean shirts."

"How much? The regulation five pounds?"

"Well… a bit more than that. Say eight or nine."

Harris groaned. "Serve you right. Oh well, I don't suppose you'll see them again."

"Do they know who the racketeer is?"

"No. And speculations aren't my business."

It was about ten o'clock that Harris left the hotel and set out across the snow. He felt thoroughly disturbed and uncomfortable, and his conscientious mind was worrying about what steps he ought to take. In his own mind he was anxious to avoid reporting these thefts to either hotel manager or police until he had considered the situation a bit more closely. It was all too easy to say, "It must be one of those foreigners," when he had no evidence to go on, save that it went against the grain to believe that any of their own party could be a thief. But Harris was a very fair-minded man: he had known thefts to occur in very respectable surroundings, in public schools, in reputable clubs, in sports' pavilions, in the residents' quarters in hospital. Sometimes the theft had been of a pathological nature, the kleptomania which can possess the adolescent or maladjusted mind. In one case it had been quite inexplicable—a theft by a fellow who had no conceivable need to thieve. Harris thought of all these things as he walked over the silent snow beneath a sky whose stars seemed brittle with brilliance, sharp splinters of light which might crack into myriad scintillas of radiance. Then, a little way behind him, a man's voice began to sing *"Heilige Nacht"*. Softly the traditional air was lilted, murmured rather than sung in a deep bass voice and inevitably the English words came into the Englishman's mind: "Stilly night, starry and bright..."

Keeping pace with the music, Frank Harris walked up to the front door of Robert O'Hara's chalet and rang the bell. Before the door was opened the singer had joined him on the doorstep, and Harris recognised a tall fair young German who was a noted skier. They exchanged greetings in German, and when the door was opened by stout Fraulein Braun, Frank explained that he had come to see Mr. O'Hara. It was likely that Mr. O'Hara was not yet in. Could he wait for him? The German woman knew Harris as one of the English party at the Kronebergerhof and she said at once that the Herr Doktor could go up to Herr "Harror's" room (the name O'Hara completely defeated her) and that Herr Schmidt would show him up. It was number seven.

Harris thanked her and went upstairs with the polite young German, who was delighted to find an Englishman who talked fluent German.

"How many visitors are staying in this house?" asked Harris.

Young Schmidt considered: "My sister and myself, and… one, two, three Englishmen. Five, that is. You have one very good skier in your party, Herr Doktor."

"Have we? I thought we all did a lot of tumbling about, though O'Hara is better than most of us. He is an Irishman."

"He is a good skier," replied the other. "If he tumbles, it is to encourage the beginners, perhaps."

O'Hara's bedroom door was not locked. Not that it would have made any difference if it were, thought Harris, because Robert had left his window open. You could hardly blame him for that, for the central heating was overpowering to an English mind, but leaving windows open was very unpopular with German hausfraus, as there was always a chance that the water pipes might freeze. Harris glanced round the clean commonplace room. The usual feather bed, with the inevitable "duvet," the huge top eiderdown which they all hated. If it stayed on the bed you were much too hot, but it always came off and left you struggling with an inadequate sheet. The furniture was new, of the same variety as English "Utility" but, apart from the elaborate fixed wash-basin, even more gimcrack. There was a combined hanging cupboard and shelves with a door which did not fasten properly, a bedside table and two chairs. That was all. O'Hara's suitcase was under his bed, and Harris pulled it out. It was locked, but one of his own keys turned the locks. He went quickly through the suitcase and then closed it again and replaced it under the bed. Sitting down to wait until O'Hara should come in, Harris looked round for something to read. He could find nothing but an old newspaper, *The Morning Mail*, which had apparently been used for packing, but the crossword puzzle was intact. Harris got out a pencil, and happened to glance at some of the paragraph headings. "Cat burglar on snow-covered roofs," he read. "Daring climb ends in sordid crime." Harris yawned. The room was hot, even with the window open. He had been ski-ing all day, and dancing since dinner, and he thought longingly of his bed.

4

It was not until after eleven that Robert O'Hara came in.

"Sorry to have kept you. We got dancing reels," he said, and Harris replied:

"All right. I've been doing a crossword in your paper. Can I keep it?"

"Lord, yes. I don't want it. I had it for packing something."

"Right. Now I'm sorry about all this to-do, Robert. Will you tell me exactly what happened, from the word go?"

"There's not much to tell. We arrived here on Tuesday. In the evening I changed a traveller's cheque at the hotel: several of us did."

"Yes. I did myself. I changed one for two pounds only. Yours was for ten pounds, wasn't it?"

"Yes. I produced my passport, signed the cheque, and bunged it over to the manager—the blond type—and he handed me the Austrian notes and I shoved them in my pocket—"

"Can you remember who was beside you at the time?"

"One of the girls, I think, but I'm not sure. We were most of us there, and the lounge was packed, everybody milling around. Anyway, we went and danced for a bit and went to bed pretty early. Tim Grant and Ian and I walked back here together, and Tim told us about flying to Zürich and the plane charter company he works for. When we got here we unpacked and mucked around in each other's rooms—they're all much of a muchness and hot enough to suffocate you. I put the notes in my suitcase, and I thought I locked it."

"Was anybody in here when you did so?"

"Yes, both of them, I think—Tim and Ian. I remember Ian was cursing because the wardrobe in his room doesn't shut properly: neither does this one, and there isn't a lock on anything. So I said I'd better put the notes in my suitcase. And that was that. I didn't go to it again until last night. The notes were there then, at least I think they were. I'd put them in an envelope, and those hundred schilling notes make quite a wad. But when I went to get them out this morning, they'd gone."

"What about your English pound notes?"

"Well... I had five to start with, but I spent one on the meal in the train and drinks on the boat, and I changed one on the train in France—some of the others had got more French currency than they wanted—so I've only got three left. They're tucked in my diary in my pocket, together with my traveller's cheques and some small Austrian notes I got on the train—change for a French note I paid for a meal with. The International Dining Car people accept any European currency you like to pay in."

Harris nodded. "Yes. Well, I'm glad you've got your English currency accounted for. Now look here, Robert. Say if you open that suitcase and go through everything carefully. I've known chaps who complained they'd lost something when they'd simply mislaid it. And you don't seem the world's tidiest creature, from what I can see of that wardrobe. Start with the suitcase, and then go through everything else and make sure."

"Well, dash it all, I'm not a kid," said Robert indignantly. "I may not be tidy, but I know where things are and what I've got."

Harris sat in silence for a moment or so: then he said: "If I have to let the police know about this, Robert, the first thing they'll do is to ask you to go through your belongings in their presence. I've had experience of this sort of thing. It's much wiser to make absolutely certain beforehand. If you'd rather not, say so."

The Irishman sat on his bed and stared at Harris with a stare which was very far from being amiable. Robert was a big dark fellow, who looked as though he might well put on weight with increasing years, and his dark eyes sometimes looked aggressive.

"Are you suggesting this is a put-up job, Harris?"

"No. I'm not. I only want you to make certain you've got the facts right before we volunteer information to anyone else," replied Harris patiently.

After a moment or so of hesitation, Robert plunged under his bed and drew out his suitcase.

Chapter IX

1

It was a very commonplace suitcase, reinforced fibre with worn corners of leather, such as you see by the hundred at any main-line station. Robert fumbled in his pockets and produced a commonplace key and set the lid back. He had said he had unpacked, but the process had been a very partial one. Clean pyjamas, spare sweaters, vests and pants, books and writing materials and an old tweed jacket were jumbled up with packing paper, maps and medicaments. Robert stirred the whole lot into even worse confusion, saying crossly, "I told you it wasn't here."

"That's no good, my lad," said Harris. "You take things out one by one and shake them, and I'll fold the garments up when we're both quite sure that envelope isn't in one of those pyjama legs or something."

Robert glowered at him, but did as he was bid. Pyjamas and underwear were shaken out and then folded up methodically by Frank Harris. Handkerchiefs followed, a fair isle pullover, a seaman's jersey, ties and scarves. Again O'Hara said: "I told you it wasn't there."

"You take out every single thing in it," said Harris.

The Irishman was beginning to lose his temper now. He flung things pell-mell on the bed, and threw a book across the room towards the bedside table. He missed his aim and the book flew open. It was a new copy of *Popski's Private Army* and as it fell on the floor, crumpling the clean leaves, some English pound notes fell out of it.

There was a sudden dead silence. Robert O'Hara's face flushed a dusky red and his eyes seemed to bulge as he stared at the crisp slips of greenish paper. Then he turned to Harris. "Those aren't mine," he said.

"Is the book yours?"

"No. It's Dexter's. He lent it to me on the train. He'd got another one."

"Better get him in," said Harris. "He told me an hour or so ago he'd only got five English pound notes, and he'd got those on him, in his coat pocket."

Flushed of face, O'Hara said: "Is this a frame-up?"

"I don't know what it is," said Harris. "Better fetch Dexter. Perhaps he can explain."

The Irishman went to the door, and a moment later Harris heard him banging on the adjacent door, followed by Ian Dexter's voice expostulating: "Here, steady on, Robert. You'll be waking the whole house up if you make so much row."

"You come along in here," said Robert wrathfully.

Ian entered the room and stared, as well he might, for Robert had thrown the odd items out of his suitcase all over the floor, and paper lay crumpled up on the bed, giving the room a debauched air.

"Is that your book?" demanded Robert angrily and Ian retorted:

"Yes, it is, and it's the last time I'll lend a book to an Irishman. It's a filthy way to treat a book." He advanced to pick it up and then saw the pound notes, scattered on the floor. "Good lord, whose are those?" he demanded.

Harris got up. "Better shut that window and draw the curtains," he said prosaically, "and don't let's make a row. It's past midnight."

He went and closed the window. Ian Dexter, looking very young and slim in a tailored silk dressing-gown, stood with his back to the door, his face a study in bewilderment. "Is he drunk?" he said to Harris.

"No, damn you. I'm not drunk," said Robert furiously.

"Getting excited about it isn't going to help," said Harris. "Dexter, there was a sheaf of pound notes in that book. Robert says they're not his. Are they yours?"

"No. They're not. I've only got the regulation five. I told you so."

"All right. Let's sit down and think this out. We'd better have Tim Grant in here as well. Go and fetch him, Ian."

Tim—he whom Pippa had described as a "dark disharmonic young man"—came into the room with Ian a moment later. He, also, wore a silk dressing-gown, rather gaudier than Ian's, and above it his dark thin face looked brooding and troubled.

"Sorry to rout you out, Tim, but we've struck a spot of bother," said Harris, his calm resolute voice deliberate and sensible. "Sit on the bed. Robert can cope with the damned duvet later. It's like this. Robert reported to me that ten pounds' worth of Austrian notes had gone from his suitcase. I asked him to go carefully through the suitcase, examining everything in it. Ten English pound notes were tucked inside that book of Ian's."

"Good lord! Neville says he's lost his English currency," said Ian.

The remark was hardly a fortunate one, and Robert turned furiously on Ian, but Harris interrupted him. "If you'll kindly let me get on with what I'm saying, we'll deal with things in order," he said resolutely. "The first thing that occurs to me is that one of you chaps may have been staging a rag. At the moment Robert's lost ten quid's worth of Austrian notes and been presented, unknown to himself, with ten quid in English notes. If anybody has been being funny, it's time he said so."

"I haven't," said Ian at once. "I'm not above ragging anybody, but rags connected with money don't strike me as amusing. I have neither touched Robert's money, nor left any English notes in Popski."

"Neither have I," said Tim. "I agree with Ian. Rags about money wouldn't seem much like rags to me: quite the reverse." He turned to Robert, who sat glowering on a chair. "I'm sorry about this, Bobs. It's a pretty foul thing to have happened, but it's also quite bats. Thieving is one thing. Everybody who gets around knows there are plenty of travel thieves. You find them everywhere. But thieves don't replace one sort of currency with an equal amount of another."

Harris was relieved to hear Tim Grant's quiet sympathetic voice, and his use of the nickname which had been promptly bestowed on Robert brought a more friendly atmosphere into the room. O'Hara's face was no longer flushed: he still looked angry, but he was rather white.

"The whole thing's filthy," he said. "You've nothing but my word for it that I did lose my Austrian notes, and for all you know I may have pinched Neville's English ones."

"All right," said Tim equably. "And you have nothing but Ian's word and mine that we didn't snaffle your Austrian currency and replace it with English pound notes, which may be dud ones for all you know. Likewise we've nothing but Neville's word for it that he's lost his English money. It seems to me to be more sensible to believe each other. We've no earthly reason to suspect each other of telling lies. Personally, I believe every word you've said, Bobs."

"So do I," put in Harris quietly, "and it's time we got everything on the square. I tell you straight that I haven't been behaving too sensibly myself. When Robert told me that he'd lost those notes out of his suitcase, two things occurred to me: the first was that he might be mistaken. I know from experience that it's quite possible to get things jumbled up in a suitcase, and I'd seen enough of Robert to know he's quite good at 'losing things' which have merely got put in the wrong pocket."

"That's true enough," said Tim equably. "Bobs lost his passport, his ski-school tickets and his ski-lift season at least twice each in the last two days—and they were all safely on his person all the time."

"So I observed," said Harris. "Well, here is my 'own-up'. When I was in this room, before you came in, Robert, I opened your suitcase. I've got several keys on my ring which would undo the locks. I opened the suitcase and looked for the Austrian notes. Instead I found the English notes, almost at once. I then shut your suitcase and when you came in I asked you to go through it. You did so. Now you may consider this a very discreditable way for me to behave, but it's settled one point, so far as I am concerned. You obviously did not know those pound notes were there. If you had done, you'd either have refused to open the suitcase, or else taken care that I did not see the notes."

"I quite agree," said Tim, but Robert put in angrily:

"You'd no right to touch my suitcase, Harris."

"That I acknowledge, and I offer you an apology for having done what seems to you a shabby trick, Robert. But do try to remember this. Thefts of this kind are no trivial matter, and I'll ask you all to believe that I'm not taking this business light-heartedly. Very far from it. The issues involved are too unpleasant. To begin with, I don't like the idea of coming to a foreign country and accusing either the hotel employees or fellow guests of theft. Austria is technically an ex-enemy country, and it's up to us to be particularly scrupulous in our behaviour to the Austrians."

"I entirely agree with you," put in Tim. "The Austrians are being wholeheartedly friendly to us; they're all glad to see the English here again, and as tourists in their country it's up to us to behave decently to them."

"No one has suggested that the Austrians have had any hand in this," said Ian, in his quick, impatient way. "It's idiotic to suppose they have. What Austrian would plant English pound notes in a suitcase after having pinched a corresponding amount of their own currency? It's the craziest story I ever heard. Sounds much more like an Englishman with a perverted sense of humour, if you ask me."

"Or an Irishman," put in Robert O'Hara sullenly.

"Let's leave that out of it, Robert," said Harris. "The next thing to consider is the effect on our own party. I don't know how you fellows stand, but I do know that some of the girls in this party have made a considerable effort to save their money for this trip. It's something they've been looking forward to for a long time, and I don't want it spoiled for them. If there's any suspicion of ill will, the confidence and enjoyment will go sky high, just blown up, and we might as well all pack up and go home. I don't want that to happen."

"Well, I'd better go home," said Robert. "It all seems to be my fault."

"I don't know what you're grousing about, Bobs," said Tim placidly. "So far as I can see, you're no worse off than you were before. You've got your ten quid back, even though it is a mystery how it happened. Technically, I suppose you haven't been robbed at all. You're all square."

Ian Dexter turned to Harris. "Frank, who first told you there was some funny business going on?"

"That I can't tell you," said Harris. "I was told that there might be a thief about. I spoke as I did at dinner because I wanted to warn everybody not to be casual over leaving money in bedrooms. It's an elementary precaution when you travel to keep your cash on you, or else hand it in to be put in a safe. There are very few suitcases which have good enough locks to resist a thief, and the furniture in rooms like this offers nobody any security. Leaving money in bedrooms is simply likely to cause bother for honest landladies and hotel servants. That was the point I wanted to make when I spoke to you after dinner."

"That's all right, Frank," said Tim. "Contents noted, so to speak. I bet we'll all be a bit more careful after this. But the point is, where do we go from here?"

Robert O'Hara said at once, "Better give those pound notes back to Helston. It's he who's lost English notes. Not me."

"Well, there's that," said Ian. "But who the hell's been playing the goat? What's the point?"

"There is only one point. To do the dirty on me," said Robert furiously. "Don't pretend you're too thick to see that,

Ian. Somebody loses their pound notes and they're found in my suitcase."

"I wonder if your Austrian notes are in Neville's suitcase?" put in Tim. "That seems to be the logical conclusion to me. If so, who's the poltergeist?"

"Well, that's an idea," said Ian. "What about going and routing out Neville?"

"A bit late for that tonight," said Harris soberly, but Ian replied: "This isn't an English village. We're on the Continent. Nobody expects us to keep English hours. They go on dancing until about three o'clock in all the hotels. I reckon we'd better go and ask Neville to see what surprises he's got in his outfit. Come on, Bobs. You'll feel better when we've made Neville look fishy."

Robert suddenly grinned. "I certainly should. It'd be jam to find his suitcase packed with Austrian currency."

"Better leave it until tomorrow morning," said Harris, but the Irishman turned round on him in a flash.

"All right. You leave it till tomorrow morning, Frank. I'm not going to. I'm the one with the grouse. I've had my Austrian currency pinched, and my suitcase searched with no permission asked. I've had several lectures from you and I'm not taking it all lying down."

"All right," said Harris resignedly. "I admit you've a right to resent the way I behaved, and you've also a right to tell me that I had the opportunity to plant those English notes on you. Incidentally, have you got a pair of gloves? Mine are still wet with snow."

"Yes, but what for?"

"So that I can collect those notes without leaving fingerprints all over them," replied Harris.

Tim whistled, and then asked: "Where do we go from here?"

"The answer to that one is that I don't know," said Harris and he spoke very soberly. "I call everybody to witness that none of us in this room has touched those notes. Robert chucked the book across the room, but he didn't touch the notes. I did not touch them, neither did Ian or you."

"That's quite a point, old sober-sides," said Tim, and Ian put in: "Fingerprints… Cripes. I didn't think of that one. It doesn't sound too good."

2.

The four men went out into the starlit night. Frank Harris deliberately slowed Tim down, so that Ian and Robert were a little ahead.

"Look here, Tim, this is a silly business," said Harris. "Robert's lost his wool completely, he's spoiling for a scrap. Neville isn't what I should call a patient chap and we don't want a row."

"Agreed, but I shouldn't bother too much," said Tim. "The place Neville's sleeping in is up that steep slope away towards the pine woods. It's as slippery as a glacier and Robert hasn't got ski-boots on, and he hasn't got ski-sticks either. You wait and see what happens. It's surprising how fed up a chap can get with falling off a track into deep snow. Ian won't help him, he's got too much horse sense. Look, toss number one. It's amazing how slippery these tracks get after sunset."

"Well, I hope you're right," said Harris resignedly, and Tim went on: "I've got an idea, Frank. Do you remember the incredible yarn in that book about Constantinople in war-time, when a valet pinched diplomatic papers marked Top Secret, sold them to Ribbentrop and Co., and got paid in forged pound notes—dud sterling?"

"Yes, I remember."

"Well, is there a chance that some of those English currency notes the Nazis forged are still about?"

"I don't know—but I think I can guess what you're getting at," said Harris.

"Somebody—enemy alien of some kind—unloading them on British tourists, hoping to discredit sterling when the Bank of England repudiates them?" hazarded Tim.

"Doesn't sound very probable to me," said Harris. "It'd have to be on a colossal scale to have any effect, and although I know that war-time stories are crazier than any that a thriller merchant would dare to put over, I tend to fall back on common sense now that we're not actually at war."

"I was trying to find an explanation of what's happened to Robert," said Tim. "It's dotty enough, in all conscience, although, technically, I suppose he hasn't been robbed at all. What are you going to do about those pound notes, Frank?"

"I've sealed them up in an envelope, as you can bear witness. I shall put the envelope in the hotel safe tomorrow. If we don't have any more incidents—and I hope to God we don't—I shall give them to Robert on the boat, when we go home. Incidentally, Ian was perfectly right about the hours they keep in this place. There are still lights on everywhere, and they're still dancing at the Schneiderhof—you can hear the band when the door opens."

"You can—and I wouldn't mind betting some of our lot are having a final dance before they turn in, Neville included," said Tim. "Look, they're just getting to the steep bit—what did I tell you?"

"They're both down," said Harris. "I thought Ian had his ski-boots on."

"He has—I expect Robert grabbed him and pulled him

down as he slipped. Watch your step. It's as treacherous as what not."

The steep slope which led to the chalet by the pine wood was easy enough to walk up in day-time, when the sun had softened the trodden snow sufficiently to give boots some purchase, but after dark it froze to a condition when it was almost unnegotiable in smooth-soled shoes. An additional difficulty was caused by the impossibility of seeing the track in the starlight—the snow seemed to gleam in an unbroken sheet. Robert and Ian had fallen together, glissaded off the path and landed in a snowdrift below. It appeared to be a deep snowdrift, judging from the amount of scuffling which was going on. Ian's indignant voice was heard in a muffled shout: "Here, chuck it, Robert. What the hell do you think you're doing? Let go my legs."

"What the hell did you sit on my head for?" demanded the Irishman furiously, and Tim called: "Chuck it, you two— you'll start a minor avalanche next. There's tons of snow on that bank. Here, Ian, give me your hand and I'll haul you out. It's deeper than I'd realised." As though to give point to Tim's warning, an overhanging crust of snow from the ledge above fell with a thud on O'Hara's head and neck, just as he was struggling to his feet. Ian had regained the hard track by this time, and together he and Tim hauled the floundering Irishman out of the drift.

"That's about enough foolery for this evening," said Harris tersely. "This isn't the sort of temperature to have a snow fight in. You can get straight home, both of you. By the time the snow on you has melted, you'll both be wet through. Come on, Robert. You don't want to get pneumonia."

Rather surprisingly the Irishman turned back with Harris, while Tim stood for a moment, beating the snow off Dexter's clothes. None of them was in ski-kit, and snow can be surprisingly penetrating when anybody rolls in it in ordinary clothes.

"Cripes, what a muck," said Ian, stamping and shaking himself. "Did you see that happen, Tim?"

"Yes, more or less. Robert slipped—I knew he would, that path's impossible in ordinary shoes. As he slipped, he grabbed at you, and you went down too."

"He pulled me over," said Ian.

"Of course he did. It's instinctive to grab at anybody when your feet go from under you," said Tim. "He fell sideways and pulled you down with him, and if my guess is anywhere near right you landed on his head. Result, he was convinced you meant to land on his head. So would anybody else have done in the circumstances. You can both reckon you were lucky you didn't hurt one another."

Ian grunted, and they trudged on together, both more wary than they had been on the outward journey.

"Well, it was a damn' silly business," said Ian at length. "But what do you make of the other racket, Tim?"

"I don't know—and I don't think I want to know," said Tim slowly. "Better leave it to Harris to deal with. He's got plenty of common sense, and if we're going to keep this party in trim, common sense is what's needed. It'd be an awful pity to muck it up, Ian. It's the nicest party I was ever with. Everyone's enjoying themselves, and everyone's fun to be around with."

"Yes. I agree—but there must be some explanation of this schemozzle over Robert's currency."

Tim walked along for a while in silence. Then he said: "I think Robert's a muddler. I don't mean I don't like him. I do. But I think he loses things, or thinks he loses them, and forgets where he's put them, and then gets excited. The whole show is probably just a muddle."

"And what about Neville—d'you think he's a muddler?"

"No, but if he left his English pound notes tucked under his clean shirts, he's an ass. Now, for the love of Mike, let's leave it alone, and if Robert tries to come and argue any more tonight, take care your door's locked and don't answer him. Somehow I don't think he will. Snow's very deflating stuff when it falls on you in bulk and he had as much rough and tumble as he wanted, and not much fun with it. So forget the rest."

"O.K.," said Ian. "I'll try. I'm sleepy enough to snore the clock round."

Chapter X

1

When Rivers left George Bell at Harpenden, the C.I.D. man drove straight back to London, as fast as visibility permitted. It was a disgusting evening, pondered Rivers, as he left the lights of St. Albans behind and accelerated on the first long straight stretches of the Barnet road. Wet snow drove depressingly against the windscreen and slush flew out in dirty cascades from the wheels, while mist tended to settle in the hollows. Into Rivers' mind there flashed a visualisation of crisp, dry shining snow on the Scheidegg-Wengen slopes, hot sun and the hiss of skis flying on a delectable unbroken surface of glittering whiteness. He swore softly as a huge northbound lorry threw a small avalanche of dirty slush right over his own car. Snow?—heaven save the word!

It took two hours to drive into central London—and all the patience which Rivers possessed. He drove to the public library mentioned by George Bell, interviewed the deputy librarian and drove back to Scotland Yard with *The Times*

Atlas safely in the back of the car. That huge and heavy tome was not used a great deal, the librarian had told him. It was in the reference library, and anybody could consult it, but its weight discouraged the frivolous.

Having turned the atlas over to the fingerprint department, Rivers went up to his own office and rang through to the canteen for coffee and sandwiches. He was shortly joined by Detective-Inspector Lancing, who looked cheerful enough despite his greeting:

"Good evening, sir, and of all the foul, filthy and ineffable evenings I've ever met, this one wins easily."

"They call it snow," said Rivers. "Let's forget it. Have some coffee. I've known worse."

The two detective officers made an interesting contrast to anyone who cared to study physique and physiognomy. Rivers was a tall fellow with big shoulders which he could hunch in a convincing imitation of lethargy, but there was a lissomeness in his movements which told of physical control and training. His fairness was untouched by grey, his eyes surprisingly blue—when he really opened them—and his ears well set back, flat, against a good skull. "Sleepy-looking" was often a first reaction to his casual glance and off-hand manner. Lancing, nearly twenty years younger, was four inches shorter, dark, compact, with lively eyes and lips which tended to curl up at the corners. If he sat or stood still, it was a disciplined stillness, for mobility was the essence of him. Rivers had once said that Lancing faced life on tiptoes, and the phrase suggested the zest innate in the younger man.

Lancing fetched another cup and helped himself to coffee, and as he lit a cigarette he said: "I reckon Victoria's a safe guess, sir."

"I'm delighted to hear it," said Rivers dryly. "Duty is duty, but a line heading southwards seems less revolting than a line heading east or north. And the North Sea must be a poem tonight. Don't mind me, Lancing. Tell me all the bits and pieces. Had a good day?"

"I've had a perfectly revolting day, sir. I've been beating around Southampton Row, Holborn, Kingsway, Waterloo Bridge, and Victoria Station for about ten perishing bleeding hours. 'London, thou art the flower of cities all.' There are moments when I think anybody who chooses to live in the place must be meet for Bedlam." Lancing cocked his dark eyebrows and grinned at Rivers' unsympathetic face. "It was a postman who gave me the first dope," went on the younger man. "Seven-thirty a.m. on New Year's Day—and you remember what sort of morning it was, sir. Between seven and seven-thirty's a good strategic time around Southampton Row. Too early for the black-coated, too late for city chars and market porters. Sort of pause in the day's occupation, if you ever learnt Longfellow at school. I think our bloke must have wrapped up his skis in newspapers, neatly tied round with string. The postman didn't think they looked much like skis, but he saw a chap with a parcel about eight feet long balanced on his shoulder. It didn't look much like anything else, either. The chap crossed Holborn to Kingsway, heading south."

Rivers suddenly grinned. "Good for you, Lancing. How many chaps did you tackle before you froze on to the postman?"

"About a hundred," said Lancing modestly. "Nobody'd ever believe the amount of plain donkey work we do. I lost track of the bloke with the parcel in the Strand and wasted a coupla' hours. Then I thought of Waterloo. I reckon he went there for breakfast, complete with parcel. About ten o'clock he left the parcel in the cloakroom, together with a workman's tool bag. The chaps in the left-luggage office thought the parcel was planks, and the bloke who left them said he was making a chicken run."

"Description of bloke?" inquired Rivers.

"Tallish, dark, youngish: talked like a good cockney. A dirty raincoat 'over all,' as the heralds say, and regulation cloth cap. About as remarkable as some million or so other blokes in Greater London. He came back for his planks at twelve o'clock or thereabouts. I spent the whole afternoon dodging round the taxi-ranks. About twelve-thirty p.m. on New Year's Day a quite personable young gent, complete with suitcase, rucksack, skis and ski-sticks took a taxi from the Waterloo rank and was driven to Victoria, continental side, where ski-sticks are about as noticeable as flowers in May. The boat train left at one o'clock."

"Description of personable young gent?" inquired Rivers.

Lancing cocked his brows again: "Want a lot from your underlings, don't you, sir? The operative word was 'gent'. A nice bloke, apparently: dark eyes, tall, nice grin, very good teeth, friendly manner. Dressed in tweed topcoat, gaudy wool scarf—club colours, says Jehu, but same not specified. 'Victoria,' says gent, 'and make it snappy, unless the end of the world catches up with us before we get there.'"

"How much of this are you making up?" asked Rivers morosely, "or are you expecting me to believe a taxi-driver on a main-line rank remembers the conversation of the fare he picked up the day before yesterday?"

"It was New Year's Day, sir—and was it a day! Did it get dark round about noon or didn't it?"

"Yes. There's that," agreed Rivers. "Go on."

"And the bloke with the skis in the taxi wasn't the only

one who suggested it was either the end of the world or an atom bomb on the outer suburbs. Cripes! That was a day, that was. They got held up in a traffic block at the approach to Westminster Bridge, and the laddie got restive. 'Cut out of it and try Lambeth Bridge,' he said. 'If I miss that train I'm kippered. I'm travelling with a party.'"

"Was he, by gad," said Rivers, suddenly waking up, his blue eyes very bright.

Lancing grinned. "I thought there might be a reaction to that one," he replied. "Well, the taxi-man said, 'I can't bloody well cut out. Here we are and here we're stuck until something obliges by moving on.' And the next bit takes my fancy," went on Lancing. "''E didn't 'alf swear,' said the taxi bloke to me, 'and 'e went on with some piece about smoke of hell and blanket of the dark.'"

Rivers' eyes were very much awake now. "'... pall thee in the dunnest smoke of hell,'" he quoted: "'That my keen knife see not the wound it makes, Nor Heaven peep through the blanket of the dark to cry "Hold, hold!"'"

"Yes," said Lancing. "*Macbeth*. Act I. Scene v. Not inappropriate when you think what the nice bloke had just been organising—if your guess is right, sir. And the dunnest smoke of hell just about hits off the atmospheric conditions on New Year's Day at noon in London, when that taxi was jammed in a traffic block on Westminster Bridge. But he caught his train all right, with about three minutes to spare."

2

Lancing paused in his narrative and took one of Rivers' cigarettes.

"Thank you, sir. Well, I didn't get going at Victoria until

after six, by which time the bloke I wanted had heard the hooter and gone home. As you probably know yourself, British Railways, in their paternal benevolence, give preferential treatment to parties of people who travel abroad together, particularly ski-ing parties."

"Yes. I did know that," said Rivers. "If the party consists of a given number—fifteen, isn't it?—a rebate is granted sufficient for one free ticket if desired, but the party must travel together—en bloc—to satisfy the conditions."

Lancing nodded. "And the party is traceable, because one person generally makes himself responsible for arrangements and payment and so forth."

"That's why I came to when you mentioned a party," said Rivers. "It looked a much better proposition to locate a party than a single skier."

"It was the largest grain of comfort I derived in the whole sodden perishing day," said Lancing. "It's funny, on the few occasions when I've been lucky enough to go abroad, I've regarded Victoria Station as the gates of paradise. Today, it was as the gates of Avernus: hell, but a cold hell. Cripes, what a climate this one is!"

"Cheer up. There's quite a prospect we may both get out of it for a few days," said Rivers. "So you'd better see to it that your passport is in order."

Lancing's grin extended from ear to ear, his good white teeth flashing in his dark face. "Would the department run to skis, sir? I reckon I've earned them today."

"Depends how good you are—at ski-ing," said Rivers. "Incidentally, how good are you?"

"I've seen worse," said Lancing: and then added modestly, "I've also seen better. But I'm off the leading strings. At least I can stop when the driving-test bloke says 'stop,' which is more than I could my first year. I could go like hell, but an emergency stop was simply beyond me. My own theory is…"

"Say if we get back to the matter in hand," said Rivers firmly. "I gather you spent another two hours at the mouth of Avernus, or in your cold hell, being Victoria Station, continental side, on a January evening. What did you do there?"

"Yes, sir," said Lancing submissively. "I talked to porters and ticket inspectors and platform inspectors: I talked to the *'baggage enregistré,' 'bagaglio spedito in transito'* blokes, and to anybody else who was fool enough to stand about on platforms to be talked to. A ski-ing party did leave by the one o'clock boat train on New Year's Day. To be really truthful, several parties did, but I expect we could sort them out a bit when we get on to the bloke who booked them. Anyway, the probability is that they went direct to Basle." Again Lancing chuckled. "Do you think the department will give us a roving permit, sir? Inspect ski-ing resorts from Zürich to St. Anton? I reckon they won't have gone farther than that. Austria's cheaper than Switzerland, but there's no object in going too far, and once you get beyond the French occupied zone you strike all the extra trouble involved by the Russians. I've been looking at maps, and I reckon—"

"I've no doubt you do," interrupted Rivers. "Since you're talking shop in your free time, or what ought to be your free time, I'm not justified in being too departmental, but we're getting ahead of our facts, Lancing."

"'Too many facts chasing too little belief…'" murmured Lancing. "Do you know who said that, sir?"

"Yes. I do: and you haven't got the quotation in full," said Rivers, "and it's not relevant to detection, anyway. You can't

have too many facts in our job, and they don't chase belief…
or do they? Damn, don't bring in red herrings, Lancing."

"I've been chasing belief all day long, sir. The belief being
yours. And it's all based on the print of a ski-stick in snow
which melted the day before yesterday."

"It isn't. At least, not altogether," said Rivers. "You're not
the only chap who's been working overtime. And now you can
ring down to the fingerprint department and ask if they've
got any results for me yet."

Lancing picked up the inter-departmental telephone, and
Rivers sat drawing patterns on his blotter. His patterns were
jagged and ridgy, and he knew quite well what was the motive
behind his pencil as peaks and saddle-backs formulated themselves on government blotting paper. Lancing's voice recalled
the Chief Inspector to the matter in hand.

"Bill Brown's bringing his prints up, sir. They're not dry
yet, but he says he's got them identified all right."

"Luck's all against this chap," murmured Rivers. "So far,
everything's gone wrong for him, all because he forgot one
thing. Or perhaps he didn't forget, but there was nothing he
could do about it."

"The coins in the slot meter?" asked Lancing, and Rivers
nodded.

"Yes. I wonder if he thought about them? But he couldn't
do anything. He was staging an accident. Just one of those
accidents which happen to chaps who get so drunk they
fall over a gas fire. If he'd forced the coin box of the slot
meter it wouldn't have looked like an accident, would it? Of
course, that wouldn't have mattered—the fingerprints on
the coins—if he hadn't dropped that cigarette carton on the
roof. Rule one for cat burglars: don't carry anything loose in
your pockets."

3

Bill Brown had come and gone. A series of photographs, still wet from the rinsing water, lay spread out on Rivers' blotting paper, and Rivers and Lancing were studying them with magnifying glasses. There was no guesswork here: across Map 36 in the *Times Atlas* were the same fingerprints which Records had listed as found on a cigarette carton and on the coins in the slot meter box at 13 Lioncel Court. Gray had been studying the *Times Atlas* all right, and the map he had concentrated on was that showing eastern Switzerland, part of Austria and the north of Italy. On the closely printed smooth surface of the map the fingerprints had been brought up with white powder and in the enlarged photograph the tell-tale chalk showed up surprisingly white and clear. The man who had studied this map had done what most people do when looking for tiny place names on a closely printed map; he had pressed his fingertips on the surface of the paper, and the clearness of the prints indicated that his fingers had been damp—"with excitement," Lancing hazarded. "Like mine are now, sir. But he wasn't interested in the Bernese Oberland. No prints on the Scheidegg-Wengen area. It was Austria he was after."

"Yes," said Rivers. "He traced the railway route from Zürich right across Switzerland... Sargen, Buchs, Bludenz—"

"Yes, and on to Langen and St. Anton," exclaimed Lancing, "and farther south, what is it—?"

"Villach," exclaimed Rivers. "Villach—that's a junction, between the Vienna line and the Adriatic ports, Trieste and Fiume. You can get to either of them from Villach."

"Where do we go from there?" asked Lancing, his dark eyes dancing.

"Anywhere in the wide world," said Rivers soberly, "and English currency notes are accepted anywhere on the Continent."

4

"What have we got that is cold, indisputable fact, leaving surmise and attractive theories out of it?" asked Rivers. He had moved the photographs out of the way, and pushed aside the big maps which he and Lancing had been studying. "A man, who called himself Gray, lodged in Mrs. Stein's house. Gray is young, tall, dark and a man of education. He may—or may not—be an Irishman. He knows a lot about ski-ing, but denied that he could ski. It can be presumed that the fingerprints found on the coins in the slot meter were Gray's fingerprints. These fingerprints are the same as those on the cigarette carton I found on the roofs above the post office. The man who achieved the climb over those roofs was an athlete. The body found in Gray's room at Lioncel Court was that of a young man, five feet eleven in height, of dark colouring: the only things which were presumably in his pockets which survived the fire were some coins, a petrol lighter, the nib of a fountain-pen and the front door key of 13 Lioncel Court. We have no means of proving that the body is, or is not, Gray's. Finally, Gray's typewriter has disappeared, and there was the print of a ski-stick in the porch."

Lancing promptly put in: "Gray had been studying a map showing the Swiss-Austrian frontier, concentrating on the ski-ing resorts of Vor-Arlberg, and tracing out the route to Villach. He speaks fluent German."

Lancing rubbed his dark head. "We've had many a case which offered us less to go on, sir. It all fits."

"It fits a damn' sight too well," said Rivers. "In fact the appositeness of the whole thing is almost hypnotic. You have dug up the fact that a tall dark fellow carrying a parcel which may have been skis was seen not far from Lioncel Court on the morning of the fire, and a tall dark fellow who was undoubtedly carrying skis took a taxi from Waterloo to Victoria to catch the one o'clock boat train on New Year's Day. But we've no proof that that man was Gray. How do we get proof?"

"A print, a print, my kingdom for a fingerprint," said Lancing. "No use trying the taxi—they clean them too well. Do they sign anything for registered baggage?"

"He wouldn't have had time to register any baggage," said Rivers, "but is there a hope from his railway ticket? You remember the little books they give you for tickets—one page for each stage of the journey. Don't they collect the first page at Dover? There's just a chance he might have fingered that page. That would be proof all right. I'll try the railway for that. Anything else?"

"Nothing of any immediate use, sir," said Lancing, "but may I have a smack at the whole jig-saw? Isn't it true that you've got to the stage when you're saying to yourself, 'I've been jumping to conclusions. Now I've got to go into reverse, start again from the beginning, and prove, or disprove, every step?'"

"Quite true," said Rivers. "It's an inevitable and salutary stage. I'm not running down imagination and its value in detection. Imagination is often the motive power which sets detection going. You're faced with a set of beastly facts—a partially incinerated corpse, a cracked whisky bottle, snivelling people and an obvious explanation of accidental death. If, at that stage, a detective doesn't use his imagination, he simply leads up to an obvious and probably wrong verdict. But once having used imagination as the fuel to drive his own mental engine, he's got to cry Halt, and reverse—as you suggested. And it's at this stage that the whole set-up gets tiresome."

Rivers paused to light a cigarette, and then went on: "I indulged in a possible hypothesis based on the ascertained facts: that Gray, knowing if he were caught he would be charged with homicide, killed another man whose corpse might pass as his own, took that man's ski-ing outfit, foreign currency, tickets and passport, and got abroad. It's an idea, and in given circumstances it might work. But the minute you analyse it, you're faced with equally possible variations. Gray, as a known bad lot, may have driven another man to murder him. That corpse may still be Gray's. And the adenoidal Syd may have murdered Gray when the latter was drunk, stolen what he could lay hands on—including the post office loot—and fired the house. Passed to you, please. 'Interpret it your own way.'"

Lancing grinned. "You've quite a knack for picking out the conversational bits from contemporary poetry, sir. You've never got over the effect of coping with Rollo Tempest. There was a poem of his in last month's *Apollo*. But about Gray. There's one point which convinces me that your first hypothesis is the true one. Gray told George Bell he could not ski, after George Bell had overheard a conversation which convinced him that Gray was an expert skier. Why did Gray say he couldn't ski? There's only one answer: because ski-ing was involved in Gray's plan for getting out of the country. Gray didn't want George Bell to say to the police 'Gray was an expert skier,' because no detective would have disregarded that one."

"Yes," said Rivers. "It's a point worth considering. It's also worth considering that if George Bell is a liar, the whole set-up looks very different."

"Oh, my God!" groaned Lancing. "Sorry, sir—but we can sort George Bell out easily enough. Chaps don't suddenly change their characters. I know characters do change, but it's over a period of time."

"I agree with you there," said Rivers. "Gray's character must have changed, but over a period of time, as you say. And there's another thing. You and I have got to be almighty careful that our own recollections of ski-ing don't father the thought that our quarry is probably to be found in the mountains in blazing sunlight and dry crisp snow: in the very conditions we'd both give a damned lot to be in, away from this filthy slushy mess of an English winter and the dunnest smoke of hell in this loathsome city."

Lancing chuckled. "Yes. And can't you imagine Gray saying that to himself? 'If I could only get away from all this, start afresh in decent conditions doing something I can do, and leave all this filthy tangle behind and start all over again'—as you do when you take a ski-lift up to the top and the jolly world's all yours." He broke off, and added more soberly: "I'll take you up on that one about facts chasing beliefs, sir. It's the other way round. You've made me believe in your original hypothesis, and that belief is going to make me chase the facts."

Rivers laughed. "Thanks for the vote of confidence. But there're a lot of variations to be sorted out. Don't imagine it's going to be easy."

"I don't," said Lancing, "but we're on the way."

Chapter XI

1

It was Mrs. Stein who found the typewriter. She had been having a wretched time. Anybody who has had a fire in the house, and fire hoses played on the flames, knows the heart-breaking state to which the two elements of fire and water can reduce domestic arrangements. Mrs. Stein had plenty of courage, and she was a hard worker, but she admitted to her sister Gert, who had nobly come in to help, that she almost wished the fire had "made a job of it and done with it".

"Don't you talk silly, Mabel," replied Gert. "There's not all that harm done, and some of your things is real good. You'd never get such a nice home together again, what with the price of things and that there utility. Real trash most of it is, and yours is good solid ma'ogany."

It was Gert who took all the blankets to the public wash-house. ("Don't you never trust good blankets to no laundry," she urged.) It was Gert who helped to drag sodden blackened carpets out into the yard, saying a little snow might help to clean them up, while Mrs. Stein stoked up the kitchen range and got the copper going for the sheets, and sent Syd on errand after errand to the dry cleaners. ("And see you get it out of the insurance," admonished Gert.)

The basement kitchen had suffered least from the debacle. It was stone-flagged, and for once in her life Mrs. Stein was thankful for those flagstones. Once mopped up, the stone dried at once, and the scrubbed kitchen table and dresser were soon got to rights. With Gert at the washhouse and Syd out on errands, Mrs. Stein sat down for a rest by the kitchen fire. There were men upstairs fitting a tarpaulin over the roof, and the rest of the house was cold and stinking and miserable, but the kitchen was warm and clean and homely. Mrs. Stein plumped down into her ancient arm-chair by the kitchen fire. It was an awful old arm-chair, whose springs had long since gone and been replaced by webbing, filled up with a variety of old flock cushions which had escaped inundation. Mrs. Stein had sat and cried in that chair when her husband "had been took". She plumped down into it thankfully, but said, "Law! This chair's gone dotty. Hard as a board, it is." She heaved herself up again and pulled off the cushions—two plush-covered, one crazy patchwork and the others best not described. At the bottom of all the cushions was a portable typewriter in its case, with a typed label still tied to the handle: "w. r. gray."

Mrs. Stein stood and looked at it, her face flushing dark red. Then the flush faded and she went a pasty grey. She had no doubt at all as to how the typewriter had come there, and she was badly frightened. She covered it up again quickly with the cushions and sat down on a hard kitchen chair to think.

Mrs. Stein, as George Bell had said to Rivers, was honest. It was natural to her to tell the truth, and she was thoroughly uncomfortable if she told a lie. She had told lies—and she faced it: the lies had been told for Syd. Mrs. Stein was a mother before she was anything else and if the only way to help Syd was to tell lies, well, she'd tell them. "Syd pinched that typewriter," she said to herself, and after that she dared not go on thinking about Syd. She had to think about the typewriter.

Before Mrs. Stein had been married she had been cashier in a shop. Typing had not been required in those days, but she knew how to fit a sheet of paper into a typewriter—she'd played about with a machine in the office—and an idea came into her head. It was true that the police had inquired if Mr. Gray had had a typewriter and she had said, "Of course he had. It was on the table in his room." But she could say she'd got all muddled up with the bother and everything, wasn't it enough to muddle anybody? Mrs. Stein sighed. Muddle? Wasn't she in a proper old muddle? Dare she say she'd asked Mr. Gray to lend her his typewriter to type a business letter, and gone and forgotten all about it with all this bother of the fire and that? It had been in the sideboard cupboard all the time. "If I go and tell the police myself, they can't say I tried to steal it," she argued to herself. About one thing she was quite determined. Syd wasn't going to be in on this. Mrs. Stein would deal with her son in her own way, but she wasn't handing him over to the police.

With resolve in her heart, she found a duster and a bottle of meth. Mrs. Stein knew all about fingerprints—'the Sunday paper and that' had told her all there was to know. She set to work and cleaned the typewriter with conscientious care, every key and lever, every bit of metal work and every bit of the cover. She was a careful cleaner. The cleaning finished, she shoved the typewriter under the ironing blanket in the big middle drawer of the dresser and sat down to think. If the police came in sudden like she'd got her story all pat. Of course she'd cleaned it—she was cleaning everything, and sakes alive, didn't everything need cleaning?—and she was ever so sorry she'd forgotten, but with the way things was, it'd be a wonder if she didn't forget her head.

Inevitably, Mrs. Stein made herself a cup of tea and wondered if her story were waterproof. It'd be a bit awkward if the police asked her to type something, she didn't really remember how the thing worked. If only she could put it back in Mr. Gray's room... but the door was locked, and anyhow they'd know the typewriter hadn't been there in the fire. Where else could she put it, so that it looked natural? Then she had another idea. She was busy cleaning up Mr. Rawlinson's room—that was the one on the first floor, just below Mr. Gray's. No end of a mess it was in, and she'd turned a lot of the things in it out on to the landing, and brought some of his books down to the fire to dry. There was that cupboard on the landing, too, where Mr. Rawlinson kept some boxes, and his heavy boots and some of the things he'd had when he went abroad last summer. She could clean them up, too, and turn the cupboard out, and if she put the typewriter back in that cupboard, who was to know that Mr. Gray hadn't used it to store some of his things, same as the other lodgers had always done?

The next hour was one of intense activity for Mrs. Stein: she pounded up and down stairs, her arms full of bedding and curtains: she put a whole pile of dry books into a big old tablecloth and dragged the bundle upstairs by its corners, bumping it against the stairs. She turned the contents of the cupboard out on to the landing, and began to clean everything up. When Syd came in she gave him a list of shopping as long as your arm and told him to go out and stay out, and he'd better have his dinner at Tod's snack bar, seeing she couldn't get any cooking done with her hands full like this. Syd being disposed of, Mrs. Stein made confusion worse confounded by beginning to turn George Bell's room out, too.

It was about midday that Inspector Brook rang the front-door bell, and Mrs. Stein, her face smudged with soot, her overall dirty beyond description, went to the door.

"I'm sorry to bother you, ma'am," began the Inspector, but Mrs. Stein put in:

"I'm past caring. You must take me as you find me, and if ever you have a fire you'll know what it's like. I never would've believed—but there, I mustn't run on. Gert's come along to lend a hand and Gert's a tower of strength. Was you wanting to go upstairs? I've been turning out on the first floor, but you can get by if you're careful. The men's working on the roof, so you'd better give them a shout if you're going up."

The first floor landing was complete chaos: big old-fashioned bedroom toilet sets were piled up amongst books and boots and boxes: pictures and photographs and orna-ments were stacked on bedroom chairs and tables.

"It do look a bit mixed, don't it?" said Mrs. Stein, "but all that lot's clean, inside *and* out. I don't want my gentle-men to think I didn't do my best. And seeing you're here, I wonder if you'd give me a hand shifting Mr. Bell's wardrobe away from the wall? Weighs a ton that wardrobe does, and my Syd's out shopping, not that he's any good with weights. Delicate, Syd is."

The inspector helped to move an outsize in Victorian wardrobes clear of the wall, and was warmly thanked by Mrs. Stein.

"How I'm going to remember where all this lot came from's just nobody's business," she said shrilly. "Still, I do know they're clean, and the young gentlemen can change things over themselves if I gets anything wrong, can't they? They all use that cupboard on the stairs to keep their oddments in. Fair old mix-up it looks, don't it?"

Brook was just agreeing that it did when he spotted the typewriter, lying on the floor beneath a heavy pair of nailed boots, some boxing gloves and a pair of skates. Brook picked off the irrelevant items, while Mrs. Stein exclaimed, "Be careful, do. I've cleaned all that lot."

"Where did you find this?" asked Brook, pointing to the typewriter.

"That? Law, how should I know? In that cupboard's likely as not. Them boots was in the cupboard. And the boxing gloves. Mr. Bell's, they are. I've given them a good rub. They all use that cupboard for their bits and pieces. Now was it in the cupboard, or was it in one of the bedrooms? It was the cupboard, I fancy, but I'm not swearing to nothing. I'm past being certain of me own name. Only thing I know is that I cleaned everything. Soot? You'd never believe the way it seeps inside everything."

The Inspector lifted the typewriter from beneath the climbing boots and the skates, glanced at the name on the label and said: "This is Mr. Gray's typewriter—at least it's labelled with his name. We asked you if he had a typewriter in his room."

"So you did," said Mrs. Stein, "and I told you he had. Generally kept it on the table near the window. I suppose he put it in that cupboard, or maybe he lent it to Mr. Bell. I don't know, I'm sure."

"But you must know where you found it," said the Inspector. "You've turned all these things out this morning, haven't you?"

"Yes, I have, and there's no must about it," said Mrs. Stein tartly. "If you'd been working as hard as I have, turning every room in the house upside down to get rid of the filth, and dragging mattresses and carpets and books and curtains and clothes and goodness knows what downstairs to get them dried, you'd know what being in a muddle feels like. If you expect me to remember exactly where all them things came from, you're expecting too much, and I tell you so straight."

And with that she slumped down on the stairs and sat there, wiping her eyes with her dirty overall, while real tears ran down her flushed face. "I'm sorry I'm shore," she added huskily. "It's not that I want to be unobliging and that, but I'm fed up. It's just got me down, and it's no use you expecting me to be all bright and helpful. I've just about dropped my bundle, and for two twos I'd walk out and leave the lot. It's bad enough to have me home all mucked up without being badgered by police when I'm doing my best."

"Now look here, nobody's badgering you," said Inspector Brook. "I'm sorry about all the trouble you're in, and I realise it's enough to upset you, but I only asked you a perfectly simple question. You've found that typewriter somewhere this morning: you knew we'd asked you about Mr. Gray's typewriter—surely you said to yourself, 'There's that typewriter. I wonder how it got there.'"

"Well, I didn't," said Mrs. Stein, "and it's no use you expecting me to do your job as well as my own. My job's to get this house clean, and I've been working at it a sight harder than the police ever work at anything. Look at all this stuff, d'you think I can swear to just where I found it when I've been working all out to get it shifted and cleaned up? I can't and that's flat. I've told you I thought it was in the cupboard, but it may've been in one of them bedrooms and I tell you so straight, and it's no use you bullying me. I tell you I'm past caring. And I'll thank you to get off my landing and leave me to get on with my work."

It was at this moment that Gert let herself in at the front door and heard Mabel's shrill voice complaining about being bullied. Gert had a great sense of family solidarity and no affection whatever for policemen. Clutching her umbrella firmly, Gert came pounding upstairs like a war-horse scenting battle from afar and pawing terribly.

"What's this, Mabel?" she shouted: "What's this about bullying?"

"It's the police, Gert," wailed Mrs. Stein. "Come and help me, do. It's not that I'm being awkward, but I tell him it's no use him expecting too much. I know I'm all muddled and maybe being silly with it, but how can I remember just exactly where I found all this here? It's the typewriter, Gert. You was here when I turned the bottom of that cupboard out. Was the typewriter there or wasn't it?".

"That's torn it," thought Brook. "A fine time I'm going to have with the pair of them. I've seen this sort of combination before."

Gert was on to her cue like knife. She and Mabel had always backed each other up when they'd been girls together. If Mabel had seen fit to mention the cupboard, then the cupboard it was.

"Of course it was there, Mabel. I saw you take it out," said Gert, "and you'd think this policeman might find something better to do than to bully an honest woman who's in trouble like you is." She turned on Brook in righteous indignation. "Ought to be ashamed of yourself, that's what you ought to be," she cried.

"Now, madam, there's no need to get worked up," said

Brook. "I've got my duty to do, and I've only asked Mrs. Stein a civil question."

"As good as told me I was telling lies," sobbed Mrs. Stein, feeling that a good scene might relieve her feelings. She was really feeling very unhappy about the whole thing, and her own sense of guilt was relieved a little by being able to blame other people for their shortcomings. Gert turned on the Inspector in righteous wrath, her bosom heaving dramatically.

"That beats everything," she proclaimed. "My sister Mabel, and a widow at that, what's worked her fingers to the bone and is known to everyone as being honest and truthful to a fault, and you comes into her home and calls her a liar. Policeman you call yourself—I reckon Mabel ought to have the law on you."

Brook tried to intervene, but Gert was in full spate, her vocal power carrying all before it. "I'll tell our Minister," she said, and Brook wondered whether she meant the Home Secretary. "Him what's known her from a girl and married her, too. Taking away our Mabel's character, I'll tell him—"

"Now don't take on so, Gert," sobbed Mrs. Stein. "It's only that I can't swear to what I'm not sure of, and I'm that muddled and bothered. I thought it was in the cupboard, but I can't be sure. Now was it under Mr. Rawlinson's bed, Gert, with his suitcases?"

"No. It wasn't. You said it was in that cupboard and you was right," declared Gert stoutly. "Not that I'm surprised you don't remember, seeing how higgledy-piggledy those young men put their things away. What with their boots and their boxing gloves and what-nots, it's enough to muddle anybody, but I'm not going to stand here and let no one call you a liar, Mabel, that I'm not."

Brook had to give it up. If he'd let them go on, Gert and

Mabel would have talked all day, backing each other and making confusion worse confounded with every fresh suggestion they made. He left them to it, and went to the Yard, hoping to see Rivers. Brook took the typewriter away with him, his ears still echoing with Mrs. Stein's quavery bleat, "I cleaned all that lot, inside and out."

The fingerprint experts at Scotland Yard gave Mrs. Stein full marks for her cleaning powers. Sniffing the well-polished machine when he had taken its cover off, Sergeant Higgins said, "Meth…what a hope." Higgins tried all his wiles, but the result was nil. "Clean as a whistle," he said.

Brook went into the canteen and waited for Rivers, a sadly disgruntled man. Somehow those two—Gert and Mabel— had diddled him and he knew it.

2

Meantime Rivers and Lancing had been having a busy time at Victoria Station. Their first inquiries were made in the office which books for parties travelling together, and here they met their first set-back. There was no record of any party travelling to Austria on that particular train: Switzerland, yes: several parties. Reservations all in order. Austria, no. Then one of the clerks said:

"What about that nice young lady who was fixing up a party to Langen? She couldn't arrange for the cheaper rates because they couldn't all return together: there were some schoolmasters or doctors in the party who had to come back before the others, so we couldn't do anything for her up here and she booked separate tickets. I think I've got a note of her address somewhere."

The other clerk nodded. "Yes. You're right. Two girls there

were: they came trotting back and cadged some couchette reservations when they couldn't get fixed up downstairs. That was on the 17.30, Calais-Basle express, January 1st."

The younger clerk fumbled among his papers: "Her name was Manners," he said. "I remember that, because I thought she'd got the prettiest manners I'd met for a long time. The manners some folks have got these days'd disgrace a pigsty. Bridget Manners. Half a mo'. I'll find it some time."

"There's no proof they went on that train, though," replied the other clerk carefully. "Booking separate like that they could travel as they pleased, go by the morning train or what not, but they'd have been together on the Basle express—at least a dozen of them would, because they paid for those couchette reservations."

"Got it!" exclaimed the other. "Miss Bridget Manners 7 Hamilton Gardens. South Ken. I knew I'd kept that address."

Hot on the scent now, Rivers and Lancing worked their way through the complex of departments at Victoria Station. Miss Bridget Manners had reserved fifteen places on the one o'clock Dover boat train on New Year's Day, and Miss Bridget Manners seemed to have got what it takes to cause busy booking clerks to remember some people when they forget others. Whatever that was, it lightened the job for Rivers and Lancing, so that the latter said: "I'd like to see this girl. There must be something about her."

Eventually the two detectives learnt that the same train crew were on the one o'clock boat train today as had worked it on New Year's Day, and that the train would shortly be in the station.

"Might as well try," said Rivers, "but it's too much to hope that anybody on the train will remember anything about them."

"I'm not so sure," said Lancing. "Belief chasing facts, remember. Come to think of it, we've had a chain of facts, all the way through. It's only a few links that are on the weak side."

"Missing links," murmured Rivers, "and one missing link invalidates the whole chain."

But luck was still with them: after having interrogated porters, guards, platform men and restaurant car men, they came on a rather startled hair-brained boy, the newest recruit to the restaurant car staff. His name was Tom Jones, and Tom remembered serving lunch to a party of fifteen on the boat train on New Year's Day. He remembered the party because one of the gentlemen broke a bottle of rum—or a bottle of rum got broken. "It rolled off the table when I was serving," said Tom, "and the gent blamed me and said I ought to pay for it. Not half a scare it gave me. Costs money, rum does."

"It certainly does," agreed Rivers, and Tom went on:

"It was the lady took my side, sir. 'Don't be an ass,' she said to him. 'It was your own fault, Ian, not the waiter's.' I wasn't half grateful to her."

Slowly and patiently Rivers got from the boy all he could remember of the party. It wasn't much, an impression of happy, prosperous care-free people, "off for a lark". "'It won't half be fine when we gets there,'" he quoted. "'Out of this ruddy climate.' And I thought how lucky they was, what with the fog in London and all," sighed Tom Jones.

But one thing did emerge from his ramblings. There was an Irishman with the party, a big dark chap. They'd been ragging him because he nearly missed the train.

"Here a little and there a little," said Rivers.

Chapter XII

1

When Rivers eventually heard Brook's sad story about the well-cleaned typewriter, the Chief Inspector sat and stared at the blameless machine for quite a while.

"I'm quite satisfied in my own mind about what happened, sir," said Brook. "That Syd pinched the typewriter and his Ma found out about it, and she palmed it off amongst the other junk and said she couldn't remember where she found it. That's one of the statements that leaves us standing. You can't do anything with 'I can't remember'. There just isn't an answer to that one."

Rivers nodded. "I quite agree. It's the person who swears to a thing who is the detective's best friend. All the same, I'm puzzled, Brook. If Syd did pinch the thing, why did he leave the label on it? Surely the first thing he would have done would have been to take off the label with Gray's name on it. If he'd done that and cleaned all fingerprints off the machine as well, we should have had our job cut out to prove it was

Gray's typewriter. Second-hand typewriters are changing hands all over the place."

Brook scratched his head. "Yes. That's a point," he said slowly, "unless Syd's so half-witted he didn't think of it."

"From what we know of his record, Syd isn't half-witted," said Rivers. "He's sly and smart and on the spot in the matter of petty larceny, but he hasn't been actually caught at it. If he were half-witted, he'd have been caught."

The Chief Inspector sat thinking and then said: "Oh, hell. If I'd only got time to sit and chew it over, I've got an idea somewhere at the back of my mind. But I've got to get on with tracing this party who went on that train. Look here, Brook. Write me out a detailed report of your search in that house: the order in which you searched, and so forth. I'll come back to Syd later. Bring him along here about six o'clock this evening unless I phone to the contrary, and see to it that the report your chaps are making is ready for me."

Rivers and Lancing set out for Hamilton Gardens when the dreary day was closing in to a premature evening: an evening of which the most optimistic could say nothing better than that it was no worse than the day which it closed.

"The house which Miss Manners lives in is a residential club," said Rivers to Lancing. "It's quite probable we shan't be able to get any information about the party."

Lancing, as usual, was more optimistic. "Some of her girl-friends probably know a lot more about that party than her parents do," he said. "Girls of today are generally very cagey with their parents, but they talk to their pals in a residential club all right. This is one of the occasions when a policeman's handicapped. If I could go my own way about it and no questions asked I bet I could get the make-up of that party with no difficulty at all. Whereas you will approach the lady superintendent, on the highest level, I take it."

"You take it aright—cutting out the bit about the highest level," said Rivers. "My inquiry will be on familiar lines—a witness to a traffic accident. We don't want the lady superintendent wiring to Miss Manners that the police are taking an interest in her party."

"Quite," murmured Lancing, "but couldn't you make it an inquiry about stolen property, or property we suspect has been stolen? These girls are always losing their handbags or what-have-you."

"I'm going to do it my own way, and you're going to keep quiet for once," said Rivers.

Lancing had to admit that the Chief Inspector did his stuff remarkably well. Quietly courteous almost to the point of diffidence, Rivers handled the lady superintendent very ably. Having apologised for troubling her, he inquired if a Miss Manners were a resident in the club: on receiving an affirmative answer he spoke of an accident near South Kensington Station on the morning of New Year's Day. The police were seeking witnesses—a stolen car was involved—and a newspaper vendor who knew Miss Manners by sight had said that he thought she was passing by at the time, another young lady being with her. This reason given for the presence of two C.I.D. officers was accepted *in toto* by Miss Hammond, the lady superintendent. As Lancing said afterwards: "Innocent people are very innocent. They just swallow the bait at a canful and ask no questions." Far from asking questions, Miss Hammond obliged with quantities of information. Miss Manners had gone to Austria with a ski-ing party, to a place called Lech. She had left England on New Year's Day, by the afternoon boat, but she had been in London on the morning of that day: "Yes, and she did go out to the shops," said Miss Hammond, "because she bought food for the journey. Meals on the train are so dear abroad."

"Have you any idea who was with her when she went shopping?" asked Rivers.

"No—but Joyce Ellison might know. She and Bridget Manners are great friends. I think Miss Ellison is in. I'll send for her."

Rivers murmured something about being grateful for such valuable co-operation and Lancing said straight out: "How I do envy Miss Manners! The thought of getting away to Austria and sunshine almost hurts when your job keeps you in London in weather like this."

"I couldn't agree with you more," said Miss Hammond cordially. "How I should have loved it, and it sounded a delightful party, sixteen of them, eight girls and eight men—and how hard Bridget worked to get it all fixed up. It's very difficult to get sixteen people to agree on times and terms and all the rest. Oh, here is Miss Ellison. Joyce, this is Chief Inspector Rivers, C.I.D. He is trying to find witnesses to a traffic accident last Monday morning, and it seems that Biddy Manners was passing at the time. Do you know what time she went out that morning?"

Rivers, on his feet, bowed to the girl who had just come in and she beamed at him cheerfully and then beamed at Lancing even more cheerfully.

"Biddy went out as soon as the shops opened," said Miss Ellison. "Just before nine, that is. You see, she was going abroad for a fortnight so she'd got rations to spare and she collected ham and eggs and butter and all that. She met Jane Harrington just outside South Ken. Station. I know that, because I walked to the station with her."

"Now isn't that satisfactory," said Miss Hammond happily. "Of course, Miss Harrington has gone to Lech, too, but is there anybody in the club now who might have seen Miss Manners after she'd been shopping?"

"I don't know," said Miss Ellison, and turned to the two detectives with an endearing grin. "Say if you both come into the common-room and talk to us all," she suggested. "If you'd like to, that is. You always like to get evidence at first hand, don't you?"

"We do indeed," said Rivers. "It's an excellent suggestion."

"Come along then," she said. "You needn't be afraid. There's only three or four of us, not a monstrous regiment."

"Never let it be said that we lacked courage in pursuit of duty," said Rivers, and Joyce Ellison chortled happily as she led them out of the room.

"You are honestly C.I.D.?" she asked.

"Honestly," said Rivers. "You can see our warrants."

"I'll take them as read. Glory, this is the best thing that's happened since I came back from the Christmas hols, what with the lousy weather and Biddy going off ski-ing, blast her. I tried all I knew to get leave, but my boss is one of those people. Still, this is quite a story. Come on. I don't suppose any of them can tell you a thing, but you could tell us quite a lot to brighten a dreary evening."

2

Joyce Ellison led Rivers and Lancing across the entrance hall into a big cheerful room where a group of girls were chattering around a huge fire. One or two of them glanced up as Joyce came in with the two visitors, but the majority took no notice of them until Joyce announced: "Here are two officers of the

Criminal Investigation Department of Scotland Yard. They are seeking witnesses to a traffic accident outside South Ken. Station last Monday morning."

There was a general scramble as the lasses on the rug jumped to their feet, and a very fair, very young person said:

"That's wizard. Come and sit down. You'll find these chairs quite comfortable. Are you going to caution us that anything we say can be taken down in writing and used as evidence?"

"I hadn't intended to do so," said Rivers, looking down into a pair of limpid blue eyes. "We generally keep that one for persons whom we suspect of being involved in misdemeanours and whom we may have to charge—but if it would give you any pleasure to hear me recite that bit, I'm quite willing to do so."

"*Please*," begged the blue-eyed imp, and Rivers obliged imperturbably.

"Having got that over, I'll just mention names," said Joyce Ellison. "Anne Carey, Mary Somers, Ruth Elliot, Mifanwy Jones: meet Chief Inspector Rivers and... sorry, I don't know yours."

"Detective-Sergeant Lancing," said Rivers and both men bowed and accepted the chairs offered them. Joyce promptly went on:

"Let's get business over first. Did anybody see Biddy when she came in after shopping on Monday morning? It's she who's supposed to have seen this car smash."

"Well, she didn't," said Anne Carey—the fair infant. "I saw her when she came in and all she said was that it was the foulest day on record and ham had gone up to 12s. 6d. a pound. If she'd seen a spectacular smash she'd have told me." She looked meditatively at Rivers. "I'm quite sure Biddy didn't see any smash, but even if she had, she'd have looked the other way and passed by on the other side. You do see that, don't you?"

"I'm not sure that I do," said Rivers.

"Oh, but you must. Think you're Biddy, on Monday morning. After weeks of hair-tearing gruelling effort, and months of skimping and saving, she'd got this thing fixed up, a complete properly balanced party all ready to go to Austria, tickets and reservations in her pocket, and herself panting to be off like Puffing Billy. Would she—I put it to you—*would* she have gone rushing up to the nearest cop and said, 'I saw that. I'm a star-turn witness, and please may I come and give evidence at the inquest? I was going to Austria, ski-ing, but that doesn't matter now. I'm only panting to assist the law and I'll cut everything else out.' After all, a girl has a life of her own, hasn't she, and no one can make you say you saw a thing if you say you didn't. Actually, I'm quite certain she didn't see anything of the kind, but you do see what I mean, don't you?"

"Strictly off the record, perhaps I do," said Rivers, "especially as I'm rather keen on ski-ing myself, but we're not so inhuman as you seem to think."

"Oh, I don't think you're inhuman at all," replied the imp, "but I'm afraid it's no go. She just didn't see anything but ham and eggs and the beastly weather and she simply came hurtling back to borrow my best Thermos. Do tell me, have you ever been to Lech?"

"No, but I've been to St. Anton, which is quite near Lech," said Rivers, and Lancing put in:

"Did they have a lot of bother in getting the party together?"

"Bother!" exclaimed Joyce. "It was agonising. Someone got married and wouldn't go, and someone went broke, and someone wouldn't go because his best friend couldn't go and I said I'd go and couldn't get leave, and someone got appendicitis at the last moment, and honestly it was the final moment of the final hour that the last man sort of tumbled into the party—so it was all a bit wearing for poor Biddy, but they did get off, so everything in the garden's all right. Hallo, here's Rachel Swift. Ray, love, wasn't there a letter for you from Biddy this morning? We've got Scotland Yard here, trying to involve her as witness to a car smash on New Year's Day."

"Good heavens! Biddy wasn't in a car smash, I'm certain she wasn't," exclaimed Rachel, a tall dark slim creature. "The most frightful thing's happened," she went on. "I woke up late this morning, and I simply had to rush and I didn't even look to see if there were any letters, and now I've found one from Biddy with a pound note inside and signatures from everybody, and she asked me to get some flowers for Nigel from all of them and be sure I got them to his nursing home before he woke up after his appendix. I know all this is nothing to do with car smashes, but she honestly wasn't in a car smash and what can I do about the flowers? All the shops are shut."

"Never mind. Send them in the morning," put in Joyce. "Nigel will be feeling much too sick to notice flowers. They only did him this morning and he'll be feeling too foul for anything."

"But Biddy asked me to be sure to get them for him today. I bet Pippa was at the back of that, she's all maternal over Nigel," wailed Rachel. "Whatever can I do?"

It was then that Rivers put in: "If you really want some flowers left at a nursing home, I expect we could manage it for you. We do far more difficult things than that in the course of our duty."

"Ask a policeman!" cried Anne. "I think that's marvellous of you—just terribly kind and chivalrous and old world. Do you go and dig up Covent Garden?"

"No. It's so easy I'm almost ashamed to explain," said Rivers. "Several of the big hotels and restaurants have flower stalls, and I've got a car and it's a beastly night. I'm not allowed to give you a lift in a police car, but regulations can't stop me delivering flowers and a letter at a nursing home. You've all been very nice in trying to answer my questions, so I shall be only too happy to help in return." ("The Lord forgive him!" thought Lancing, piously if unofficially.)

"I think that's utterly charming of you," said Anne, wide-eyed and breathless, "and I do assure you that Biddy did *not* see a smash or a grab or anything, not a ghost of one. You do believe that, don't you?"

"I do indeed," said Rivers, and Rachel asked:

"Would roses be right?"

3

When Rivers and Lancing left the club in Hamilton Gardens, the Chief Inspector was in charge of a note which had been posted at Basle Station. "Just to let you know we're all thinking of you and wishing you good luck and nice nurses," it ran and the message was followed by sixteen individual scrawls: Biddy, Jane, Pippa, Jill, Kate, Martha, Meriel, Daphne. Frank, Malcolm, Tim, Ian, Neville, Derrick, Robert, Gerald. This was the note which was to be tied to the flowers which Rivers had undertaken to deliver at the Beaumont Nursing Home, for Nigel Carstairs.

It wasn't until the car moved forward cautiously through a fog which now reinforced the sleet that Rivers said: "I feel like Herod, slaughtering innocents."

Lancing snorted. "Well, sir, you needn't. Anything less like innocents than that rosebud garden of girls I never met. That fair infant could leave Cleopatra standing, pipped at the post. I was thankful to get out of it. If it hadn't been for the slightly batty Rachel and her gift of roses, you and I might have had a thin time. You see, we didn't know the answers, and if they'd got us into separate corners the whole little illusion would have had some rough handling."

"You mean they didn't believe the traffic-accident gambit?" said Rivers, beginning to laugh.

"Of course they didn't," said Lancing. "What d'you call her, the girl with the good ankles—Joyce—she's as sharp as a needle. Your stuff was all right for the lady superintendent, because she is innocent."

"What you'd call a really nice woman," murmured Rivers, and Lancing went on:

"Yes, but she's fifty if she's a day, and niceness of that kind isn't found in anyone born later than 1920. I should know. Miss Hammond would believe anything which you chose to tell her, because she recognised you as a pukka sahib, but Joyce and Anne both wondered what a Chief Inspector, C.I.D., was doing trotting round about traffic accidents. They both looked about twenty, but I'll lay any money they'd served in the Forces and what they don't know is hardly worth knowing. I admit it panned out quite incredibly well, because they were so taken with your handsome offer that their analytical faculties were short-circuited, *pro tem*, but I hope they don't go and put a continental call through to Lech to warn Biddy the narks are after her. The only thing is that it costs quite a lot to get through via Vienna and they're all extravagant wenches, so they're probably careful in small ways. Hell! This fog's thickening up. Is that Knightsbridge or isn't it? It might be anything."

"And a fog is just what we don't want," said Rivers.

"Is it?" said Lancing, and there was a world of hopeful inquiry in his voice.

"When we get back to the Yard, you can ring up the Savoy or the Dorchester or the Café Royal and ask them if they've got a nice bunch of roses," said Rivers. "You can then detail any one of your more reliable friends to go and collect said roses. You thus employed, I will ginger up the fingerprint department to do their stuff in record-breaking time. This artless missive in my pocket has been signed by each member of Bridget Manners' party. When people sign their names, they nearly always hold the paper steady with the other hand. If there is even a fraction of a print which tallies with Gray's, I think it's all Lombard Street to a China Orange that the Commissioner will advise that I go out to Lech. And if I go, you go. And the fog's getting thicker every minute."

"Glory!" said Lancing. "If only... it's all right, sir. I'm not hitting it. Everything under control."

"You may be: he is not," said Rivers disgustedly as a large and opulent car waddled broadside on across the road in the fog. "Put your top light on, Lancing. We don't want to be turned into road casualties just when we're getting a little evidence together."

"And if Gray's prints aren't on the chit, sir?"

"You can have the pleasure of taking it, plus the roses, to the foul-feeling Nigel," said Rivers. "I hope he's a nice straight-forward case. Have you ever had your appendix out?"

"No, sir. 'Fraid not. No first-hand information to offer, but some of the modern surgeons are very snappy at it and their victims wake up feeling nothing to notice."

"Depends if they're sick. I don't suppose they'd let me see him until tomorrow and if they did it wouldn't be much use," said Rivers. "He'll be all dopey. The last thing he'll even want to remember is the ski-ing party he's missed, and he probably doesn't remember a thing about it at the moment. Anaesthetics are like that. And in the meantime, I'm willing to bet that Gray is the life and soul of Bridget Manners' party, and they're all saying: 'We're so glad you managed to come.'"

"Pretty grim... if what you believe is true," said Lancing as he swung the car round the Hyde Park roundabout and nosed his way into Constitution Hill with visibility almost nil. "If this sort of thing is widespread, there won't be a plane leaving any airport tonight," he went on. "If there were, Zürich's about the nearest... I'll bet any money you'll find enough evidence on that chit to justify us going out after Gray. I'm all bitten with your beliefs this trip."

"Normally speaking, I shouldn't expect a thing, but there's a sort of deadly fate attendant on Gray," replied Rivers. "The mark of that ski-stick in a patch of mud noticed by an inquisitive constable and recognised by the one officer in E Division who knew it for what it was. There's something abnormal about this case."

"I don't know," said Lancing. "Gray's an opportunist. He took a chance. In the main it seemed to work. He's probably got away and thinks it's all marvellous, but he challenged your wits in doing it and you saw the possibility of another side to the picture. Once the set-up was queried, it didn't look so good."

4

Rivers took Biddy's chit into the fingerprint department and waited there while the experts "treated it". He saw the confused jumble of fingerprints on it emerge after the excess of finely pulverised dark powder was blown away: saw the paper stretched beneath arc lamps and camera. He waited patiently while the films were developed and dried, with a swiftness almost unbelievable. Each step in the process was carried out with an expert skill which cut out every redundant movement. The enlarged prints were studied by men who could eliminate the inessential at a glance. They had their identification print pinned out for comparison, type, whorls, loops all numbered and measured, and they worked as mathematicians work, precisely.

"Well, there it is—tip of the left thumb only, on the edge of the sheet," was the verdict of the senior officer. "I doubt if any jury would hang him on it, but I'd say that there's an overwhelming probability that that thumb tip is identical with the specimen."

"Thanks. That's good enough for me to tackle the A.C. on," said Rivers. "Incidentally, you've got some reasonably good forgers here. Get that chit copied for me, and see to it the signatures look as bad as the real ones."

"Written in the train, was it?" asked the other. "We'll wobble the table for verisimilitude. Who's it for?"

"A blameless lad who's just had an appendix out when he should have gone ski-ing," said Rivers. "I doubt if he'll be in any state to criticise the signatures, but do your best for him."

It wasn't until Rivers left the fingerprint department that a sergeant came and asked if he still wanted to see the witness Brook had brought along, and Rivers remembered Syd.

"Won't do him any harm to wait a bit longer," said Rivers. "How's he shaping?"

"Like a jelly in midsummer, sir. However, we're keeping an eye on him. We won't let him pass out on you."

"Bad as that?" inquired Rivers.

"He's badly frightened, sir, and he's a neurotic sort of chap, but we'll see he's there when you want him. Choice sort of evening, isn't it? Even the buses have given up. All over the south of England, too."

"It would be," said Rivers. "What a climate!"

Chapter XIII

1

"There's something about the whole set-up I don't like, Kate," said Frank Harris.

They were out sleighing together, their vehicle drawn by a shaggy decrepit-looking horse whose appearance was deceptive: given its head, the improbable-looking creature liked to gallop and it had a surprising turn of speed, so that occasionally the sleigh swayed madly from side to side along the beaten snow-track. If you wanted to exchange confidences, thought Kate, two people could not do better than go for a sleigh ride through the snow-laden pine forests. The young Austrian who was in charge of the outfit was as shaggy-looking as the horse, but he was a very clever driver and he did not understand a word of English. In that white world of glistening snow, miles away from other human beings, with the sleigh bells tinkling an obligato as a background to conversation, you could say what you liked without fear of eavesdroppers.

"I'm reminded of that cryptic phrase they use on the stock

markets—'loss of confidence,'" went on Harris. "Industry may be booming and the country in good fettle, but once a whisper goes round indicating loss of confidence, stocks fall. That's our trouble, Kate. Loss of confidence. We all set out feeling supremely confident. Everybody liked everybody else. We didn't all know one another, but everybody was vouched for by somebody. So and so's friend, he's O.K. Now we feel we've got a snake in the grass and we don't know who the snake is."

"Isn't it fairer to say that we're afraid we've got a snake in the grass?" asked Kate. "What you say about confidence is perfectly true. Come to that, our whole lives are based on acts of faith. Aren't you being too quick to suspect everybody because of one idiotic incident which may be due to one person's muddle-headedness?"

They had emerged from the pine woods now, and were in bright sunlight again, travelling up a wide valley shut in by snowy crests, the intense whiteness confusing distances, so that the valley seemed a vastness of immeasurable untrodden snow, stretching from the track to the mountain tops, the horse and sleigh dwarfed to insignificance.

"You may be right. I only hope you are," said Harris. "I admit that at the present moment, in this alpine valley, other people's idiocies and even the international situation seem curiously unreal, and Austrian schillings and English pound notes seem equally meaningless and valueless. Snow and mountains are the only reality and in spite of their beauty there's an element of terror in them."

"I feel that the whole time," said Kate. "I think it's part of the attraction. The whole elaboration of the winter sports racket is almost an impertinence in the face of this serene immensity. Frank, do you think altitude affects people more than they realise? Can people's judgment be affected by it so that a person given to doing irresponsible things can become more irresponsible without realising it?"

"Not to my knowledge," he replied. "Altitude affects some people physically, especially if their hearts aren't sound: it affects asthmatic persons occasionally and some with respiratory troubles. Otherwise, apart from a feeling of exhilaration, I don't think people's minds are affected by it." He broke off, and then added: "I grant you there was a marked degree of levity among us all, but that's just a holiday feeling. We all said what a relief it was to get away from rationing and news bulletins and exhortations to work harder and spend less— but I don't think that accounts for last night's performance, Kate. What are you trying to get at?"

"Well, it all started with Robert, didn't it? He said he'd lost his Austrian currency. You, very sensibly, wondered if he'd just mislaid it in his usual haphazard way. I still think that may be the explanation."

"All right. It's quite possible, but I don't see how those English pound notes turned up in Ian Dexter's book."

"Doesn't the fact that Robert's an Irishman make a difference? Most right-thinking English people have a sense of responsibility about the economic position. We all curse the rules and regulations, but we do abide by them, by and large. An Irishman doesn't have the same feeling of responsibility. I can well believe that Robert thought he was justified in bringing as much money out of England as he chose. And when you faced him with it—got him into a corner by discovering those notes in his suitcase—he said the first thing that came into his head to get him out of an awkward situation—that the notes didn't belong to him. And having said it, he stuck to it."

"You mean he's an ordinary damned liar? It takes a bit of swallowing, though I've known plenty of liars in my time," replied Frank resignedly, "but that doesn't explain away the fact that Neville Helston says he has lost a wad of pound notes, and I have a hunch that the ones which turned up in Robert's case are probably the same ones which Helston lost. Something damned odd has been going on. Not ordinary theft. Something more like the mischief which a maladjusted mind is capable of committing. There's something unbalanced about the whole thing."

"That sounds pretty beastly," said Kate. "Oh, look, that must be Zug church, with another of those lovely onion cupolas. Isn't it marvellous how the buildings compose with the mountains, they're always so perfectly placed. I wonder if the others will get there before we do?"

When Kate had said she was going to have a sleigh ride out to Zug, six other members of the party had said they were going to get a guide and ski over from Lech. It was a noted run, in which the skiers reached the upper slopes by ski-lift and came down to Zug by a series of slopes which were not too difficult to negotiate.

"Robert will get there first, then Neville and Ian," said Frank. "Incidentally, Robert's an unusually good skier, Kate. That young German who's staying at the Braun chalet spoke of him. He said he was really good."

"I'm surprised," said Kate. "I always think Neville's much the better. He doesn't take so many tosses as Robert does, anyway."

Frank chuckled a little. "The German lad said, 'If he tumbles he does it to encourage the beginners.' How's that to add to the sum total of our perplexities? That young German is an international skier, remember. Kate, how was it that Robert came to join the party? You're friends with Jane and Biddy, so you ought to be in a position to give information."

"A review of who's who," murmured Kate. "Well, if you want to know, I think I can tell you."

The track was on an up-gradient now, and the shaggy horse had its work cut out to pull the sleigh, so they went slowly and silently while Kate went on: "The party started with Biddy and Jane and Martha and myself, plus you and Gerald, whom Biddy already knew, and Derrick, whom Jane knew; then Raymond and Charles and Nigel tagged on, and Charles said another friend of his would like to come. That made seven men and four women, so Biddy asked Pippa and Daphne and Meriel to even it up and they all jumped at it. That was how it stood at the end of November, when Charles suddenly decided to get married, and Raymond's new car was delivered unexpectedly and he backed out, so there were two men short and Biddy was rather fed up, and wrote and told Charles and Raymond they were platers and couldn't they suggest substitutes for themselves. She'd booked fourteen rooms, you see. Well, Charles phoned back that he was doing his best: he's a casual sort of creature and never writes a letter if he can help it, but he said he'd mentioned it at his club—he belongs to a flying club in Sussex somewhere. A week or so later, Tim Grant phoned Biddy, and said he'd heard she was organising a ski-ing party and could he come, mentioning Charles's name en passant, and she said he sounded all right, and they fixed it up, though he said he'd go to Zürich by air because he could get a lift."

"I see," said Frank. "So Tim's just a casual, so to speak, someone who heard of the party at Charles's flying club."

"That's about it," agreed Kate. "Malcolm was the next applicant. He'd heard about the party from Charles, but I gather they only met once at a dance... Incidentally, I like Malcolm, Frank. He's got an interesting mind and he's less obvious than the younger hearties. It might be worth while discussing this problem with him: I think he'd regard it with the sort of disinterested interest which is characteristic of him."

"Possibly, but I don't think I want to discuss it with anybody unless I'm perfectly certain who they are," said Frank.

"Schoolmastering is an eminently respectable profession," said Kate, half laughing. Then she added: "Don't let's get this thing out of proportion, Frank. And above all don't let's fancy ourselves as detectives. I'm not going to do any prying or probing. I'd rather pack up and go somewhere else. But let's finish describing how the party got itself arranged. The two Dexters were the next to materialise: they appeared just before Christmas, quite vaguely. Somebody at Biddy's club met Jillian at a party, and she was very peeved because she and Ian had been going to Norway with relations and somebody got messed up in a car smash, and when Jillian heard of Biddy's party, she rushed round and asked Biddy if she could get rooms for herself and Ian and there were more frantic telegrams and that was that. Then on Boxing Day Nigel got ill, but he was awfully decent about it and routed out Neville, whom he'd known for years. Neville had got some leave owing to him, or managed to wangle it, as these Civil Servants always do wangle things. I think it was the same day Neville phoned to say he could come that Robert rang up out of a blue sky, and said Raymond had told him about Biddy's Lech party and could he come as he was mad keen on ski-ing and preferred to go with a party, especially with people who liked dancing. That balanced the party, and Biddy was delighted to get it squared up."

"The whole set-up was pretty casual," said Frank, and Kate put in:

"What are you fussing about? If you go on a tour, you don't ask for references for all your fellow tourists. You just regard them as part of the entertainment. We agreed to start with it'd be more fun to have a party, with varying degrees of skill and experience in ski-ing, so that beginners and more practised people should have somebody to keep them company, rather than to have just three or four people. Biddy was the only one who took any risk, because she got tickets and reservations. Everybody has paid up for their train and boat and all the oddments, and each person pays individually for hotel and all that. So I don't think you need fuss about its being casual. In fact until there was this to-do about Robert losing his money, we were an exemplary party, everybody behaving beautifully. Look, that's the hotel at Zug. I believe we've got here first. I shall be jolly glad of some hot chocolate, Frank. It's amazing how cold you can get even with all these rugs."

"Yes. It always makes me marvel how the Russians used to survive whole days of this sort of transport," said Frank, and then added: "Well, what's the upshot, Kate? Leave it as it is?"

"Yes. I think so. You've warned everybody to be sensible. That was all I wanted. I don't think anybody else will leave money or valuables in their bedrooms. If they do, it serves them right if they lose it. But it'd be intolerable if we all began suspecting each other of theft or playing detectives. We've just got to leave it alone."

2

It was pleasant to get out of the sleigh and go into the tingling warmth of the small hotel. Frank and Kate found themselves the only occupants of a homely lounge, whose polished wood floor seemed to ask to be danced on. Cups of steaming chocolate, heaped high with whipped cream, appeared promptly, and the two sat down in the sunshine by one of the double windows and watched for the appearance of the skiers on the slopes above. Frank said:

"I think you're right, Kate. The only thing is to leave it alone, though it goes against the grain. I feel there's mischief about."

"Perhaps there is," she replied, "but you've given fair warning to the mischief-maker, if one exists, and also to the party as a whole. Several of these girls haven't been abroad before, and don't realise that you've got to be more careful of your belongings than you have at home."

"The point that interests me is this," went on Frank. "You and I say 'leave it alone,' but will Robert leave it alone? He was pretty mad last night, swearing that it was a frame-up."

"Well, he was quite calm at breakfast this morning," said Kate. "In fact he looked a bit sheepish. Did Neville say anything more to you?"

"Oh, he came along after breakfast and said he realised it was his own fault he'd lost his money," replied Frank Harris, "and he didn't want to make any official complaint. He added, perfectly reasonably, that people do go in and out of those chalets, calling on their friends, and the owners can't be held responsible for everybody."

"Very sensible of him," said Kate. "I had the fright of my life yesterday. The first and second floors at the hotel are identical, and I went to my own bedroom, as I thought, and starting washing my hands and suddenly realised I wasn't using my own soap. I'd gone into a room on the first floor instead of on the second floor without thinking, and any thief could give the same explanation. I just rushed out with my hands dripping, as fast as a scalded cat. Look, that must be our lot, just coming down from the crest."

Frank jumped up and looked at the distant figures. "Yes. There they are. Well, they haven't made much speed. Malcolm's leading—I can see the colour of his sweater—and Jane's with him. Jolly good for her. Who's next?"

"Ian and Tim. They're not so tall as the others, and Robert and Neville and the guide last. Let's order chocolate and cakes for them. They'll be starving after all that trek."

A few minutes later the skiers came into the lounge, laughing and exhilarated, as people always are after ski-ing: they set to on the hot chocolate and ordered drinks to follow, as cheerful a crowd as could be imagined.

"I don't think you broke any records that trip," said Frank Harris. "Kate and I expected you to get here before we did."

"Neville fell into a snowdrift and we had to go back and rescue him," said Tim.

"Neville?" asked Kate. "I thought he was the one person in the party who knows how to avoid falling into snowdrifts."

"Well, he landed into a beauty this time," said Jane. "We organised the party carefully. Malcolm and I set off first, because I'm the slowest and Malcolm came to keep me company in case I got into trouble. Then Ian and Tim set off, with the guide, so that he could keep an eye on all of us, and Neville and Robert started last, because they're the fastest. We'd got nearly to the crest above Zug when Ian and Tim caught up with Malcolm and me, and we heard the guide yodelling behind us. He'd stopped to look out for Neville and Robert, and he was worried because he'd lost sight of them. So we all went back a bit and found Neville and Robert floundering in deep snow. However, all's well that ends well—but it'll be a long time before I risk ski-ing by myself. It's too jolly easy to get out of control."

"What happened, Neville?" asked Kate, and he laughed rather ruefully.

"I suppose the simple fact was that I made a fair-sized ass of myself," he replied. "Robert was leading, going very well. There was a dip which was obviously a place to avoid, and Robert avoided it, taking an upgrade with the velocity he'd just acquired, and coming to a stop a bit above me. I just tried to be clever. I'd got the deuce of a speed up and I thought I could jump the bad patch. Well, I mucked it. I came down in the mushy stuff instead of clearing it. That's all."

"You were lucky you weren't scuppered altogether," said Tim. "There's a ravine there—the surface shows it quite plainly. It's that eiderdown look."

"I know, I know. Don't rub it in," said Neville, "and then poor old Bobs came floundering in to pull me out and we were in a proper muck, like two rhinos in a quagmire."

"Well, what did you expect me to do? Leave you to submerge like a submarine that's had it?" demanded Robert indignantly. "I know your jumping's very snappy when it comes off, but when it doesn't it's just a mess."

"I can't make out why you didn't swerve or stop, Neville," said Tim. "You must have realised it was no sort of jumping proposition—not enough gradient for a take off."

"Yes, I did realise it," said Neville, "but ski-ing's a funny business. There's something hypnotic about it. I just couldn't stop. If it had been a precipice I should still have gone over it. But it's not going to happen again, so don't think I'm making a habit of it. Anyway, it was good practice. We're going over to St. Anton tomorrow if the weather holds."

"Who's going?" asked Kate.

"Robert and I are ski-ing both ways: Ian and Tim and Jane are coming, but they think they'd rather come back by train from St. Anton to Langen, and out to Lech by bus. Malcolm's still considering it."

"You're being a bit ambitious, aren't you?" put in Frank. "It's a stiff trip."

"It's easy enough," said Robert defensively. "I've looked the route up pretty carefully. We take the bus from Lech to the road-fork at Steuben, and from there we shall have to walk to the top of the Arlberg pass. It's only three kilometres—about an hour's climb, or less—to St. Christoph. I believe there's a very old inn or hospice there, where we could get a drink. From there you can ski down to St. Anton, about seven kilometres. Coming back, we may get a lift to St. Christoph and from there we could ski back to Lech. It sounds pretty good to me. It's stupid not to try a good run when we're here."

"Better take advice about the weather before you start," advised Frank. "If it starts snowing, and the track disappears, coming down from the Arlberg pass won't be easy."

"Cautious old stick, aren't you?" laughed Neville. "I'm looking forward to it. It'll be a jolly good trip."

3

It was after lunch at the Kronbergerhof that Pippa said to Jane: "I got through to Joyce this morning. I promised I'd phone once while we were here. It's an awful thrill getting a phone call from Austria."

"I call it sheer squandering," said Jane. "How's Nigel, anyway?"

Pippa blushed—and she was a girl who looked very pretty when she blushed. "He's doing frightfully well, an absolute star-turn case. Rachel got Biddy's chit all right and sent the flowers. I still can't make out what happened. Joyce said they'd had two C.I.D. officers round, asking about a car smash you and Biddy saw on New Year's morning when you were out shopping."

"But we didn't see a car smash," said Jane.

"They told them you didn't see it. Joyce said the C.I.D. were perfect lambs. There was a perfectly foul fog, and they offered to leave Nigel's flowers at his nursing home. Terribly nice of them."

"Well, it just sounds crackers to me," said Jane. "You couldn't have heard it right. C.I.D. men don't cope with traffic accidents."

"I know. I thought of that. I expect it's something to do with Anne. She does vamp the most extraordinary people. What's she got that you and I haven't got, Jane?"

"The sort of face that launched a thousand ships," said Jane, "and yet her face isn't all that when you really look at it. But I'm a bit puzzled about this C.I.D. racket, Pippa. I don't quite like the sound of it. Why did they pick on Biddy and me?"

"I can't think," replied Pippa. "I don't terribly want to think, either. I know it's neither of you."

"What isn't?" demanded Jane quickly and Pippa said helplessly:

"Collecting the C.I.D., or attracting them, or whatever it was. Jane, don't go getting agitated about it. You can't spoil the party."

"Well... I think that's a bit steep," said Jane indignantly. "Anyway, if the C.I.D. want us, they obviously know where to find us."

They were standing outside the hotel, both holding their skis, and Tim came up behind them. "What's this about the C.I.D.?" he asked.

"I'm writing a detective novel," said Jane promptly. "All about this party."

"Well, after last night I don't wonder," said Tim, his melancholy dark eyes studying Jane's face rather too intelligently. "Is all discovered, Jane? All over, bar the handcuffs?"

Jane suddenly shivered: she suddenly realised that Tim's dark eyes had an expression in them which she couldn't fathom, and she strove to answer light-heartedly: "Of course it isn't. Handcuffs come in the last chapter. I've only just finished chapter one."

"You've got it all wrong, Jane," put in another voice: this was Gerald, generally the quietest of the party. "You've missed out the nine o'clock walk 'to be taken from the place where you are...' I always think there's terrific drama in the judge's lines."

"What a loathsome subject to discuss on a gorgeous day," protested Pippa. "Come on, everybody. We shall lose all the sun if we hang about any longer."

Gerald and Pippa shouldered their skis and went on towards the bridge which led to the ski schools area, and Tim said, "Coming, Jane?"

"No. I'm waiting for Biddy. You go on," she replied, and turned back into the hotel.

Chapter XIV

1

After his consultation with the fingerprint experts, Chief Inspector Rivers wrote a brief report, embodying the salient points of the evidence which he and Lancing had collected that day. He then telephoned to the Assistant Commissioner, who was at his home in Chelsea, and entrusted Lancing with the job of taking the report to the A.C., and of answering any questions which the latter might propound.

"As to how you get to Chelsea, G.O.K.," said Rivers. "The fog is thicker than ever and it's now freezing hard again, so that the roads are glazed. The tubes are the only sane way of getting anywhere, and the old man lives about as far from a tube station as is possible. Can you find your way southwards from South Kensington Station?"

"Not me," said Lancing promptly. "It's not my beat. I know my way better in Whitechapel. On a night like this South Ken. gets me guessing. If it's all the same to you, sir, I'd rather walk all along the Embankment. It's only about a coupla' miles to Cheyne Walk and at least you can't go wrong on the Embankment."

"As you like," said Rivers. "I wish you joy of it whichever way you go."

"What about those roses for poor Nigel?" grinned Lancing.

"Bradey's seeing to that," said Rivers. "I promised those girls I'd get them to him, and whatever aspersions you may make about the Cleopatra's innocence or lack of it, I'd have it on my conscience if I didn't do as I promised."

"Bradey's out for promotion anyway," grinned Lancing. "This assignment's just up his street. I'll bet you any money he tries to contact poor Nigel's nurse."

"Well, I'm going to contact Syd," said Rivers, "and if he's not poor Syd before I've done with him I shall be surprised."

Syd Stein was brought to the Chief Inspector's office by a uniformed constable. Looking up at that young man, Rivers thought he had never seen a poorer specimen. Pallid, grubby, furtive and trembling, Syd looked a wastrel—but not, to Rivers' mind, a desperate criminal. With Syd standing before him, the Chief Inspector spoke curtly:

"You stated in evidence that on Monday, January 1st, you stayed at the house of your friend, Monty Smith, in Euston Passage, until you set out to meet your mother at the corner of Southampton Row. You met her there at four o'clock. I'm giving you the chance of reconsidering that statement. Do you wish to alter it in any way?"

Syd gulped. "No, sir. That's right."

"How did you get to Southampton Row from Euston Passage?"

"I walked along Euston Road to St. Pancras and got a bus by the church—a No. 73 bus it was. Goes straight to Southampton Row."

"What time did you get there?"

"About quarter to four it was. I didn't know for sure what time me Mum was coming, but she said she'd be back by tea-time and I reckoned I could take her out to tea. I hung about a bit by the bus stop there. Perishing cold, it was."

Rivers looked steadily at the slovenly loose-lipped youth and then pulled a file towards him. "You say you walked to St. Pancras from Euston Passage: that would have been about half-past three?"

"That's right. I left Monty's soon after three. I spoke to him before I left."

"It won't do, Stein." Rivers' voice was quiet enough, but it made the wretched youth dither. "You were seen by a police constable as you got off a bus at the corner of Gray's Inn Road and Theobalds Road shortly before three o'clock on January 1st. You were seen by a hawker who knows you by sight in Red Lion Street just after three o'clock, and you were walking towards Lioncel Court." Rivers turned to the constable. "Give him a chair," he said. Syd was swaying on his feet. The constable shoved him on to a chair and Rivers went on: "The man whose body was found in a bedroom in your mother's house was murdered. I haven't cautioned you, because on the evidence I have at present I have no intention of charging you, but I give you this piece of advice. Don't tell lies. They're quite useless and they will only land you in worse trouble."

"I don't know nothing about it," slobbered Syd.

"Then why did you say to your mother, when you met her in Southampton Row, 'You're insured'? The constable who helped to pick your mother up after she slipped heard you say so."

Syd was silent now. His wits had given out: he was much too frightened to think. "I'm giving you a chance to tell the truth," went on Rivers, and his voice had a quality in it that had made tougher youths than Syd feel apprehensive. "You went home that afternoon. You knew your mother wouldn't be home until later, because you knew when to meet her. Why did you go home?"

Syd had no means of knowing that Chief Inspector Rivers was feeling his way along, trying out a theory which seemed reasonable. From much experience with lying witnesses, Rivers was pretty good at guessing when he had knocked the nail on the head. Before he was a policeman at all, when he was a young naval officer, Rivers had noted that startled look on a silly face when he himself had stated what seemed to him likely to be true: it was the witness who often informed Rivers when he was right, not in words but in that dumb animal look of resentful surprise.

"I'm asking you *why* you went home?" persisted Rivers. "Was it to get tea for your mother?"

To the Inspector's immense surprise, Syd blurted out "Yes," before he had had time to think: then he added, "I mean no. I didn't go home before I met me Mum."

"I'm not asking you if you went home. I'm asking you *why* you went home," persisted Rivers, who was pretty certain by this time that he was on the right lines. "You were very near home when the hawker saw you. His name is Joe Lime and he has a fruit barrow. He knows you quite well, doesn't he? It was only just after three o'clock when he saw you. He'd packed up early because it was too cold to do any business." Rivers paused, to give Syd time to realise the mess he was in. Then he went on: "You've told lies about what you did during the afternoon. You were seen very near your home about three o'clock. You met Mrs. Stein, less than five minutes' walk away, about an hour later. You tried to persuade her to come out to tea rather than to go straight home. You told her something that startled her so much she slipped off the kerb and fell down, repeating the word 'Insurance'. Do you know what cross-examination means, Stein?"

Syd remained silent, his lips working tremulously, and Rivers went on: "Nobody is going to believe the story you've told. I'm not trying to catch you out. If I believed you had committed murder, or even been accessory to it, I should have had to caution you. As it is, I'm giving you perfectly honest advice. Tell the truth. You went home because you'd arranged to meet Gray. Did he tell you to meet him there at three o'clock?"

Syd gave up: he was sick with fear, and he realised the mess he was in. His lips trembling so much that he could hardly speak, he said, "Yes." Then he blubbered. "I went upstairs and saw that there," he said. "I knew the cops'd say I done it. What could I do? What the bleeding 'ell could I do?" he sobbed.

"Get him a drink," said Rivers patiently.

2

Syd produced his story in spasms of hiccoughs and self-pity, and the story seemed to Rivers to fit in very well with the assumptions he had made about both Syd and Gray. Syd had done a good many errands for Gray. Some of these were concerned with street corner betting, Gray having an instinct, apparently, to avoid contacting betting stooges in person. Sometimes Syd had obliged by obtaining whisky at black market prices (plus a percentage for himself) from his flash friends. It was on the morning of December 31st that Gray had told Syd to come along to his (Gray's) room at three o'clock on New Year's Day with a bottle of whisky which Syd had undertaken to collect. This suited Syd very well, as he knew his mother would not be back much before four o'clock. He had left Monty's flat about one o'clock, got a meal in a snack bar in Euston Road, gone on to see a friend in Gray's Inn Road (only the friend was out) and had gone back to Lioncel Court via Theobald's Road and Red Lion Street. He had entered No. 13 by the basement door, to which he had a latch key. He told Rivers he hadn't noticed anything wrong when he was in the basement. It wasn't till he opened the door at the top of the basement stairs that he had smelled the smoke and something burning. Even then it hadn't occurred to him that the house was on fire. He went upstairs, and by the time he got to the top landing even Syd's slow wits and adenoidal incapacity to smell anything had been startled into an awareness that something was wrong. "The door of 'is room was shut, see, and 'e'd got Mum to put an 'eavy curtain over it to keep the draught out," said Syd.

He had pushed the door: it had stuck at first and then flown open, and Syd had found himself looking into a representation of a small concentrated hell. The heavy curtains were across the windows and the room was lit by the glare of the gas fire, which was full on. Rivers realised, as the wretched Syd stuttered and sobbed out his story, the full hideousness of what the youth had seen. A corpse lay with its face almost against the glowing gas jets: the clothes and carpets were smouldering red and the room was dense with clouds of hideous smoke. "Then all of a sudden it blazed up, like's if you'd chucked petrol on it," sobbed Syd. Likely enough, thought Rivers: a bottle of petrol or paraffin left by the door to be overturned when the door was opened. Syd had slammed the door to on that small inferno and gone pounding downstairs as though furies were after him. He said the next thing he remembered was standing by the kitchen sink drinking the whisky which he still carried. Then he was sick. He put his head under the cold tap and at last he began to think. That was a corpse upstairs: a stiff. They'd say Syd had done him in. "They always put the blame on me," he sobbed. Then he thought that no one knew he had been in the house. Get out quick and nobody'd ever know. Keep his Mum out of it for a bit. Let the whole ruddy house burn.

Rivers knew his story was true. Syd had seen what he had said he'd seen. With a vocabulary of a few hundred words, and a dreary sameness of epithets, he had described that horrible scene with a vividness which he had not the imagination to invent. The picture of that smouldering room, its fetid smoke illumined by the glare of the gas fire, was burnt on to Syd's mind, but he could give nothing in the way of detail. It was a corpse, and what had been its face was against the glowing gas fire.

3

Syd was eventually taken to the infirmary, and the E Division men went through the fog to tell the nearly frantic Mrs. Stein that her son was being looked after and no charge had been made against him. By the time Rivers had finished questioning him Syd was in a state of collapse, practically falling asleep as he sobbed out his helpless denials: he had hardly slept at all since he had opened the door of Gray's room, and when he had slept in uneasy snatches he had dreamt horribly of hell fire and evil-smelling smoke. Once his story was told, he fell asleep almost automatically.

"Doesn't realise how lucky he's been," said Rivers, talking to one of his C.I.D. colleagues after Syd had been trundled off between two policemen. "He was cast for the scapegoat if anyone smelt a rat. If he'd been a tougher sort of malefactor we might have accepted him as the *fons et origo*, but a backboneless worm like Syd would never have dared to tackle Gray. I'm not even prepared to believe Syd would have tried to rob him; those spineless ne'er-do-wells are frightened to death of potential violence."

The other nodded: he was a grey-headed inspector, senior to Rivers in years but junior in rank. "You're right there. There's a sharp demarcation line between the tough and the sneak. You seem to have done some very pretty guessing in this case, if I may say so. Do you reckon you've spotted the winner?"

Rivers laughed. "It's the hell of a queer set-out, Charles. I've got the bloke's fingerprints. I'll bet my shirt I know just what he's done. I know where he is. I don't know what his real name is, or what name he's using now. He's one of eight chaps staying at Lech am Arlberg. I've got the names of all eight. I've had the continental telegraph system just about sizzling because I won't risk a slip-up on phone calls. We can check up on all eight men here in England—respectable professional young men they are, doubtless. And all we can learn over here is as much use as a sausage, because one of them is bogus. He's using another man's name and identity. And this qualified climate of ours has shut down on transport for tonight. Planes grounded, trains sitting, Channel service cancelled. Damn and double damn."

"Can't the Austrian police check-up on fingerprints for you? Call in their passports. It's often done."

"I won't have it done," said Rivers, banging the table with his fist. "Once that chap who called himself Gray senses the least smell of trouble, he'll be off. He's a skier, Charles. For all

I know he's up to international status. Once he's off, he may be able to cock a snook at all of us."

"But if they call the passports in, he can't get far, Julian. Particularly in Austria. You're stuck at the frontiers of the international zones if your papers aren't O.K."

"Damn it, can't you see he's probably got two passports?" snapped Rivers. "We've never caught him, Charles. We don't know who he is. He's probably got one passport under his own name, Smith, Brown or Robinson or Vere de Vere, complete with visas for the lord knows where. I'm not underestimating his brains. I dare not underestimate his brains. He's clever, and I know it. Lech is an Austrian village, away in the mountains. There'll be village policemen there, as there are in English villages. If they collect the passports of that party of sixteen skiers, my chap smells trouble. He'll beat it, using his own passport: he'll become any one of the few thousand Englishmen who are goating about on skis anywhere from the Bernese Oberland to Carinthia. Look at the map, Charles. Gray's looked at it already. Anybody can get a travel permit on the Vienna line, via the Semmering or via Villach. I've no doubt he's thought it all out very carefully. Well, I'm thinking, too. I'm not going to let any Austrian village policeman go asking for Gray's fingerprints, nor letting them try to impound that party."

"I see," said Charles slowly. "You've been doing quite a bit of thinking."

"Like hell I have," said Rivers inelegantly. "I told you I don't know who he is. I've got Henry Fearon badgering the Foreign Office, checking up on private secretaries to High Ups, finding out if any nicely mannered young hopeful's been sacked recently or taken French leave or what have you. Gray's hitched himself on to a party of skiers. It's not often I claim a bouquet, Charles, but I wasn't slow off the mark this time. All the same he'd got to Austria before I got a smell of him. And if he's got as much valid information as will go on a sixpence, the Russians will embrace him with open arms and not give a damn how many people he's murdered en route."

"Quite—but they'll probably murder him too when they've sucked him dry."

"Maybe. But that's not my pigeon. I want to get him. I want to go to Lech and get on skis myself and have the pleasure of seeing him perform. He's a tourist now: well, I'm going to be a tourist, too."

The older man chuckled. "Well, I hope he'll wait for you. Seems to me it's a bit chancy."

"Perhaps it is," said Rivers. "Perhaps... Ever been on a jaunt like that, Charles?"

"Not me," said Charles emphatically. "My dad was a grocer. I've worked hard since I left school at fifteen, and ski-ing was as much my cup of tea as playing polo. I'm married and I've brought up five kids on a policeman's pay. Ski-ing? Ask me if I'm a member of M.C.C. or the Jockey Club."

"You're exaggerating," said Rivers. "Anybody can go ski-ing. Lancing's done it. I've done it and neither of us is in the stud book. We've just spent our pennies that way instead of rearing a family. But, Charles, you don't know what you feel like when you get there. I do. It's as though the mountain air goes to your head. You forget everything else. I tell you Gray's enjoying himself. I bet any money he's enjoying himself. He's with a party of light-hearted youngsters, pretty girls and his own idea of nice chaps—fellows who went to good schools and have had a good time. He'll be the life and soul of the party for a few days. Think of the contrast between Lioncel Court and an Alpensports hotel at Lech, the sun, the snow, the exercise and good food: and he'll be admired as a fine athlete, which he is. No. My bet is he'll stay put for a bit, enjoying it all, establishing his new personality."

"Well, you do freeze on to some rum cases, Julian. They say a chap attracts the events which belong to his own ego or id or whatever the dotty jargon is. I get the robbery with violence blokes and the con men. You get the blighters who beat it on skis. It's the way we're made. No criminal I ever contacted took to skis. Thank God for it. I should have been nowhere."

"Hallo, here's Lancing. What's the latest met. report?" said Rivers eagerly.

"Anticyclone solid over France, Low Countries, Channel and G.B.," said Lancing. "That means less snow and more fog—not a breath of wind for miles. But there are complex depressions in the Atlantic and there's been heavy snow in eastern Switzerland. They're having some trouble getting the Vienna express through and the St. Gothard's got a hold-up. It doesn't sound too good, but Barron has got a report in for you. He's interviewed ninety-seven witnesses in the last two days and he's struck it lucky at last. Shall I bring him in?"

The report from Detective Barron was brief and correct: he described none of the disheartening routine work when for two dreary days he had followed up reports of ski-carrying travellers: he came straight to the point when he had got some information which seemed relevant to the case. At 9.30 p.m. on Saturday, December 30th, a young man carrying skis had been seen at Liverpool Street Station. It had been a wretched evening and very few taxis arrived at the station rank. The young man with skis had hailed a taxi and asked to be driven to Southampton Row. The driver, an old man who owned his own taxi, had refused to take the fare. He said he had only got enough petrol to get him home and he lived at New Cross, and would only take a fare in that direction. It was a booking clerk who heard the ensuing altercation, the young man saying that it was illegal for a taxi-driver to refuse a fare. The taxi drove off and someone in a private car called out, "I'll take you as far as Kingsway if that's any good." The young man with the skis had got in gratefully.

That was as far as Barron had been able to get. His informant, could tell him nothing about the private car except that it was definitely a private car and not a taxi.

Rivers seized a note block. "Chit for the B.B.C. Tell 'em it's priority. They can bung it in at the end of the nine o'clock news if they're snappy."

Lancing snatched the telephone, dialled, and began to work his way through departments. "Scotland Yard. Criminal Investigation Department… The Duty Officer…" while Rivers scribbled, "Will the owner of a private car who gave a lift to a traveller at Liverpool Street Station and offered to drive him to Kingsway on Saturday, December 30th, at 9.30 p.m., please report to Scotland Yard…"

"Why not mention the skis?" put in Charles.

"Not for the gold of Ophir," said Rivers. "They don't generally tune in to London in Austrian winter sports resorts. English people are generally only too glad to get away from our nice cheery news bulletins—but they might. Or Gray may have a portable. I'm not giving away more than I must. Lancing, you'd better go home and pack a suitcase with your ski-kit. Then come back here—to sleep or not to sleep. As soon as this fog lets up, we're moving. They won't get any planes up tonight, but we'll be ready to try for the first Channel port which can get a boat across the Manche."

Lancing grinned and made for the door.

"What about your kit?" Charles asked Rivers, and the latter chuckled.

"I've got it here. I felt in my bones this would happen. Here's a précis for you, Charles, and if I prove to have been wrong you can laugh at me for the rest of your life. When Gray realised he'd killed the chap who saw him come down from the roofs, he thought he'd better get out of the country. I'm assuming he'd got a passport, but he didn't want to go rushing off immediately in case the main-line stations were being watched. He didn't know how much we'd got in the way of a description of him, to say nothing of fingerprints, if he'd missed his packet of fags. He lay low. Then he met some chap he knew, and the latter said he was off to Austria with a ski-ing party, although he didn't know a single member of the party. Everything was fixed up. It was a chance, and Gray took it. He asked the bloke to spend the night with him in London before he went abroad."

"Might be," mused Charles. "It fits. What did the pathologist find, by the way?"

"I've just got the report. A thumping great dose of barbiturate in deceased's organs. Probably mixed with his whisky. It was easy, Charles. It's always easy to kill an unsuspecting victim. The chap whose remains we found just went to sleep and stayed asleep. Next morning, Gray wrapped up the skis and took them to Waterloo. Came back some time in the morning to an empty house—luck was with him there—changed, fixed his funeral pyre and beat it. He'd arranged for Syd to come home at three o'clock, so that Syd could shoulder the blame if suspicions were aroused, and Gray had also arranged some funny business with his typewriter, I imagine, to prove that Syd had been doing a bit of looting. I'm pretty sure Mrs. Stein found the typewriter, leapt to the wrong conclusion and confused the trail. Well, that's my story and I claim I've got something in the way of solid evidence for every step of it. Not that the evidence will ever be entered as such. Gray's own fingerprints are all that's needed. Once we've got the chap who left his fingerprints on a cigarette carton and the coins in the gas meter, we don't want any of the fancy bits."

"Fancy bits," said Charles slowly. "Fancy... imagination... guesswork. That's one way of looking at it. The other is to call it interpretation of unrelated details. Detection, in short. It's one of the best imaginative efforts I've met in the detection line, Julian, because you've got the essentials—the bits of evidence which dovetail into a whole."

"Thanks for those kind words," said Rivers. "I'm still prepared to admit there may be some factor we haven't got. Something which changes the whole equation. I don't know, but like the mongoose, we're going to find out. If it weren't for this qualified fog we'd have been over France by now. I'm going to ring Dover again. I wonder if the Admiralty would help. They kept moving in the war... It's enough to drive a chap mad."

Chapter XV

1

"Are you really going to St. Anton today, Robert?" asked Kate. "The sky looks a bit ominous. I believe it's going to snow hard."

"Personally I think it will hold up for today," replied O'Hara. They were sitting over their coffee at breakfast, making plans for the day. "I've been talking to one of the guides who knows a bit of English, and he says it won't snow before evening. I'm keen to do the trip today because time goes so quickly. We're nearly at the end of our first week and we haven't made a single real expedition yet, just practice runs. The second week always flies and it's a mistake to leave things too late."

"I think Bobs is right there," put in Ian. "Besides, we may have snow for days once it starts, and not be able to get over the Pass. What do you think, Neville?"

"Well, I think it looks pretty grim, and it'll certainly be perishing cold," replied Neville, "but if Robert's set on it, and the others want to go, I'll go too. If the weather turns dirty, we can all come back by train to Langen and come out in the bus."

"He's funking ski-ing down from St. Christoph," grinned Robert. "I knew he'd back out eventually."

"You wait and see, Irishman," retorted Neville. "I've said I'll go to St. Anton. After that, a little common sense is indicated." He turned to Kate. "And we've got to find out about the homeward journey some time. I'm trying to book a sleeper. That couchette business is the poorest sort of entertainment I know."

"Oh, heavens, don't start talking about going back yet," groaned Daphne. "We've only just about settled down."

"I've got to get back before you others," said Malcolm. "Incidentally, have you heard they won't take Austrian currency at the railway station for registered luggage going back to England? You've got to pay in Swiss or English money. I call it a bit steep. Imagine Victoria Station refusing to accept English money when you're sending registered baggage abroad."

"I think it's a mistake to complicate life by bringing too much baggage," said Robert in his assertive way. "Take what you can carry and carry it yourself. If I'd had any baggage to register I should never have caught the train at Victoria—I cut it pretty fine."

"Not so fine as Neville did," put in Bridget. "I'd given him up for lost. What a foul day it was, like an eclipse of the sun."

"It wasn't so bad outside London," put in Neville. "I came from Berkshire that morning, and the sun was shining at Maidenhead. It wasn't till Slough we ran into the fog, and then we got hung up so long I thought I was scuppered. Well, we may have snow over the Arlberg Pass, but we shan't have fog. There's a wind which fairly takes the skin off your face this morning."

"How many of you want packed lunches?" put in Frank Harris, who often tackled the practical matters which the flightier members of the party forgot. "The hotel people like to know definitely, in good time—and do remember if you order a packed lunch you're not expected to have the hotel lunch too, unless you pay for it."

"It's not much of a day for picnicking," said Jane, but Neville put in:

"I'd call it a hungry day. You can eat your packed lunch as you walk up to St. Christoph and have a hot meal when you get to St. Anton if you're feeling hungry again by then, as you probably will do."

"Yes. That's sensible. Count me in," said Jane. "Neville, Robert, Malcolm, Ian. Tim, are you coming?"

"Yes. If the rest of you think it's good enough, I'll tag on— but I'll join the train party coming back."

"Six packed lunches. That the lot?" asked Harris. "Biddy and Kate? You not going?"

"Not to St. Anton," said Kate. "I might go in the bus and walk back. It's too cold to sketch, so I'll have lunch here. Let's go outside and see what it feels like. Biddy, why not come as far as Steuben and walk back with me? It'll be much nicer walking than ski-ing today, and you haven't seen anything except the Lech nursery slopes since you got here."

"Perfectly true," said Biddy, as they got up from the breakfast table and strolled towards the lounge. "Ski-ing becomes a sort of mania. One wants so terribly to get better at it. It just gives me a pain inside when I see other people doing it faultlessly, skimming down like angels at goodness knows what dizzy speeds, while I still flounder on occasions, flapping like a fish on dry land."

"But you don't flap any longer," said Kate. "I was watching

you yesterday and I thought you looked very efficient, not to say stylish."

"Oh, I've got on a lot, I feel that. I'm not being modest or anything," laughed Bridget. "I just made up my mind I'd stick to the ski-schools this trip, and work right through everything, so that next time I get the luck to come out I can feel independent."

They went outside through the double doors of the lounge, pulling on coats, and stood looking up at the mountains. It was intensely cold and very clear. To the west and south the sky was blue behind the snow peaks, and the visibility had an intense quality, so that Kate felt helplessly that here was something you could not express in terms of paint. There was no gradation, no near and far, just a vast crystalline clarity. To the east the sky was grey and great cloud banks were piling behind the mountains: it gave a queer effect because the severe little church with its rococo cupola was lighter in tone than the sky, shining with the reflected light from the south and west. Once again Kate realised that there was an element of terror in this mountain loveliness: the massing clouds and the snow slopes made the wooden houses seem puny. Only the gaunt stone church standing abrupt on its little plateau seemed to have any quality of strength, as though, if the village were submerged, the stone tower and steep roof of the angular Gothic building might survive above it all. It was a purely visual impression, something realised with the eye of a draughtsman, not a religious implication, but Kate thought to herself, "That's why they built it there: something that man has made which can compete with the mountains… something to rest the eye on…"

"Goodness, it is cold. It bites," said Bridget, "and the snow always comes from the east here, along the valley. It looks lovely, though. I think I'll come with you in the bus to the Steuben turn, Kate, and we can watch the others toil up the Pass."

"Do you know, I think my courage is failing a bit," said Tim's voice close behind them. "What is there about this morning? I've always found this place friendly before. Today it looks portentous, as though it's despising us."

"It's neither friendly nor portentous: it's just objective, unaffected by human beings and their frantic scuttlings and ski-ings," said Kate. "It could submerge us all in tons of purest snow, smooth as a cloud drift, and never show any humps where our bodies lie buried."

"Well, I'm dashed! You're a cheerful one, Cassandra," said Tim indignantly. "I'm not all that good at this ski-ing business as you call it, and I've said I'll ski down to St. Anton from St. Christoph, and all the encouragement you can give me is to assure me the snow will make a nice smooth blanket over me after I've perished."

"It's not Kate who has frightened you, Tim. It's yourself," said Biddy. "Do you feel that your sins are finding you out?"

"My sins! I like that!" he said indignantly. "Why pick me as the sinner? I know there have been a few odd happenings of late, but you needn't pick on me. Any more news from the C.I.D., Biddy?"

"I shouldn't tell you if there were," she laughed. "Come on in, Kate. We'll need all the clothes we've got. It's no morning for standing about: you could freeze as you stood, oh so easily."

"And become a pillar of salt, Mrs. Lot," said Tim. "You'd make a very handsome one, to set up as a warning to scoffers."

About half an hour later they set out in the crowded bus, which carried skiers and returning travellers, those whose holiday was over and who were going to Langen station to return to various parts of Europe: French, Germans, Italians, Belgians and a few British. It was Malcolm, sitting next to Jane, who said: "Somehow it astonishes me every time I realise the number of places you can reach by rail from that small station of Langen. It's a very small unimportant-looking station, but just think of the network of communications it's part of."

Jane nodded. "I was thinking rather the same thing," she said. "All these people, all talking different languages, going back to different countries on the Vienna-Basle express."

"To Vienna and Salzburg and Munich: from Innsbruck south down the Adige Valley to Verona and Padua and Venice: from Villach down to Trieste and Fiume, from Buchs to Zürich and Basle," said Malcolm.

It was Robert who put in: "Are you thinking of doing a trans-continental tour? In the old days you could go on from Vienna to Budapest and Bucharest and Constantinople... and the golden road to Samarkand. Nowadays you're less fortunate. Still, the good old Vienna express does catch the imagination."

"Have you ever been right across Europe, Robert?" asked Kate. "To Constantinople and the gateway of Asia?"

He grinned. "My people got around quite a bit when I was still a kid, in the palmy thirties. I'm willing to take Malcolm on on the subject of European railway communications and how to get where, and I agree the Vienna express does offer opportunities of reaching most places."

"But the opportunities are illusory these days," said Neville, leaning forward in his seat to join in the conversation. "At one time a man could leave England and say the world's mine oyster. He could work his way or pay his way. Now you can do neither. You're limited on the one hand by the restrictions on currency, on the other by trade unions and permits and visas. You can neither pay your way nor work your way. While you've got money to spend you're welcome as a tourist and nothing's too good for you. But you're like a ticket-of-leave man all the time: you've got to go back."

"Yes. *You* have," said Robert. "But if *I* wanted to stay abroad, I'd manage it somehow."

"How? Who'd employ you?" said Malcolm. "Neville's right there. The minute a foreigner gets a job there's a howl from the unions. We know that in England. What *could* you do? You couldn't even get a seaman's job, nor yet a waiter's nor a farm labourer's. Austria's poor, Italy's poor—and got any number of unemployed—and so has France. If you were stranded here tomorrow, you couldn't get a job anyhow. You'd just be repatriated, sent home like a returned empty."

It was Tim who put a word in next: "It depends on what you can do. A skilled mechanic or technician can get a job almost anywhere in the world. This is the age of engineering. Every country is expanding its mechanical potential, whether in transport, agriculture, mining or industry. If you can service an engine, you can get a job. Engines have got to be taken down and overhauled, and there aren't enough good mechanics in the world to do the world's mechanical jobs."

"How earnest he sounds," laughed Kate, and Neville put in:

"He's an optimist. Malcolm's right and Tim's wrong. National unions are all solid against foreign labour. This is Zurs. It's going to be a fine day after all."

2

The party of eight alighted from the bus at the road fork at Steuben: Jane, Malcolm, Tim, Robert, Neville and Ian shouldered their skis and turned left towards the Pass: Kate and Bridget waved them on their way and then turned back towards Zurs.

"It's perishing cold," said Bridget. "It wouldn't be a bad idea to go into one of the hotels at Zurs and get some coffee and wait in the warm until the bus comes back from Langen. It'll get us back in time for lunch. I think they were rather asses to go for that long trip today. The wind's like a knife and getting cold isn't funny at this altitude."

"They'll soon get warm climbing that gradient," said Kate, "and there's plenty of them. It's lone skiers who ask for trouble. Malcolm will look after Jane, he's a sensible soul: Ian and Tim will stick together, and Robert and Neville can go their own pace, and bicker together as they always do."

Bridget nodded, and they swung down the white road at a good pace. To their right, the pine-clad mountain slopes rose steeply: to their left, the sheer drop was in part concealed by the wall of snow piled up by the snow ploughs at the edge of the road. "It's an amazing road, but I should hate to drive on it," said Bridget. "I have the feeling that there's nothing but the snow wall between you and perdition. If you skidded against it, would it hold, or would you go over in a sort of avalanche?"

"I'd rather not try. I've thought the same thing about skiing down it," said Kate. "If you mucked a turn you'd be for it. There's such a small margin between being safe and not being safe."

Bridget laughed. "That's part of the attraction. What do you think of our party, Kate?"

"I thought that was coming," rejoined Kate, "or perhaps I hoped it was, when I persuaded you to come for a walk. The party would be all right if it hadn't been for that silly business over the pound notes. What Frank Harris says is true, it undermines one's confidence. It makes you take note of things which you wouldn't otherwise have noticed."

"I know," said Biddy, "and it's a pretty poor feeling. It makes me ashamed of myself."

"Who told you about it—the pound note racket?" asked Kate suddenly.

"Tim Grant did. I realised there was an atmosphere at breakfast yesterday and I tackled Tim. He and Ian are in the same chalet as Robert. I thought it was Ian and Tim being mischievous. There's something about Ian, you know. Not malicious, just mischievous, as though he'd never grown up. And Robert gets his goat. I can quite imagine Ian deciding to get a rise out of Robert. And then Frank Harris has been so sensible and high-minded over everything. Do you know what I mean, Kate? A lad like Ian might have thought, 'If Frank wants to play detective, let's give him a mystery to detect.'"

"Yes. I know what you mean, but Ian did tell Frank quite soberly that he hadn't been ragging and that he hadn't had anything to do with taking the notes. And it isn't only the money of Robert's that's in question. Neville's lost his English notes, too. Biddy, what did you make of that message from Joyce, about the C.I.D. men calling at your club?"

"It sounded just crazy to me," said Biddy. "I rang through to Miss Hammond on the quiet yesterday evening: she's the club superintendent, and she's a sensible business-like creature. I could only afford a three-minute call, but the line was excellent and I could hear every word. It's quite true that two C.I.D. officers did call. One was Chief Inspector Rivers—I'm certain I've heard or read about him. He was inquiring about a car smash, one of the cars being a stolen one, that's why the C.I.D. were on the case. Someone had told him that I'd seen the smash at South Ken."

"Did you see a smash, or hear anything about one?"

"No. Nothing of the kind happened when I was out. Neither do I believe that's what they went to the club for, Kate. That was only a sort of routine excuse."

"Well, why do you think they went to the club?"

"To find out about this party. I've been thinking and thinking, Kate. I know it's nothing to do with me, nor with Jane. But they're interested in one of us—unless they've got on to the wrong party. That's the most probable explanation."

"What do you mean, exactly?"

"Well, things are so abnormal with all this Cold War and Iron Curtain business. The Government's fed up with physicists who go abroad and vanish, and they're very cagey about allowing people to go to these communist peace rallies. My own opinion is that someone has gone abroad, making winter sports an excuse, and the Government's set the C.I.D. on to trace them. If you did want to get abroad without being noticed, a ski-ing party's a very good way of doing it. And we are in Austria, quite a short distance from the Russian occupied zone. Look, we're just getting to Zurs. What about some coffee or chocolate or something?"

"All right. It'd be quite a good idea. I believe it is going to keep fine, Biddy. I'm glad. I shouldn't like to think of the others getting caught in a snow storm on the Pass."

3

"I did an awful lot of worried thinking about this C.I.D. visitation, Kate," said Biddy, as they sat over their coffee and croissants in the pleasant heat of the Zurs hotel. "At first I thought it might be me they were after and I hunted through all the secrets of my murky past. Of course I was on Special

Duties in the Wrens—but they can't be trying to line up all the lasses who were trusted with war-time secrets. Then I was secretary to Brown Stacey, when he got into Parliament. He was very hot on aircraft design at one time, but things go out of date so quickly they can't imagine I'm a menace, even if I'd understood enough to know what to pinch, which I didn't."

"But Biddy, that's ridiculous. Why should the police be interested in you?"

"I'm quite sure they're not, but I've heard some odd rumours about Security, as they call it. Anyway, my guess is that the Security racket's at the bottom of all this. Someone's gone abroad whom they don't want kidnapped, and the police are checking up as far as they can. They probably inspected the parties department at Victoria—they could get names and addresses. It's true we didn't travel under the parties scheme eventually, but I did try to fix it that way. You see, there must be some reason why that Rivers man went to the club and asked for me by name. I've been trying to remember if any of the people I play around with could be of interest to the police—important enough to bring the high-ups in the C.I.D. after them, I mean. Of course, I do know some communists: we all do. I've gone out of my way to meet some of them, because I wanted to understand what it is that makes intelligent people believe in communism. But I can't believe that any of the people I know are important."

Kate stirred the thick cream into her coffee slowly, enjoying the simple fact of being able to pile whipped cream on to fragrant black coffee. "I didn't think of communists," she said. "I thought of much more commonplace things—forged cheques, currency offences, common or garden theft. Biddy, how many of this party do you know well enough to be able

to say to yourself, 'I *know* they're honest. I'm so certain of it
I'd risk my life on it.'"

"It depends on what you mean by honesty, Kate. If I were
asked if I'd risk my life on the orthodoxy of their political
opinions, I'd say I only knew three or four of them well enough
to be perfectly certain. You see, the terrifying part of communism is that some of them keep it dark. Of the men, I'm
certain Derrick Cossack is exactly what he seems to be. I'd
put my life on the fact that the Navy has no dark horses. I'd
say the same of Gerald, because I've known him for a long
time, and I think I'd risk my life on Malcolm being just what
he seems to be."

"Surely you'd say the same of Frank Harris?"

"I suppose so—but I don't know what goes on inside his
head. He seems so obvious on the surface, kindly and responsible and matter-of-fact, but he never gives himself away. He's
a much more complex creature than he appears to be."

Biddy sighed as she refilled her coffee cup. "You said
just now that this sickening business over losing money had
made you suspicious, and I said it had made me feel ashamed
of myself. I couldn't help realising that Frank Harris could
have cooked up the whole situation if he wanted to rouse
suspicions."

"I admit that, so far as the facts go," said Kate, "but I'm certain Frank is straight. I don't go all out to admire the medical
profession. I think they're excessively conservative, out to
obstruct progress and often self-important, but their profession does develop integrity. Some of it may be self-interest
and self-protection, but it's there. I'm sure we can leave Harris
out of it, whether 'it' is communism or larceny."

"All right. That leaves us with four men of whom we know
nothing, and three girls. I'll back Jane, you, Martha and Meriel.

That leaves Pippa, Daphne, and Jillian. All light-hearted, very young and out for a good time. Nothing doing in the sinister line." Biddy suddenly laughed. "We are being *awful*, Kate. All because two idiots have left their money around, and the C.I.D.'s being officious about the wrong party."

"Yes. In a way, we are being awful, Biddy, but do tell me this. Have you noticed anything, about any member of our party, that made you say to yourself, 'But that's impossible. Either you're very inaccurate or you're deliberately telling a lie for purposes of your own'?"

"No. I haven't got anything specific at all," said Biddy. "Do you want to tell me—or not?"

"No, I don't think I do want to tell you at present," said Kate. "If nothing else happens this trip, I'll tell you when we get home. I'm devoutly hoping nothing else does happen."

"All right," said Biddy. "Let's leave it at that. There's the bus. It'll get us back in good time for lunch."

Chapter XVI

1

When Kate and Biddy got into the bus, they found it fairly full, occupied by travellers who had just arrived at Langen station and were coming on to Lech to take the places of those who had left that morning. Scrambling over hand baggage to a seat at the rear, Kate murmured politely *"Bitte schon"* to indicate that she proposed to sit down on a seat which held various impedimenta, and a young man woke up from a deep meditation and looked up at her with lively dark eyes.

"So sorry…afraid I was dreaming." He moved his things hastily. "You are English, aren't you?" he asked apologetically.

"Yes. I am. Have you just arrived?" asked Kate.

"Yes. We're indefinitely late. I've lost count of how much. Theoretically we should have been here last night."

"What was it? Snow or fog?"

"Both. Fog in England. Fog over Channel. Fog in France. Snow in Switzerland. Real snow, not the English variety. What sort of weather have you been having here?"

"Lovely. This is the first day we haven't had blazing sun."

"Sun! what a wonderful thought," he replied. "You can't imagine what the weather's been like in London."

"I can imagine it all too well," said Kate. "We only came away on New Year's Day, if you happen to remember what that day was like."

"Do I not!" he laughed. "I'm going to Lech. Do you know it?"

"Yes. We're all going to Lech in this bus. It's the only place the road goes to."

"Is it a good place to go to? I've never tried it before."

"I think it's a very good place," replied Kate. She turned slightly to look at him. A personable young man, already in ski-kit, obviously not shy and yet not excessively friendly. He had a clear, clipped voice, a well-set head, and was not so young as Kate had thought at a first glance. "I suppose you mean is it a good place for ski-ing," she went on. "According to the experts, yes, it is. They have the International Ski Races at Lech—they're fixed for the day after tomorrow and the place is about full to capacity with every nationality under the sun."

"Are there many English people staying in Lech?"

"They're in the minority at present—as you'll guess for yourself when you see the cars. Opulent cars of every nationality save English."

"Opulence isn't the characteristic of most English cars of today," he laughed, "but I'll hand it to them for staying power. My father's got a real vintage product, 1932. It still goes, and he generally gets there."

Kate, who was interested in all human beings, found there was something very likeable about the young man beside her. He chattered with an ease indicating that he was used to talking to strangers, and his eyes showed a lively intelligence and interest, though he refrained from the usual exclamations about the scenery to which newly arrived travellers are all too prone. As though aware of her scrutiny he turned and looked at her, and Kate risked putting into words the speculation which flashed absurdly across her mind.

"Is your father the rector of a large and struggling country parish?" she asked. She noted the amused surprise in his dark eyes and the twitch of his lips.

"Yes. He is," he replied. "Was that telepathy, guesswork or information received?"

"None of them. It's just awareness of the fact that country parsons often have very old cars and manage to keep them going—by faith, I suppose."

He laughed. "Perfectly true. They can't afford to buy new ones. Doctors, business men and farmers all manage to get new cars. You could have added retired schoolmasters to your category, and perhaps retired colonels."

"They haven't the faith which moves ancient automobiles," said Kate. "This is Lech, and I believe you're going to have a fine afternoon. We all thought it would snow. Good-bye and good ski-ing."

"Thanks very much," he replied.

2

Kate and Biddy went into the hotel, leaving newly arrived travellers to sort out their skis and baggage.

"You seemed rather taken with your young man," said Biddy.

"Yes. I liked him. He's got an unusually intelligent face," said Kate, "and he reminds me vaguely of somebody I've seen before."

They got rid of their coats and went into their own dining-room and sat down to wait for the rest of the party, who hadn't yet come in.

"What did you place him as?" inquired Biddy. She and Kate often played the game of attributing occupations to the fellow countrymen they encountered abroad.

Kate considered. "Not a schoolmaster," she said. "Not a Civil Servant. There's a touch of originality about him, and he's very much aware of people. He's older than he looks at a first glance, probably about thirty, and my guess is that his job is concerned with people and dealing with people in some way or other. He might be a personnel manager, but he's got the build of an athlete. He comes from London and his father's a country parson. He's more probably in one of the Services. Not the Navy. They tend to be rather silent with strangers. This one enjoyed talking. Not the R.A.F. They nearly always slip in a word of jargon. That leaves the Army."

"Did you notice the man in front of me?" asked Biddy.

"No. I didn't have time to notice anybody else."

"They're travelling together," said Biddy. "I saw them for-gather when they got out of the bus. The one in front of me was a big fair fellow, forty-fiveish, silent and rather sleepy-looking, but he woke up once and had a good meditative look at you." Biddy broke off and then added: "I've probably got the C.I.D. on the brain, but I asked Hammond what those two officers were like, the ones who went to the club. She said they were both 'perfect gentlemen'—she would. One was a big fair fellow with a quiet voice, and the other was much younger, a dark boy with lively eyes, very coming on."

Kate groaned. "Oh lord!" she exclaimed. "Biddy, let's pray it's not one of our lot… How utterly sickening."

"Hoi, don't go jumping to conclusions," protested Biddy. "I was only being silly."

"You weren't. You've got it in one," said Kate. "I knew something he said rang a bell. He was just blethering in the bus to an unknown Englishwoman and he let out a word of his own jargon. 'Information received.' Like a schoolmaster saying 'last term' or a soldier, saying 'operations' or the Navy 'proceeding'. I swear you're right... a job dealing with people: very much aware of people..."

"But any of us uses that phrase," protested Biddy. "We pick it up from detective stories."

"So we may, but I always believe that jargon becomes so much second nature that it slips out when you're having a casual conversation with a stranger," said Kate. "I've noticed it again and again. Are they staying at this hotel?"

"I don't know. I was very careful not to show undue interest," said Biddy. "It would have been so tempting to say, 'Chief Inspector Rivers, I presume.' After all, it was me they trailed in London. Look here, do we tell Frank and the others that we suspect the C.I.D. has arrived?"

"No," said Kate, "after all it's only our private hunch. We've no proof: and as you say, we may be tending to get a thing about it—an obsession."

"All right. As you say. But if you see that very passable young man around after lunch, you can speak to him and ask him his name. You say he reminds you of somebody you know."

"He reminds me of a portrait I've seen, and I can't place it. It's those wide-set dark eyes. Hallo, here's Frank and the others. Thank goodness. The appetite one gets in this place is unbelievable."

Frank, Derrick and Gerald came in, followed by Daphne, Meriel and Pippa.

"The weather's held up for them after all," said Pippa. "If Jane says it's not too stiff, I shall try to do that jaunt before we go home. I believe there are some amusing shops in St. Anton, and I must get some presents to take home. The great advantage of St. Anton is that you can come back by train and you haven't got the awful feeling of another long ski run at the end of the day when you're tired."

"My own belief is that they'll all come back by train," said Derrick. "Robert was the only one who wanted to ski back. I can't see Neville being persuaded to do anything he doesn't want to do, and he was certainly in favour of coming back by train."

Martha and Jillian came in and settled in their places at table, and Martha put in: "It depends if Robert insists on skiing back. They won't let him come back by himself. Neville was only saying this morning that it's idiotic for tourist skiers to do long runs alone. Accidents are always happening, and if you broke a leg you could easily freeze to death before you were found."

"Oh, don't be so jolly cheerful," said Jillian. "I know people break their legs and bust their ankles ski-ing, but there are very seldom fatal accidents. It's not like mountaineering. Biddy, have you noticed what lashings of people have arrived today? Some of the cars outside make me green with envy. I think it's amazing the way they risk such swell outfits on these roads, and they never seem to freeze up, like cars do in England. How do they manage it?"

"They're used to these temperatures, and used to driving on snow," said Harris. "The reason we get into a mess in England during heavy snowfalls is that we don't cater for it. It always takes us unawares."

"It's a wonder the cars don't get stolen," put in Meriel.

"They seem to leave them around in the most casual way in the world, parked in some neat little recess dug out of a snow mound."

"Steal them? What a hope!" said Derrick. "They're all plastered with their national origins, and the elaboration of auto club badges is simply dazzling. You never see one of our own plain unidentifiable tin lizzies here, they're all tricked out like Jezebels. Besides, where could you take one to? You'd be at some sort of frontier post in an hour or so."

"That's about it," agreed Frank. "Passports and car permits for the Swiss, for the Germans, for the British zone, for the Russian zone, and they just about strip the car at every customshouse. We do a bit of grumbling at home, but it does cheer me up to remember I can drive from Lands End to John o' Groats without having the bonnet opened and the boot emptied and the upholstery pulled about by zealous gendarmes."

"That's quite an interesting reflection," said Kate. "When we came away, we all bawled 'Freedom!'—freedom from restrictions of every kind—and the real fact is that we can't move more than a few miles in any direction without Passport barriers and Customs barriers and all the rest."

"Moral: if you want to do a bolt, don't try Austria," grinned Gerald. "The chances of stealing a car seem to be nil: the chances of hiding under a rug in the back of a car are minus: the chances of avoiding the Passport hounds are minus-nil."

"We ought to have Robert here. He could explain how to avoid these small lets and hindrances, probably by ski-ing over the mountains and carefully avoiding frontier posts."

"Well, in fairness it's got to be admitted that some chaps did it in war-time," said Derrick. "Not many, but some. So I suppose it's only fair to admit that Robert's ideas aren't absolutely impossible."

"I hear they're reinforcing the police here," put in Frank. "There are some royal personages coming to see the International Race, and the manager says there's no end of fuss being made for security reasons."

"What royal personages?" demanded Biddy promptly. "Do you mean some of ours? Our Elizabeth and Philip or somebody really exciting like that?"

"We don't know," said Gerald. "The blond type was a bit cagey about it. I don't think it's likely to be any of our lot. Probably a grand duchess of some State we've never heard of, or some Indian rajahs or something fancy. But we just don't know. Anyway, the hotel managers are all busy checking up their lists and seeing if they can account for all the various nationals."

"It sounds a bit phony to me. If royal personages were really coming here, everybody would know about it," said Jillian. "If they're getting more police in, it's far more likely on account of the thefts that have been happening. Frank, if you've any inside dope, I think you might tell us. You seem to be the chosen confidant of the blond type. He never tells me any newsy 'items.'"

"I don't know a thing more than I've told you," said Harris. "I think it might be a good idea for all of us to keep our passports on us: we've all got pockets, and as most of you girls don't get far in French or German, it's quite a good idea to have proof of identity if challenged."

"I don't quite see that," put in Derrick. "I'll show my passport to any authorised person, but if there are plain clothes cops sculling around, how are we to know they're pukka? 'Passport please'—and then grab it. A very easy way of pinching one, especially for a good skier. I'll chase any thief on my flat feet, but chasing one on skis on my present form doesn't seem a good idea."

Kate began to laugh: she could see just what Derrick meant, and she knew the helpless feeling of the ski-ing tyro when an expert swooped past.

"That's perfectly sensible," she said. "If asked for our passports, we say, in such languages as are at our disposal, 'I will show it to the police...*gendarme, der Schutzmann, der Polizeibeamte.* Police is almost an international word—" She broke off, as she saw the hotel manager standing at the door. He came into the room in his smooth urbane way.

"I apologise for disturbing you," he said in his admirable English, "but the maids have got muddled about the numbers of packed meals. They say that somebody has had a packed lunch and an hotel lunch as well."

"Not us!" said Derrick indignantly, but Frank put in reasonably:

"The mistake isn't here. Six of our party ordered packed lunches. Those six have gone to St. Anton. That leaves ten and there are ten of us here. You can count us."

"All right, sir, thank you very much. I was sure the mistake wouldn't be in this party," rejoined the manager. "I know the English. They are always trustworthy."

"That's why you're counting heads," said Gerald flippantly. "Is the English mail in yet?"

"Yes. I have brought you your letters," replied the manager. "Mr. Harris—yes? Miss Reid—yes? Mr. Grant? No, he is not here. Miss Dexter—yes? I have a letter for your brother, too. It is under-stamped. I will keep it for him. And Miss Manners—there is one for you. Excess postage, please. Why do the English not know the cost of continental postage? It is very odd, they are such business-like people. That is all. Thank you very much."

"Well, he counted us most conscientiously," said Gerald. "Germans do love counting people."

"He will now inform the *Polizeiamt*, Police Bureau or what have you, that six of his English party are at St. Anton," said Derrick. "Did they take their passports or shall we have to go and bail them out? Does any of them speak German? What a lark if they're quodded."

"They won't be," said Frank Harris. "This district is out to attract British tourists, not to repel them. The authorities know perfectly well that one mistake on the part of an over-zealous policeman will mean loss of trade next year. They're in competition with the Swiss resorts, and one of the great attractions of Switzerland is the feeling of security and lack of interference."

"But the blond type did count us," said Jillian.

"Certainly he did," said Harris, "and it's quite likely that the St. Anton police have been informed that a party of six Britishers from the Kronbergerhof have gone over there, but that would be to protect the party from annoyance, not to cause it. It's the equivalent of looking after them."

"What a nice mind the chap has!" said Derrick.

3

After lunch, Kate and Biddy went outside again to consider the weather. The sky was all grey now, and to the east the clouds had come down over the peaks in a heavy shapeless swaddling which meant only one thing to the weather wise— snow. In Lech Valley it was still clear and the western peaks stood out white and sharp against a grey sky. As they stood there, both feeling irresolute, Meriel came and joined them.

"Jane just rang through. I asked her to get me some of those fretwork toys in St. Anton if they weren't too dear and she says they've got some beauties. She asked how much I could run to. They had a lovely trip going and she said it was perfectly easy and you could walk if you funked the ski-ing. I gathered it's pretty steep going down from the Pass, but not too difficult."

"How are they coming back?" asked Kate.

"All but Robert and Neville are coming to Langen by train and then on the bus. They may ski down from Zurs if it's still light. Bobs and Neville have started back already because they'll probably have to walk up to St. Christoph and it's quite a climb. But they ought to be back by tea-time. Goodness, it is cold. I'd better hurry up and join my ski-school or I shall miss them. Are you two coming?" She ran off, and Biddy said:

"It's going to snow. You can feel it in the air. I wish those two idiots hadn't set off by themselves over the Pass. Robert has to wear glasses, and if it snows he'll be in a mess."

Kate laughed, but her laugh lacked conviction. "You and I are a pair of worriers, Biddy. Before lunch we were groaning about imaginary detectives: now we're bothering about snow storms. If ever there were two toughs who were capable of looking after themselves it's Robert and Neville. They're both good skiers, and in any case there's a track down from the Pass. They can walk."

"But once it snows you can't see the track. There—what did I tell you—it's beginning."

Frank Harris came and joined them, his face turned upwards as the first flakes began to flutter down, hesitantly, delicately.

"Well, that seems to be that," he said. "It means business if I'm not much mistaken. I think I shall go in and write letters. I've no opinion of ski-ing in a snow storm." He looked at Biddy and Kate with the expression on his face which Kate had described as "clinical". "What's the trouble?" he asked.

"It's a sort of complexity, Frank. We're probably being idiots, but there's one perfectly simple issue. Robert and Neville have set out together to come back over the Arlberg Pass, and it's started snowing and it's going to snow very hard. Would it be a good idea to tell the manager they're coming that way? If it gets really bad he'd probably have a guide sent out."

"How do you know they've started?"

"Because Jane phoned Meriel about some shopping, and they'd already started. Let's go inside. This is going to be a blizzard... all the mountains have disappeared. Goodness, they'll have a time up there above the big ski-lift. It's come on so suddenly."

They made a dash for the hotel doors among a crowd of skiers who had been standing irresolutely, considering the weather. When they got inside, Kate said: "Frank, come up to my room after you've seen the manager. Biddy and I may be being idiots, but we'd feel better if we talked things over and you told us we're idiots."

"I'll do that with pleasure if there's any justification," he replied.

"We'll tell you what's bothering us in the plainest possible way," said Kate.

The three of them were all in Kate's small bedroom. As there was only one chair, Biddy and Frank Harris were sitting on the bed, the duvet rolled up behind them, to make a pillow between their backs and the wall. They were in ski-kit, and looked comic as they lounged on the narrow bed. Kate began her statement: "You and I both felt worried about the money-losing business, Frank. You felt there was something seriously wrong, and were disposed to question the bona fides of some members of the party. I shouldn't have thought anything more about it if it hadn't been that Pippa phoned to

Biddy's club to ask about Nigel and was told that two C.I.D. officers had called there to see Biddy, ostensibly about a car smash which Biddy was supposed to have seen."

"Let me go on, Kate," said Biddy. "It's all my eye about the car smash. I didn't see anything of the kind, and there wasn't a car smash when I was out that morning. Also I'm certain that C.I.D. officers don't go rooting out witnesses to traffic accidents, though I've no doubt they use them as routine excuses when they don't want to say exactly what they're after. The C.I.D. went to the club because they wanted to trace this party for reasons of their own."

"That's only an assumption of your own, Biddy."

"But it's a reasonable one, Frank," said Biddy. "It's not me they're after. I made all the arrangements for the party, and I bet they got my name out of some of the Victoria Station people. I nearly lived at Victoria when I was getting things fixed and numbers kept changing and we couldn't get couchettes and all the rest. Anyway I rang through to the Superintendent at the club to ask what these C.I.D. had been after, and Miss Hammond said there were two officers, one tall and fair and fortyish, and one dark and lively and much younger. The older one was Chief Inspector Rivers. He's almost famous—and I'm certain he doesn't tote round after traffic accidents. And you might as well know the rest. It's guessing I admit, but it's a bit grim. Kate and I came back from Zurs on the bus this morning, and there were two Englishmen on it who'd just come out: they were about eighteen hours late, because there's been fog delaying the railways, and snow as well. One of these men was a big fair fellow, about forty-five, and one was much younger, dark and lively. He talked to Kate, and she's certain he's an English cop, and so am I. They've come. They're here."

"But have they asked for you, Biddy?" asked Frank Harris.

"No. Of course they haven't. They're not interested in me. It's one of the others. And we don't know who it is."

"Well, you're making some fairly tall assumptions," said Harris slowly, "but I'm not prepared to tell you that you're being idiots. I only wish I could, but things have been adding up. While it's guesswork on your parts to assume the C.I.D. are here, it isn't guesswork that the C.I.D. went to Biddy's club, and I'm prepared to agree with her that it may be in connection with this party. Now I'm going to add some facts which may be related, or may not. At lunch-time the manager gave me a letter. It's from a cousin, Keith Wilson. He's the owner of a factory which makes aircraft instruments—not on the secret list, but having a high repute for design and reliability. The firm has an air strip, and test their own products on their own light planes. There has been trouble in their district during the past few months because forged pound notes came into circulation which were traced back to the pay packets of the men in Keith Wilson's works. The police have reason to suppose that someone learnt how to open the safe where the cash was lodged on Thursday nights, pending pay day on Friday, and that bogus notes were introduced and valid ones removed."

Biddy groaned. "Oh, lord. I can see where this connects up. You were talking about forged notes, Frank."

"Yes. There are too many about. Now the police, having investigated the personnel—and it's been a long job—asked Keith for a list of any men who had left the factory in the past few months. Very few had done so, because the working conditions are excellent, but he mentioned the fellow who had been a test pilot here for a couple of years. He had a magnificent record—ex-fighter pilot. For some reason

Keith didn't like him. When this chap—whose name I won't mention—was damaged slightly in a motor bike accident, Keith was very glad to agree to the suggestion of prolonged sick leave and eventually accept his resignation. He left last November, and the police can't find him. One of the reasons Keith wrote and told me this story is that the pilot who resigned is known to be a fine skier. There you are. Take it or leave it."

Biddy gave a long whistle. "Cripes!... Do you know anything else about this pilot, Frank?"

"Keith said the reason he took against him was that the pilot was of Irish extraction. Keith's a lowland Scot and he doesn't like Irishmen."

"Do you mean he was an Irish national with an Irish passport?" asked Kate.

"I don't know," said Frank.

After that they sat and looked at each other in unhappy silence.

Chapter XVII

1

Rivers and Lancing had had a record-breaking journey across Europe: it had taken them longer than even Rivers had feared. Since the widespread fog prevented them from flying, they had jogged over the same route which Biddy and her party had followed. Rivers had taken with him *The Way of all Flesh* and *Erewhon*, by Samuel Butler, and two Anthony Trollopes, and he read his way uncomplainingly across Europe. Lancing had bought six Penguin detective novels, from which he derived much entertainment: he left them all in the train at Langen—"as propaganda," he said to Rivers.

The Austrian police knew that two members of the C.I.D. were on their way to Lech. A plain clothes officer, speaking excellent English, had met Rivers at Langen station, assured him that all sixteen persons in Miss Manners' party were still staying at the Kronbergerhof, and had proffered any assistance which the Chief Inspector might desire. After which brief and business-like expression of professional co-operation, the Austrian Inspector had promptly and tact-fully retired.

Lancing had enjoyed his bus ride from Langen to Lech. He was quite sure that the Englishwoman he had talked to in the bus was one of the party he and Rivers had been tracing: it was Kate's remark about leaving England on New Year's Day which Lancing noted. Rivers, less given to talking, had used his eyes much more than he appeared to do. When Biddy paid her bus fare, she had taken off her thick gloves and Rivers had seen the name tape neatly sewn inside. The Chief Inspector was also very well aware of Biddy's scrutiny of himself and Lancing. When they got out of the bus and collected their baggage and skis, Rivers saw Biddy and Kate go into the Kronbergerhof, and he then turned to Lancing:

"We go up to the Schneiderhof to eat, and see about beds later. It's over the bridge and up the slope. There may be a message for me at Schneider's."

They shouldered their skis and turned across the bridge and Rivers saw Lancing's delighted face as he studied the crowds of returning skiers and the long snow slopes above them.

"It's all very well for you to look so pleased, but there's still a chance we may be pipped at the post," said the Chief Inspector. "We know from the Basle cables that the club in Hamilton Gardens has had two Vienna phone calls, both incoming. It's hardly likely that Miss Bridget Manners has not heard about our inquiries at her club, and Miss Manners was sitting just behind me in the bus. She looked from you to me and from me to you as though we gave her food for thought, and she's a very intelligent-looking young woman."

Lancing halted. "But why on earth... Look here, shall I go back and hang around?"

"No. It wouldn't be any good. That hotel has got hundreds of windows and it's surrounded by snow. There are ski-lifts on both sides of the valley. We don't know the bloke we're after. That's the first step. Here's where we eat—and get some information, I hope."

It was during the course of the meal that Rivers was handed a letter. "They're being most co-operative," he murmured to Lancing. "There are ten of the party having lunch in the hotel, and six of them have gone for a trip to St. Anton. I've got the list of the chalets where they sleep. This is where we go and inquire for beds, and let's hope my German is adequate for inquiries."

They paid their bill and went out into a greying world. "It's going to snow," said Rivers. "No, don't put your skis on yet. It's all uphill. You can ski down later."

Rivers' plan was simple. He was going to ask at each of the chalets for their English occupants, whose names were on the list provided by the Lech police. In each case the English would be out, but the Chief Inspector, while asking for bedrooms for himself and Lancing would also ask to see the bedrooms occupied by other people, saying he was seeking accommodation for a party who would be coming to Lech at Easter. It was Rivers' job to hold the attention of the landlady: it was Lancing's to pick up any small object in the different bedrooms which would show fingerprints—paper of any kind, an envelope, a book, or failing that a toothbrush, soap-box, comb, nail file: any small object which would retain the fingerprints Rivers now knew by heart. Rivers did not want to round up all the men of the party, with the risk that a warning might go around and the wanted man get away in the nick of time. Seeing the lowering skies, Rivers wanted more than ever to do this job neatly, in his own way. Once he had learnt by fingerprints the name under which "Gray" was masquerading, the issue would be simple.

2

They started their inquiries at the Braun chalet, where stout Fräulein Braun was delighted to see the big fair Englishman who spoke slow careful German. The English Herren were all at the hotel, she said: they would find them there without a doubt, but of course he could see the bedrooms. She could provide bedroom and breakfast, *Schlafzimmer und Frühstück.* *"Ein warmes Bad?"* inquired Rivers and was whisked off to see the bathroom, while Lancing, quicker than most pickpockets, snaffled a "souvenir" from each bedroom shown, and Rivers painstakingly asked to see *"ein Zimmer mit zwei Betten".* They worked their way up to the highest chalet, and eventually acquired objects from each of the bedrooms occupied by the men of the party, the trophies being disposed of in Lancing's numerous pockets. It was when this part of the job was complete that Rivers said:

"Let's climb on to the ridge above and ski down to the Schneiderhof. We'd better find out if we're still efficient on these contraptions or if we muck it right away. The lord knows what we'll be in for before we're through."

It was only a short run, and Rivers found his balance at once and felt his skis true on the snow, taking the rise and fall of the surface as easily as a ship at sea, while Lancing, knees bent, ski-sticks driving rhythmically, went down the slope with a zest and speed which left no doubt of his skill. He pulled up on the slope by the Schneiderhof unerringly, his skis turned in, biting the snow in a perfect braking movement, so that Rivers grinned and said: "I've seen worse... Lord, it's going to snow, and snow plenty. But it'll bring them all in. No one's going to stay outside for long today."

"It's cold," said Lancing, and then added: "It can't have been as cold as this for long. The snow's soft underneath."

"So what?" asked Rivers.

"If they get a heavy fresh fall when the drifts are soft, that brings trouble. It means avalanche conditions," said Lancing.

Rivers took off his skis. "It also means no visibility," he said. "Let's hope our man is safely inside the Kronbergerhof. They've got a room for us upstairs here. Come and sort out the bits and pieces."

They went up to the room which had been reserved for them, and Lancing began to unload the various oddments he had collected under the very noses of the unsuspecting *Hausfrau*, while Rivers took out his insufflator and camera. It was then that a knock came at the door and a message was called through saying that Rivers was wanted on the phone. Two minutes later the Chief Inspector was back. "We've got to leave all that," he said. "There's a message come through from the St. Anton party. Four of them are coming back by train, but two are ski-ing back from the top of the Arlberg Pass. The hotel manager's sending a guide out to meet them because of the blizzard. Come on. They can't wait because the car may not be able to get through if it gets any worse."

3

In a matter of seconds they were out of the house, fastening skis and pulling on gloves. "One of the guides is a police guide," said Rivers, just before they took off, "but this isn't official. We're a rescue party, so keep mum. Only it's the very conditions a chap might pray for to stage a getaway and I dare not chance it. O.K. The car's outside the Kronbergerhof."

Lancing said nothing, he just drove his sticks in and swirled off through the snow storm. He had been dreaming of this for days and he was heedless of the stinging snow and darkening skies: he had found his feet on his skis and the world swept by in a dazzling kaleidoscope as he flew down the slope and over the bridge.

A big car was waiting outside the hotel: its engine was running and blue exhaust smoke drove the snowflakes back. Apart from the exhaust smoke and the windscreen which was kept clear by the clicking wipers, the car already looked like a mound of snow itself: windows, wings, roof and running board all covered in downy whiteness. Skis and sticks went on the racks, and four men crowded into the car: the chained wheels gripped and they moved off into a bewildering white wilderness with no more fuss than a London taxi. Lancing strained his ears and wits to hear and understand as Rivers asked in German about the chances of reaching the road fork where they would get out. So far as Lancing could make out, the driver laughed at any suggestion of difficulties on the road. The snow had only just begun. It was "*Keine grosse Sache*"—no great thing, he said, ending with the international assurance, "O.K."

How the driver kept the road neither Rivers nor Lancing could imagine. All tracks had been obliterated in the first two minutes of heavy snow and the smooth coverlet stretched unbroken, the only land marks being the tree trunks. Lancing stared out as best he could between the windscreen wipers as the car swung violently round the bends, and thanked his stars he wasn't driving. "I suppose it's what you get used to..." he thought, and heard Rivers' quiet voice beside him. "We get out at the road fork at Steuben, beyond Zurs. It's only a short climb to St. Christoph—about an hour. They say it's easy enough if you know it well, but dangerous for tourists in the snow because they miss the track. They expect to find them both safely in the hospice at the top of the Pass and they'll guide them back to the car."

"I suppose they could have turned back to St. Anton," said Lancing.

Rivers nodded. "That's what they'll have done if they're behaving sensibly. They should have turned back before the snow started. It's O'Hara and Helston."

Rivers asked no questions and Lancing made no comment. He didn't think Rivers wanted an answer. Dark shapes loomed up in the snow, splinters of light blurred the windscreen and they ran through Zurs, a deserted Alpine village with not a soul outside; then uphill again, the powerful car slowed down a bit by the snow which was deepening in the hollows. "They've got the snow ploughs out, going non-stop between Langen and Lech," said Rivers. "They say they can keep the road open for days as a rule—but it's pretty heavy. This will be the road fork. Well, this is where we do some climbing on skis. It's too soft for walking." The guides and the C.I.D. men got out and put on their skis and the car went back to Zurs. In blinding snow they started the ascent, the guides leading without hesitation up the trackless sheet. Lancing soon lost count of time and distance; visibility there was none, and although he was hot with physical effort, his hands seemed to freeze as he held his ski-sticks. Every now and then the guides stopped and yodelled, and listened for a reply. As they stood at one spot, Lancing heard a slither and a thud, not far away, and the guides turned their heads and stood dead still for a second or two. The sound had been the snow slipping from a ridge and Lancing remembered his own comment—"When the snow is soft underneath and there's a fresh fall, it makes for avalanche conditions."

4

They had been climbing for nearly an hour, stopping every few minutes while the guides yodelled out the call which came echoing back to them from the mountains, and at last they heard an answer. It might have been an animal crying, somewhere below them, far away to their left, right off the track they had been following, so far as Lancing could tell, judging by direction, for sight did not help him at all. After a brief colloquy, the guides gave Rivers some directions, and he nodded agreement. The Austrians skied down a slope on their left, paused, did a Christie turn, traversed and went on down. Rivers and Lancing followed in their tracks until a shout of "Halt!" when both stood still, listening to the yodels and the faint answers which came more quickly now. It seemed to Lancing that they stood in the blinding snow for a long time before they saw the guides again, supporting between them a staggering figure, snow-covered and grotesque. One of the guides was carrying the rescued man's skis, and these Rivers took, while Lancing got behind the party to save a backward slide if the man slipped. They got him back on to comparatively level ground, banged the snow off him, rubbed him and gave him brandy. The man wasn't hurt, so far as Lancing could see, only half frozen, and completely bemused. He got out a few sentences quite clearly: "I was nearly back at the road… realised he wasn't following… I went back to look for him and lost my way…got stuck in a drift. He's there somewhere…" Then he collapsed again. They gave him another tot of brandy and Rivers then spoke to him, clearly and sharply. "We'll go and look for him. O'Hara, isn't it? You can keep your feet if you try, we're not far from the hospice. Keep your feet, man. You'll be better if you try to move."

It was at this juncture that other voices hailed them from near at hand, and two more Austrians appeared out of the blizzard. The party got moving, shoving the rescued man between the two Lech guides. "They're from the hospice," said Rivers. "It's only a few hundred yards higher up now."

They trudged on up until they reached a level terrace and saw the dark eaves of a wooden building. When they got into the still heat inside the house, Lancing felt he could have gone to sleep as he stood, so incredible was the warm security after the snow and the biting, raging wind outside. Banging the snow off his coat, Lancing heard Rivers talking again, but the German words didn't get through to Lancing's mind because his ears were ringing with altitude and storm, his mind confused by the sudden change from outside to inside. One thing he did realise, though. It was Rivers who was now giving orders—arranging the party—and the others were agreeing. Rivers then turned to Lancing. "The police guide is staying here with this chap. The two fellows who live here are going to search again by the track we came up. The Lech guide says he'll lead me down to St. Anton. I think that's the best thing to do."

Lancing came to life again. "I'll come too, sir. I've got back into it. I don't think I shall muff it."

Rivers grinned; his fair skin was flushed red, as though it had been stung, his eyes half shut, his face swollen. "All right. You said you wanted a ski-run and you're going to get it. I reckon there's an even chance the other chap broke back and made for the railway. If we ski down we can get to St. Anton

before the eastbound train leaves. We can't do it otherwise."
He glanced at the man they'd brought in. "That's O'Hara.
The Lech guide knows him. He's an Irishman with an Irish
passport. It's Helston who's missing. Well, here's wishing us
luck. Don't overrun the guide. He won't miss the track, but
we should."

5

Lancing knew that he would never forget that ski-run. The
conditions were as foul as they could be so far as the atmosphere was concerned: snow and wind together were like
raging furies, but unexpectedly ski-ing conditions were better
than could have been hoped with regard to surface. There
was a hard smooth track beneath the newly fallen snow, and
the latter was dry and packed easily. The guide went ahead
and Lancing followed: he forgot everything but the sense of
speed, the realisation that he could do this fantastic trick of
flying down a snow slope, conscious that his skis seemed one
with himself. He was aware of the snow-laden conifers whose
trunks darkened the mountainside to his left, but his eyes
and mind were intent on the dimly seen figure of the guide
crouching and speeding in front of him. At intervals the guide
let out a yodel cry, and Lancing replied and caught Rivers'
answering call. How long the run lasted Lancing had no idea,
but quite suddenly the guide yelled a very different note.
"Yoi... oi... oi! Halt! *Achtung*! Yoi-oi-oi! Halt!" he cried, and
Lancing saw him stretch his arms out as he braked in a mad
splother of whirling snow. Lancing's ankles and knees nearly
cracked as he forced his skis to turn, grip, grind, and the wild
moment of exhilaration died out as he slowed down before
some huge dark obstacle which seemed to thrust grasping

fingers out into the whirling snow. He half fell against it and was surprised to find it yielded—and then he understood. It was a fir tree, fallen right across the track.

Rivers, close behind, managed to do a half-turn which he was proud of when he had time to think about it. He kept his balance and stood staring at the fallen tree. "Well, that's put the lid on this run," he gasped. "We can't get round that."

In the fading light the guide had snapped off a branch from the fallen tree and was using it as a flail, beating the fresh snow away, as a man might beat at a fire. The dry snow flew out all around them, and then Rivers' mind took in what the other was doing, and he in his turn seized a branch, but an exclamation from the guide checked him. From beneath the snow something that wasn't part of the tree was sticking up, something too straight for the branches of a young fir tree. It was a pair of crossed skis.

6

"He must have run slap into it—as we should have done if it hadn't been for the guide," said Rivers. "His head hit the trunk and his neck broke. He'd have been travelling at the speed of an express train and the snow was coming down so hard he couldn't see anything at all."

"He'd only come up the track about an hour ago and he knew it was a clear run down," said Lancing. "It was such a marvellous run and he'd have gone all out…"

They got the body clear of the tree and stretched it out in the snow in the lee of the branches. Rivers took his gloves off and undid the ski-coat. His hands were cold from gripping the ski-sticks and he could feel that there was still some faint warmth in the dead body—the man was quite dead, but it must be less than an hour since he died. There was a passport and note-case in a pocket of his ski-jacket—Neville Helston's passport. In an inner pocket was another passport and another wad of notes. Rivers stood up and talked to the guide. Then he said to Lancing: "He says he can get round the tree, and it's only a few minutes' run on to St. Anton. He'll bring out a stretcher party. They're used to handling casualties on the mountains. We'll stay here."

They saw the guide turn uphill to the left, negotiating the difficult ground with his skis in a way that neither Rivers nor Lancing could have done. Then his figure was lost in the whirling snow, and after a moment or so they heard him yodelling as he regained the track.

Lancing said suddenly: "Helston was Gray. I'd just got his prints out when you said we were coming out here."

"I reckoned it was. I'll tell you about that later," said Rivers. "And somehow we're going to take his fingerprints."

"Here and now?" asked Lancing.

"Here and now. I've never fingerprinted a corpse in a blizzard before, but I'm going to do it. When the gale brought that fir tree down, goodness knows how it affected that slope above it, and we've heard one miniature avalanche already."

Lancing whistled, but he said nothing. Together they crouched over the corpse in the snow, pressing the stiffening fingers on to an ink pad, then taking each print in their note-books, while the gale shrilled round them and snow found its way inside mufflers and collars and piled on their shoulders and arms. Rivers went through every one of the pockets, replacing their contents in his own, and got the rucksack straps clear of Helston's shoulders. Then he said: "We've done our best. Now we'd better get higher up the track. There's a rock wall some yards back. It'll be safe to lean against and it'll give a bit of cover."

They pulled their gloves on, collected their skis and made their way up the slope, staggering and lurching, but the movement at least got their circulation going again. With their backs to the rock wall, they swung their arms in the manner of London constables, and Lancing, numb with cold, stamped his feet furiously. "Don't do that," said Rivers sharply. "They say the least vibration can set the snow shifting."

Lancing stood still. He suddenly remembered a guide saying that even the vibration of human voices could start an avalanche when the conditions were ripe for one. Then, above the shrilling of the wind, they heard a yodel from above them, and Lancing answered it, imitating the warning cry of the guide. "Yoi…oi… Yoi…oi…i. Halt! Yoi…i… Halt!" The skier was nearly upon them when he managed to stop. Lancing heard his abrupt *"Kommen Sie… Diesen Weg…"* and then there was a cracking sound, a rustle which sounded above the wind, a groaning and then an indescribable thud and indeterminate roar as though the very mountain were moving. It was only a very small avalanche, but tons of snow and loosened rocks moved down the mountainside where the fir tree had been uprooted and buried it afresh, piling up on the tree, over the body, and down into the cleft below the track. It seemed to go on for ages, and when at last it died away, the Austrian skier said again, *"Kommen Sie… Oben, nach Oben…"*

Chapter XVIII

1

"Chief Inspector Rivers?" It was Frank Harris who spoke, at the door of the Kronbergerhof, on the day after the blizzard. The snow was still falling, but the Austrian guides had brought Rivers and Lancing safely down from the Pass. The news of Helston's death had been telegraphed through from St. Anton, and Rivers was still in a quandary as to what he was to say to the other members of Helston's party. Sitting over the fire in the hospice yesterday, after the most exhausting climb that Rivers or Lancing had ever achieved, Lancing had said: "Helston is dead. Gray's dead, too. One died in Lioncel Court, one on the Arlberg Pass. Has it got to be sorted out? Isn't it better for it to be believed that Helston died on the Pass?"

And Rivers, bemused from physical exhaustion, could only say: "Search me. That's for the authorities to sort out. It's not my pigeon. But as you say, Neville Helston is dead, he's been dead for days…"

"Much better for his people to think he died in a ski-ing accident," persisted Lancing.

"Maybe…let them sort it out among the high-ups," said Rivers. "We're lucky we're not dead, too. God, I'm too tired to think any more…"

And here was Dr. Harris saying, "Chief Inspector Rivers?" The C.I.D. man looked at the other and Harris went on: "It's partly guesswork, partly having seen a photograph of you when the Shah inspected the C.I.D. Am I right?"

"Yes. You're perfectly right," said Rivers.

"Then may I have a few words with you? My name is Harris. I'm a G.P. I'm also one of the older members of Miss Manners' party, and I think we ought to get a few points sorted out. It's only fair to us."

"Very good, sir," said Rivers, and Harris went on:

"It's difficult to find a quiet spot to talk with all this crowd in here. Miss Reid has a bedroom here: we could talk up there."

Rivers agreed and they pushed their way through the babel of the lounge and went up to Kate's room. As he knocked, and led Rivers into the room, Harris said: "This is Miss Reid. I think that she and I should tell you the various points we have noticed—if you're willing to talk to us both."

"Certainly," agreed Rivers, bowing to Kate. Harris and the C.I.D. man sat on the bed, Kate on the one and only chair.

Harris started without further ado: "We're all a bit confused, and very distressed, so I'll ask one or two plain questions first. Is Helston dead, as reported?"

"Yes," replied Rivers, and Harris went on:

"Would you tell us if you came here on duty, and if so, was it Helston you were after?"

Rivers realised exactly the nature of the problem that

faced him: looking at Harris's sensible, troubled face, Rivers thought: "I've got to face this as a personal issue, and be fair over it, no matter what the authorities decide on later." He replied aloud: "Would you tell me why you put it that way? Have you any reason to suppose Helston wasn't straight? Please try to answer that quite simply, leaving out, if you can, the fact that Helston is dead."

It was Kate who answered: "We've had some trouble over money being stolen. It made Dr. Harris and myself suspicious. We began to think out all the things we'd noticed about the different members of our party, some of whom were quite unknown to us before we set out. Frank Harris and I—in agreement with some of the others—thought we ought to get the whole thing sorted out, so that the others are cleared of the suspicion of theft. We want to be fair to Helston and O'Hara and the others."

Rivers nodded, and waited for her to go on. "It seems horrible to accuse a dead man," said Kate, "but I think I'd better say perfectly plainly why I had a reason for believing that Neville Helston wasn't what he seemed to be. When we arrived at Langen station, there was some registered luggage for Neville. It had come in our train, in the same luggage van as ours. We registered our luggage at Victoria Station before we got on the train, and it takes a little time to do it. Neville Helston's taxi only arrived at Victoria a few minutes before our train left, and he wouldn't have had time to register his luggage and get it on our train. There just wasn't time for him to have done it, and for the registered luggage people to have got it across Victoria Station and on to our train—not if he told the truth about just having come up from Berkshire on a train that was delayed by fog."

She broke off, and Harris went on: "When we arrived at

Langen station, Helston went straight to the bus. I had to tell him that there was some registered luggage of his which he'd got to clear. It seems to us, thinking it out, he didn't know the registered luggage was there. We've been worrying over this and other points until we're weary to death of it. We know you went to Bridget Manners' club. You've come out here. You went up the Arlberg Pass when O'Hara and Helston were ski-ing back. Will you tell us, in confidence if you wish, was Helston the chap he said he was, and, if so, did you come out here to arrest him?"

"Look here," said Rivers. "This isn't an easy business for me. I don't know what my superior officers will decide about the case, but you've asked me a straight question, and I'm going to answer it as an individual, not as a police officer, trusting you two to keep your own counsel—and mine. You've found the right answer yourselves, by observation and common sense. The man who joined your party at the last moment was not Neville Helston. He was known to us as Gray. We have his fingerprints and there is no doubt that he was Gray, and not Helston. The probability is that the real Helston stopped with Gray over the week-end, and registered his own baggage some time on the Sunday, and that Gray knew nothing about this." Rivers paused, and then added: "Helston is dead. He died on New Year's eve. I'm telling you this because I want to be fair to the real Neville Helston, and not let you think he was a crook who stole your money, and nearly killed Robert O'Hara by pretending to get lost on the Arlberg Pass."

"Thank you for telling us." Kate Reid's face was white, but her voice was quite steady. "I've been thinking about this all night. You see—I knew he was a liar. It was just silly little things, but they added up."

Harris said: "You think this man, Gray, killed Helston and came abroad as Helston, to get out of the country?"

"Yes," said Rivers. "I can't tell you the whole story now, because we're still in process of collecting all the evidence about Gray. I don't know how much the authorities will decide to make public, but I do know this. The real Neville Helston has a brother: he'll want to see some of you and talk about the brother who was supposed to have come out here with you. I don't want you to talk to him thinking his brother was a crook. Perhaps that sounds confused, but the point I want to make clear is that the real Neville Helston, who died in London, was *not* a crook."

2

"The whole story is a grim story, and there's no denying it," said Rivers later. He was talking to Kate, because he realised she was much more upset than her manner showed. "Think of it this way. If the real Helston had come out here, it's quite possible he would have been killed in that blizzard. You would all have felt miserable over it, but sudden death isn't a bad way of passing out. You know that, both of you. The real Neville Helston passed out without knowing anything about it. He was drugged."

Harris put in: "I know exactly what you mean, Rivers. You're saying, don't get morbid over it. You're quite right. Speaking as a doctor, I've often thought that there were better ways of dying than from old age or disease on a sick bed, though I'm usually chary of saying so."

"You're perfectly right," said Kate. "I don't think I'm given to morbidity, but the suddenness of all this has been a shock, although I had realised that if my own guess was right, the implications involved were pretty black. You see, it did seem to me eventually that Neville was an impostor."

"Could you bear to tell me what it was that first made you suspicious?" asked Rivers. "Was it the theft of money?"

"No," replied Kate. "Any of the party might have done that, so far as the mechanics of it were concerned. Robert O'Hara said that ten pounds' worth of Austrian currency was stolen from a locked suitcase in his bedroom at the Braun chalet. When Dr. Harris made Robert turn out his suitcase to make certain that the money wasn't mislaid, ten English pound notes came to light which Robert said weren't his, and then Neville said he'd lost his own English notes, which he'd left in his bedroom in another chalet. It was all very confusing and unpleasant, because neither Dr. Harris nor I wanted to suspect any of our own party, but it seemed to us that one of them must be a bad hat."

"The trouble was that there were two or three whom we knew nothing about," put in Harris.

Rivers nodded. "Yes. It was confusing—but go on, and tell me how you thought it out," he said.

"I just sat and tried to think out any discrepancies, or anything suspicious about any of them," said Kate. "Tim Grant hadn't travelled in the train with us. He'd come by air. I wondered if there was anything in that. Robert O'Hara had an Irish passport but he didn't talk like an Irishman. Ian Dexter has something impish and mischievous about him—and so on. And while I was chewing it all over, rather miserably, because I felt very mean, I remembered something odd. We'd all talked a bit about our background: Neville said his people had farmed. I noticed that because I'm interested in farming: I like going to see the little farms up the Lech Valley. Coming back one day with Neville and Robert, Neville said two things which were quite incredible from anyone who was brought up on a farm. He spoke of sending out the cows in the spring-time to pasture in the meadows."

Rivers chuckled as she paused. "Yes," he said. "I was brought up in Norfolk. No one who has lived on a farm could ever make that mistake. Wherever else the cows pasture, they're not allowed in the meadows. Meadows are for hay crops, and sacrosanct... 'The sheep's in the meadow, the cow's in the corn'—both equally shocking to a farmer."

"I should never have spotted that," said Frank Harris. "It's not my technique."

"Yet to a farmer it's an impossible thing to say," said Kate, "and he made another floater. He said his people were dairy farmers and the cows they kept were Herefords. Herefords aren't dairy cattle. They're beef cattle." She broke off, and then said: "Ordinarily, I shouldn't have thought anything more about it, except to laugh to myself because he'd such a rotten memory, but when I began to look for discrepancies, well—here was something I couldn't square up."

"That's what I'm always doing," said Rivers. "Once you've noticed one thing that doesn't square up, you just go on."

"I know," said Kate. "I couldn't stop. I thought about those Austrian notes Robert had lost. Who would steal Austrian currency? Surely, someone who wanted to stay in Austria. I knew that Neville had got traveller's cheques like we all had. The first time he changed one I was at the desk, just behind him. He'd had a fall when he started ski-ing: he and Robert got out of the bus at Zurs and insisted on ski-ing to the hotel here. We all laughed because Neville took a toss almost at once. It was then he dislocated his thumb. But Malcolm, who knows quite a lot about ski-ing, said 'He knows how to fall.'"

Again Rivers nodded. "Yes. That's interesting. One of the

most important things in ski-ing is to know how to fall—and while you can play the fool and pretend you've lost your balance, it's not easy to muff a fall. Once you've learnt how to fall without hurting yourself, it becomes a reflex, something your muscles do for you."

Frank suddenly spoke here: "That young German said to me: 'You have a very fine skier in your party.' I said, 'You mean O'Hara?' I didn't realise he was talking about Neville Helston because I don't really know enough to spot the expert, and I went on, 'But he still tumbles about a bit.' The German said, 'If he tumbles, it's to encourage the beginners.'"

"Neville was a wonderful skier, Frank," said Kate. "I don't know a great deal about it, either, but I saw him once, when he was just enjoying himself, that day I went to the farms up the valley. He was going like a flying angel. He was a marvellous sight."

"It's because he was such a fine skier he was killed," said Rivers. "He'd just come up from St. Anton. He counted on it being a clear run down, and the surface was good. He went all out, although there was no visibility, and he hit that tree trunk when he was travelling at speed. His neck was broken with the velocity of the impact."

3

"Will you go back to the point you were making about the traveller's cheques?" said Rivers a little later, and Kate went on:

"Oh, yes. Neville explained to the manager that he'd dislocated his thumb and couldn't write properly, and the manager said, 'We've got a good doctor here. Why not see him and get it properly strapped up?' and Neville said, 'It doesn't matter.

It'll soon be better.' I didn't think about that again until I got suspicious, and then I wondered if the dislocated thumb was an excuse to cover the fact that his signature on the cheque wasn't very much like the signature on his passport. He had to sign the cheque when he changed it, and although the manager contrives to look pretty casual, I think he's really very observant. I suppose the real fact was that Neville didn't want to sign any more cheques in case any comment was made, but he did want some more Austrian notes in case he had to do a bolt in a hurry."

"I see all that plainly enough," said Harris, "but why confuse things by putting those pound notes in O'Hara's suitcase?"

"Wasn't it just in order to confuse things?" said Kate. "The notes were in Ian's book which he'd lent to Robert, and it made you and me wonder about Ian—and the others as well."

"I should be interested to see those pound notes," said Rivers.

Frank Harris turned on him quickly. "Had the man you were after—Gray—been employed by a firm whose men got forged notes in their pay packets?"

"I can't tell you that at the moment," said Rivers, "but something of the kind is being looked into. I only heard about it this morning: the evidence hadn't come in when I left London. We hadn't been able to trace Gray before I came away."

4

"Can you tell us at all how you found that Gray was in this party?" asked Frank Harris.

"I can only give you a vague idea," said Rivers. "As I've already told you, I don't know what line will be taken about publishing the evidence. Possibly it will never be published. We got Gray's fingerprints from a previous job he worked. Outside his digs, after he'd left, an observant officer of E Division spotted the print of a ski-stick. We traced a man who had carried skis from Gray's neighbourhood to Waterloo Station, and another man carrying skis who took a taxi from Waterloo to Victoria about half-past twelve on New Year's Day. This man told his taxi-driver he must catch his train because he was going with a party. So we went to the parties department at Victoria and heard about Miss Manners. We got a trace of Gray's fingerprints on the letter which you all signed for Nigel Carstairs. So I came out here. I didn't know what name Gray was using, but before I left I told my department to contact the relatives of every member of the party and find out if everyone had sent a letter or postcard saying they'd got here. In my experience people always send their families a line to say they've arrived when they come on trips like this. The only one who hadn't written was Helston. That didn't prove anything, but it made me take a particular interest in Helston. I only got that piece of evidence when I arrived here—hence my determination to see what Helston was doing between St. Anton and the Arlberg Pass. And it also enabled us to fish Robert O'Hara out of a snowdrift into which he'd tumbled because he went back to hunt for Helston. I'm afraid that's all I can tell you in the way of a reconstruction."

Harris stared at Rivers in amazement. "Then your whole chase out here was started by the print of a ski-stick in London?"

"Yes. But it was an association of ideas: one thing led to another and luck had a lot to say in it. It always does." Rivers paused and then added: "I think the most unforgettable moment of the whole case, so far as I am concerned, will be the moment when the guide beat the snow away from some of the branches of the tree Gray had collided with. His skis were sticking up among the brushwood, and they were crossed. It's a synonym for disaster—crossed skis."

And Frank Harris found himself echoing the phrase "Crossed skis…"

THE END